The Dedalus Book
of Surrealism

(The Identity of Things)

edited by Michael Richardson

Dedalus

Supported by the Eastern Arts Board

Published in the UK by Dedalus Ltd, Langford Lodge, St Judith's Lane, Sawtry, Cambs, PE17 5XE

ISBN 1 873982 45 3

Distributed in Canada by Marginal Distribution,
Unit 103, 277, George Street North, Peterborough, Ontario, KJ9 3G9
Distributed in Australia by Peribo Pty Ltd, 26 Tepko Road, Terrey Hills, N.S.W. 2084

Typeset by Datix International Ltd, Bungay, Suffolk
Printed in Finland by Wsoy

Acknowledgements

Special thanks to all the translators and all the help they have given. Thanks also to Karol Baron, Isabelle Blanchard, Bona Pieyre de Mandiagues, Alastair Brotchie, Mario Cesariny, Michael Dash, Rikki Ducornet, Julien Gracq, Malcolm Green, Irène Hamoir, Stuart Inman, Abdul Kader El Janaby, Alain Joubert, Nelly Kaplan, Petr Král, Sergio Lima, Rike Lina, Albert Marenčin, Mary Low Machado, Marcel Mariën, René Ménil, Akira Okazaki, Pavel Reznicek, Carlos Felipe Saldanha, Stuart Thompson, Philip West and Rainer Wichering and to all the other people without whom this project would not have been possible.

Thanks also to the following for their help in respect of rights: Marie-Paule Cornavin, Roberta Cremoncini, Isabelle Dibie, Jacqueline Favero, Monique Guibert, Jean Mattern, Michele de Simon Niquesa Lezzerini, Isabelle Sieur, Béatrix Vernef, Gary Pulsifer and Gil McNeil.

And to the British Centre for Literary Translation and the Council of Europe for financial assistance.

List of Contents

All translations, except where otherwise stated, are by the editor.

NOTE ABOUT THE EDITOR

Michael Richardson is an anthropologist who has made a special study of surrealism.

Introduction

The aim of this anthology is to give an introduction to surrealist narrative writing though a focus on key surrealist themes. Anyone preparing an anthology of surrealist writing is faced with acute problems of selection, especially since the surrealists assert that surrealism can be defined neither epistemologically nor ontologically. How then does one determine its boundaries? There is no completely satisfactory way to answer this question and thus to define what writing can be legitimately considered within the purview of surrealism is difficult. Surrealism is a collective activity and one has to begin with the various Surrealist Groups and the activities associated with them, especially their journals. Even this needs care, though: the surrealists published work by non-surrealists and they also recognised as surrealists many writers who did not directly participate in collective activity. In considering surrealism one needs to remain sensitive to the nature of its internal intimacy: surrealism is in a very real, if rather elusive way, a secret society and it requires some form of commitment to its collective sensibility. The nature of this 'secret society' is expressed by Jean Ferry in a story entitled 'K, or the Secret Society' (which is translated in J. H. Matthews' *The Custom House of Desire*) in which a society exists which is so secret that either it is impossible to belong to it or perhaps everyone may belong to it. Nevertheless, an element of reciprocity between the writer and surrealism is necessary for a work to be considered within its frame. This has been the primary consideration in this selection. All of the writers here have made a positive engagement with surrealist ideas. My choice of stories within this context has been determined by the overall thematic concerns of the book rather than from any wish to give a representative selection of surrealist writing. Its formal limit is narrative writing, although this has been very broadly interpreted to include a study like Aragon's 'Enter the Succubi' which has a storytelling element even if, strictly, it appears to be more of a theoretical text.

To consider surrealism, the first task is to separate what responds actively to surrealism from what is merely influenced by it. The difficulty here is that within contemporary literature the position of surrealism is deceptive. We are as if faced with the bottle that confronts Alice with the injunction 'Drink me'. Taking one perspective its influence can appear so vast as to be pervasive over a wide area, from science fiction to so-called magic realism, that any specificity is lost: it comes to cover a vast hinterland which engulfs it and destroys its meaning. From another perspective it can be reduced to something so inconsequential it vanishes from view altogether. In addition, surrealism has too often been interpreted in a way that is alien and even antithetical to surrealism itself by critics too arrogant to take account of what surrealists themselves say and who rather subsume its activity to what they think it should be – thus, for example, the common misinterpretation that it transcends reality in a 'super-realism'.

To come to terms with what generally constitutes surrealism it is perhaps helpful to look at its boundaries and the influence it has had, and influence too often subsumed within the catch-all words 'surreal' and 'surrealistic'. In fact one is tempted to say that genuine surrealism can never be defined by either of these words.

In French literature, beyond being stylistically important for what has followed it, surrealism has had little genuine influence. With the rise of existentialism and structuralism after the Second World War, and the ascendency of the *nouveau roman* surrealism became very much marginal to French culture generally, and though it has continued to draw adherents to it, its influence beyond what is surrealism proper is very limited.

Its influence can perhaps be seen most sharply and interestingly in Latin American literature, where writers like Alejo Carpentier, Carlos Fuentes, José Lezama Lima, Ernesto Sabato and Julio Cortazár were certainly steeped in surrealism and owe much to it. But essentially all of them used it for different purposes, taking some of its concepts in directions that are important and of interest to surrealists, but nevertheless remain external to surrealism itself. Above all, as Carpentier himself soon realised after a brief association with the French surealists in the early thirties, what was most important for him was the establishment of identity, while for surrealism it was the dissolving of identity that was the central issue. The same thing is – loosely – true for all of these writers. The impulse underlying the 'magic realism' of Gabriel García Marquez (who displays no influence of surrealism himself) and those many writers who have followed him, who create a heightened reality using aesthetic precepts that appear close to the nineteenth century social novel, is sharply divergent from surrealism.

A greater intimacy with surrealism is seen in francophone Caribbean writers like Edouard Glissant, Jacques Steven Alexis, René Depestre or Franketienne, but again the central impulse behind the work of these writers is not surrealist, but concerned with their own identity. They too use surrealist ideas as part of their own development.

In the English speaking world it is difficult to think of a single writer who has been genuinely influenced by surrealist ideas, or is working in a parallel way. True, the superficial influence of surrealism is everywhere and writers like J. G. Ballard or Angela Carter have used it in ways that are not negligible, but again they use it for purposes quite distinct from surrealism.

Angela Carter is a particularly interesting example to take, since she was directly influenced by the writings of Breton, Aragon, Pieyre de Mandiargues and particularly Desnos. But her use of this material is purely literary and as such is a pastiche of surrealism. She neither engages with surrealism itself, nor does she utilise surrealist ideas in a different but original way, like the writers mentioned above. Essentially she appropriates these ideas for her own aims, which lie within a more traditional literary form, that is as a 'mode of expression' rather than part of the sphere of 'activity of the spirit', which has always been the hallmark of surrealism.

Writers like Octavio Paz, Magloire-Saint-Aude or Leonora Carrington and all the other writers in this anthology are different from any of these writers in that they all made a positive decision to participate directly in surrealism and align their work with its overall aims. All of them conceive their work as a process of discovery and it is this element that determines their work within surrealism as an 'activity of the spirit'. On the other hand there are other writers, like the Brazilian João Guimarães Rosa or the Guyanese Wilson Harris who have no connexion with surrealism and appear completely untouched by its influence, and yet seem very close to its spirit. Both are concerned with exactly the same sort of interrogation of reality as the surrealists and for both of them writing is undoubtedly an 'activity of the spirit' (Guimarães Rosa once said that he didn't make up stories – they came to him and told him to write them down). Neither writer should be subsumed to surrealism, but they do reveal the extent that the exigencies to which surrealism lays claim have some universal application.

Surrealism itself never sought to make its ideas exclusive; it has never desired influence or power, but seems to prefer a marginal role. Surrealism is a total activity, involving the whole body. One cannot be a surrealist as a pastime, or treat it as an ephemeral activity. It must respond to one's own internal being and not be treated as a means to an end. Perhaps it can be likened to a spring. As such it both nourishes and needs constant refreshment. While there are many who pass by and take nourishment from its waters without offering anything to it in return, there are others who contribute to its abundance without taking anything from it. It is, however, only those who both sustain themselves on its waters and offer back to it who can be considered surrealists. This is the criterion I have tried to apply to the selection of writers to be included in this anthology.

In contemporary culture surrealism is something of an anomaly. As Julien Gracq asserts, in a world in which true feelings and genuine literature are stifled by bad air, surrealism 'had the essential virtue of laying claim to express, at each moment, man's *totality*, which is refusal and acceptance mingled together, constant separation and constant reintegration, and it has been able to maintain in its heart this contradiction not [. . .] through the conciliatory and rather feeble route of a measured wisdom, but rather by maintaining at its most extreme point the tension between two simultaneous attitudes – bedazzlement and fury – that do not cease to respond to this fascinating and unlivable world in which we exist.'[1]

Refusing what Adorno called that 'comfort in the uncomfortable' taken by the fantastic, surrealism seeks to reintegrate man into the universe and its aim in literature has perhaps not been better expressed than by the Brazilian surrealist Xavier Domingo who, although prefacing the French translation of Guimarães Rosa's *Biriti*, could equally have been speaking about surrealism, when he wrote: 'In this world of Genesis man lives before the fall, and his life flows with the simplicity of a Franciscan spring or a troubadour song. The sertanejo [the subject of Guimarães Rosa's work] wakes into a fresh and renewed universe, without memory, with no future but the night to come. Here time evaporates – or rather is not yet born. What then could its transitory accidents matter? They completely elude the vision that man, an innocent and cruel demiurge, has of this Hell-Paradise that the sertao [the place in which it takes place] is, where all duality is imminent in each thing, where contrary forces, implicated in each other, engendered through each other, indissolubly devour each other (the tree of science is still intact!) in the harsh combat which is life and joy. For the sertanejo, drawn into this universal battle, only the luminous signals which allow him to stake out the land – the green stain of lizards among the pines, the bluish snouts of caimans glimpsed in the greyish mud – and always enchanting him. In this enticement of odours and music that surrounds him, in which he is born and dies, he is [. . .] only one sound, only one more colour: pure geometry, pure vibration. [. . .] And yet without going *anywhere*, without wanting *anything*, the sertanejo opens up a track – and what an admirable track! – while, at the same time, the sertao also opens up to him a route into the heart of the sertanejo, as if each of them was conscious of the other.'[2]

In other words what is sought, as Julien Gracq has pointed out, is a space in which – freed of the literary market place – the air is fresh and one can take pleasure in breathing it.

Notes

[1] Gracq, 'Quand la littérature respire mal' in *Préferences* (1961) Paris: José Corti p. 103.
[2] Preface to *Biriti* (1961) Paris: Seuil p. 10.

ANDRÉ BRETON AND PHILIPPE SOUPAULT:

White Gloves

The corridors of the grand hotels are unfrequented and cigar-smoke keeps itself dark. A man descends the stairs of sleep and notices that it is raining: the window-panes are white. A dog is known to be resting near him. All obstacles are present. There is a pink cup, an order given and the men-servants turn round without haste. A buzzing denotes this hurried departure. Who can be running in so leisurely a way? Names lose their faces. The street is no more than an abandoned track.

Towards four o'clock that day a very tall man was crossing the bridge which links up the various islands. The bells or the trees were ringing. He thought he could hear the voices of his friends: 'The bureau of lazy excursions is on the right, someone called to him, and on Saturday the painter will be writing to you.' The neighbours of the solitudes leant down and the wheezing of the street-lamps could be heard all night long. The erratic house loses its blood. We all love conflagrations; when the sky changes colour, it is a dead man's passing. What better could one hope for? Another man in front of a perfumer's shop was listening to the rollings of a distant drum-beat. The night that was hovering above his head came down to perch on his shoulders. Conventional fans were up for sale: they weren't producing fruit any more. Without knowing the results people were running in the direction of the maritime inlets. The desperate clocks were telling the beads of a rosary. The virtuous hives were organising themselves. There was no one passing near those main avenues that are the strength of towns. A single storm was sufficient. Far away or close up the damp beauty of prisons went unrecognised.

The best shelters are railway-stations since travellers never know which route to pursue. It could be read in the lines of palms that the most fragrant pledges of fidelity have no future. What can we do with the children with well-developed muscles? The warm blood of bees is preserved in mineral-water bottles. Sincerities have never been seen unmasked. Well-known men lose their lives in the recklessness of those fine houses which set hearts-a-flutter.

How small these rescued tides appear! Earthly delights flow in torrents. Each object offers paradise.

A great bronze boulevard is the most direct way. The magical squares are not good stopping-places. The slow advance is unerring: at the end of a few hours one catches sight of the pretty nose-bleed plant. The consumptives' panorama lights up. All the footsteps of subterranean travellers can be heard. But the most ordinary silence reigns in these narrow spaces. A traveller comes to a halt, perturbed. Amazed, he approaches this coloured plant. No doubt he wants to pluck it but can only shake the hand of another traveller adorned with stolen jewels. Their eyes exchange sulphurous flames and they talk for a long time about their marvellous cries. A dry moon's murmur is thought to be audible, but a glance dispels the most prodigious encounters. Nobody has been able to identify these pale-skinned travellers.

The suburbs' twilights and the sadness of travelling fairs divided them. The weather under canvas is so clement. A sky-blue mist was invading the vicinity of the glade and the miraculous plant was growing slowly. At the militant outer limits long calls were causing the shrubs to shiver; they were those of steamers leaving the isle of adorations for several years. The emigrants were already working things out and were no longer unaware of sentimental calculations. The surrounding forest was losing its inhabitants. Animals in their dens were looking at their young. The clouds were disappearing rapidly, leaving the stars to die. The night dried up.

The carefree traveller said to his companion: "I have walked ahead and I have come to understand the fatality of perpetually running about and of solitary orgies. On my right I killed a friend who knew nothing but the sun. Its rays splashed us painfully and I was so thirsty that I drank his sufferings. I couldn't help gnashing my teeth on reading in his eyes the passionate resignation of those who commit suicide. The wind tightened my throat and I was unable to tell who was talking to me all the time. Then I recognised you."

The gloomy silence of metals was browsing on their words. The traveller with ornate hands replied: "The three best days of my life have left a pale heart in my breast. The loathsome flavours of eastern lands arouse nightmares. I remember a man who ran about without seeing his hands. Today I see you again."

That was how they reached the months with an *r* in them. The day withdraws, leaving a few words of the purest kind on their lips. At this time in other years, as all bodies opened upon milky ways, they climbed into the observatories. There they pored over calculations of distance and probability. They recalled certain infallible utterances such as at a pinch those of Saint-Medard. They rarely discovered a star red as a distant crime or a star-fish.

Their soul's entrance once open to every wind is now so obstructed that they no longer offer a hold to misfortune. They are judged according to clothes that no longer belong to them. Most often they are two very elegant dummy figures devoid of both heads and hands. Those wishing to assume good manners bargain for their dresses in the display-window. When they pass by again next day, the fashion is no longer the same. The collar which is to some extent the mouth of these shells makes way for a stout pair of gilt pincers which when one is not looking seize hold of the shop-window's prettiest reflections. At night it merrily swings from side to side its label on which all could read: 'The season's latest novelty'. Whatever is inhabiting our two friends gradually emerges from its quasi-immobility.

It gropes its way forward obtruding a fine pair of stalked eyes. The body in complete phosphorous formation remains half-way between the day and the tailor's shop. It is connected by delicate telegraphic antennae to the sleep of children. The dummies down there are made of cork. Lifebelts. Those charming codes of polite behaviour are far away.

★★★★★

published in *Les Champs magnétiques* (1920) Paris: Au Sans Pareil (translation *The Magnetic Fields* (1985) London: Atlas Press)
French original © Éditions Gallimard, 1968.
English translation © David Gascoyne and Atlas Press
translated by David Gascoyne
used by permission of Atlas Press

★★★★★

ANDRÉ BRETON (Tinchebray, Orne 1896–Paris 1966) Major theorist and the central figure in the French Surrealist group from 1924 until his death in 1966. Magnetiser of surrealist energies, Breton wrote the major surrealist manifestos and is the key figure in its theoretical development. Author, with Philippe Soupault, of the first specifically surrealist text, *Les Champs magnétiques*, in 1919.

PHILIPPE SOUPAULT (Chaville, 1897–Paris, 1991) After playing a crucial role in surrealism, Soupault became increasingly distanced about 1926 and soon withdrew altogether from surrealist activities. His novel *The Last Days of Paris* has been translated into English.

MARCEL NOLL:

Dream

It was one evening in Odessa during the revolution. Or more accurately twilight, since the fading light of day had managed to penetrate here and there into the theatre in which I found myself in the orchestra stalls waiting for the second part of a play organised by the new rulers of the country. The curtain soon rose on a clearing in a forest and, from a door on my left, a beautiful young woman appeared, dressed completely in blue – a very pure sky-blue that was luminous and seemed to bathe the hall in a strange glow. My thought was that *here was a colour that overcame men's scruples*. The young woman, who I recognised as the star of the José Padilla troupe, crossed the stage with slow steps towards a hut where a man who had made a sign for her to join him was sitting alone. She went over and they spoke together. He was laughing but she was rather grave. At the moment I became conscious of this gravity expressed by the whole of this young woman's allure and expression, I was making a vain effort to try to recall the circumstances in which I had previously met her. All I could remember was that *this colour had previously been completely unknown to me*. After having smiled furtively and grasped the hand of her interlocutor, she went up a small stairway on to the stage, to the right of the orchestra. At the moment she reached the centre of the clearing and, as she was about to speak, I noticed that her colour and radiance were powerless against the *green* which permeated the landscape. She spoke, and as her discourse continued, her dress became paler and I felt that it was no more than a normal dress as worn by any other woman, a white dress with the whiteness of first communion rather than the whiteness of the rose. She spoke in conventional terms about the play they had 'the honour of presenting' and mentioned the author who could be perceived in the forest which extended as far as the eye could see behind the young woman. She trembled as she pronounced his name: FANTOMAS! She then spoke about herself and replied to questions she imagined the audience was asking. Her voice became grave–I felt that her consciousness had suddenly discovered and seized upon the most terrible image of herself – her theatrical smile turned into a desperate laugh when she held out her arm in a low, slow gesture: 'There was a little bit of me born everywhere in the world.' At that moment I had a clear view of a map of the world. The Balkans was swarming with shapeless things and I felt that obscure forces were in the process of taking shape. Asia was completely white and dazzling, with the shadow of its elevation and the silver of its rivers. Just as I was filled with a sudden sense of hope, such as one feels when a promise seems to be on the point of coming to fruition, when a pledge is guaranteed, the young woman seemed about to faint under the pressure of the great effort she had made. At the sight of her distress, I felt incredibly distraught at the sacrifice she made.

I went down a very long staircase which led me into a long and dark corridor at the end of which was a courtyard feebly lit by the moon of an agonizing night. I thought about the new day we would have to live through, I thought of the blood that had been spilled (badly spilled) everywhere and felt infinitely troubled when I considered all the scruples, all the weaknesses, remaining within me and which made my relations with men and events so disappointing. At that moment I saw the young woman of the night before going towards the courtyard. I managed to catch her up and I found her still as grave and as silent. She offered me her hand, which I shook, and for a few moments we walked side by side to the courtyard which retreated in proportion to our movement towards it. I thought of the distressed and agonized state of shock of both of our thoughts. I felt our union was irremediable, without understanding, and yet with a force of hope that I always knew would be the same. I foresaw that under other latitudes we would perhaps both have preferred indifference. . .

At the moment the young woman seemed about to take me in her arms, I woke up for reasons that had nothing to do with the dream.

★★★★★

(published in La Révolution Surréaliste no 7) (1925)

★★★★★

MARCEL NOLL (born Strassbourg) One of the mysteries of surrealism is 'Whatever happened to Marcel Noll?' A central figure of the twenties, he drifted away after the convolutions in the Surrealist Group of 1929. He apparently became a Communist Party functionary for a while and is thought to have died fighting in the Spanish Civil War.

RAYMOND QUENEAU:

Destiny

1. Translation

Old values! Old truths! This was all that emerged from long evenings of study. He's a young chap – and they say he used to be hard working, clever and rich. His name, no one knows why, is Christian Stobel. We know less about his childhood and adolescence than we do about his foetal life. But there came a day when he became subject to a conversion. An unwonted combination revealed something new to him. A pattern of life seemingly set for good was thrown into disarray. It was a fortuitous encounter, an act of chance. A journey served to confirm this restlessness.

2. Port

No longer relishing the idea of study, Christian Stobel went off to Le Havre. In the hotel in rue Racine in which he stayed people sometimes found women's corpses. For men it was a place to meet. He composed antiopes and delighted as much in the heady smell of tar from the roofs as in the rectangular length of the lines. He sought an adventure but didn't find one. He was inexperienced and besides he didn't have too much imagination.

3. Bohemians

One day he wandered out into the surrounding countryside and, tired out by the long walk, sat down and gazed at the small valley and the hill on the other side. In the distance a band of itinerants could be seen on the luminous road that came out of the depths of the wood. Four caravans advanced towards the freshness of the valley. A few men walked alongside, but they were still only indistinct forms, rather like dots of print. Impregnated with the sun's light, they again became obscure as they passed through the market town, curled-up like an old white cat at the bottom of the valley, and along the road. When they re-emerged at a nearby turning in the road they became more clearly distinguishable. They passed by and infused the ground with the sweat of their feet, the men sunburned and muscled, the women in rags, with children and some carts and horses.

"We have come from all the countries of the world and are going to Saintes-Maries de la Mer. Nomads of the enigma, we gather there each year after having carried our mystery through ordinary countryside and fluid towns. Since we become transformed by our wanderings we are despised by those who stand still and retain a memory of giant serpents and metallic green."

They vanished round the next turning. Stobel got up and left. He returned to Paris. After a few conversations with an enigmatic metaphysician who suggested a few, none too numerous, possibilities he abandoned studies, family, friends, Paris and finally France.

Comrades! My dear friends, don't you find this Stobel a diaphanous and rather transparent character? After he has passed we don't remember a thing about him. For myself I'd prefer anything to the recounting of this sort of naive story.

4. Memory

On the ship Stobel picked the husks off orange pips. He thought: "Nights of islands, nights of coasts, nights of cliffs. How I would have loved the skylights of old shacks, the luxuriousness of exotic dances, the geometry of machines! Nothing remains of the dreams of an eighteen-year-old. On streets paved with old prejudices, I have done no more than hauled along disorientated silences. The hollows in the wall no longer allow sounds to pass through.

The cross is extinguished on waylaid roads. The immortals have left for other tombs."

5. Music

Parallel scenes – an undefined swarming of innumerable Oriental multitudes, a limitless profusion of inextinguishable peoples, an infinitude of crowds (sources of races, fountains of invasions) – were superimposed in diverse ways on the initial rhythm. Some conveyed death sentences and complex luxury. Others imparted the calm of sages and the cosmic charity of Ascetics.

Paintings – with rain and mountainous perspectives that symbolised Infinity – attested it with their calligraphic designs. The music persisted in its multiple rhythms in which all individuality was lost. How could one remain *a person* in the face of the antiquity of ancestors, the infinitude of their wisdom and the multitude of individuals? Lose yourself! It was time to have done with Tradition, Race, the ancient Land, and ineluctable principles.

6. Cinema

On shores abandoned by unwholesome crabs, thoughts of inauspicious destiny gather eagerly around the mossy rocks moulded by the waves into indescribable phallic forms, no doubt serving to stimulate the reveries of the women bathers in swimsuits of blue, red, green, yellow, black or white according to whatever destiny determines their lives or in accordance with the colour of their lovers' ties.

If Stobel wanders down to the beach, among those bathers in eccentric or photogenic swimsuits, it is not that he is tormented by the desire for women nor is he enchanted by the climate. He merely wishes to fulfil the destiny he set himself. Before leaving he gazes at the mossy rocks with their phallic forms, at the thighs and bottoms of the bathers, at the greyish-white or bronzed (depending on the direction of the setting sun) sand or at the sea where

mermaids – for too long dead – seem to wake to the
breath of destinies as deep as the Pacific Ocean.

7. Navigation

Three continents had tired him out and now he has his
eyes on a yacht sailing for Oceania. He had never managed
to escape from himself. No matter what they say, the
world isn't so big. When he arrived in Manilla, his first
portent of the East, Stobel realised how his wanderings had
served only to take him to places he had already known.
He knew that even if he fled to the South American forests
or the Siberian Steppes, he would still only end up in
encountering what he had just escaped from.

These were his thoughts as he reclined in a deckchair on
the bridge of his yacht. He contemplated these tropical
lands and this sea that reminded him that he had already
sailed these seas, on a journey from Singapore to Hong
Kong.

His thoughts were hemmed in. One can only draw
curved lines on the terrestrial sphere which, as they extend,
forever meet with themselves. At such intersections we
always encounter what we have already seen. Unwilling to
return to the old ways, neither could he bow anew to the
perpetual and disconcerting civilisations of the Orient.

He thought he had been round the world and experienced all (or almost all) that civilisation and thought had to
offer. He had no wish to return, but equally he did not
want to stay.

"Through determination and wealth, I have gained pos-
sessions. I have followed my destiny, but now my will is at
a standstill. Henceforth let me be at the mercy of things!
Let me be dependent on the eventuality of circumstance!"

At Palembang he found a bar up for sale. Stobel bought
it. Then he disposed of the rest of his fortune, making a
gift of his yacht to the captain who has since traded in sea-
slugs with the gourmet-mandarins of Shanghai.

You can imagine that he might have become an opium-smoker, an alcoholic, an ataxic, or else that he might have got married and had children who would go to college in Melbourne, or perhaps be converted to the Catholic religion. It hardly makes any difference.

In any case this is a completely boring story. Fortunately it's finally over. Whether you liked it or not, I couldn't give a monkey's.

★★★★★

first published in Raymond Queneau: *Contes et propos* (1981)
French original © Editions Gallimard 1981
translated by Krzysztof Fijalkowski and Michael Richardson

★★★★★

RAYMOND QUENEAU: (Le Havre 1903 – Paris 1976) left the Surrealist Group in 1929 for 'strictly personal reasons'. Thereafter maintained a calculated silence, combined with occasional ironical or cynical asides, notably the disillusioned novel, *Odile* (1937), on the subject of surrealism. While for the surrealists he was too embroiled in establishment literary politics to entirely satisfy them, the whole of his work remains deeply imbued with surrealist ideas. He was a founder of OULIPO and Satrap at the College of 'Pataphysics.

RENÉ CREVEL:

1830

Straight lines go too quickly to appreciate the pleasures of the journey. They rush straight to their target and then die in the very moment of their triumph without having thought, loved, suffered or enjoyed themselves.

Broken lines do not know what they want. With their caprices they cut time up, abuse routes, slash the joyous flowers and split the peaceful fruits with their corners.

It is another story with curved lines. The song of the curved line is called happiness. And so, of all the years of the Christian era, 1830 was the best one in which to live. Three out of the four numbers that designated it were round.

Slender and with fine cheeks, 8 makes a bow, 3 is the number of love, not because it adds up the elements indispensable to any sentimental tale, but with its two curls it recalls, like a literary sister, the locks of hair which women in the last century kept preserved to offer as presents to their lovers. In the circle of its symbol, zero is the most comforting image of the void, since by emptiness it gives us a notion of infinity.

1830, then. Romanticism in its despair impervious to grand words and beautiful phrases, as the egg in its shell is no less rounded than the bottom of Alfred de Musset's high hat, no less rounded than the hem of crinolines, the bun of chignons, the globes of breasts and shoulders, in the evening between muslin sheets, no less round than the mouth of the pistols that on at least one night would give the young men of the day the hope of a proud death and which, grandiloquent temptation having passed, look so good on a mantle-shelf next to a sepia toned photograph in a round frame.

1830, the only year in which the lightning deigned to fall in a ball of fire and roll around the earth; 1830, when the balloons rose into the sky; when apples shone even brighter than usual on the trees in the country; 1830, and for 365 days drunkards renounced their usual zigzags and formed clever curves on the paths; 1830, and France concocted a revolution to get a more rotund king, a king whose name made the same sound in the mouth as the casks rolling along the cobblestones.

1830. The flowers that Athénaïs gathers in her garden are also round. Athénaïs is a young woman with a captivating mouth and she walks arm in arm with a near neighbour, a young man called Agénor. Athénaïs talks ceaselessly and Agénor, who is never able to get a word in edgeways, finds her truly full of life.

But what is the meaning of this sudden chiming?

Agénor interrupted the chattering.

"Athénaïs."

"Agénor"

Athénaïs does not walk but rather skips along. Athénaïs knows how to pronounce the name of her knight in a pretty way, Athénaïs rolls her eyes sweetly. Her feminine charm caused Agénor to forget the chiming which caused him a momentary start. Agénor believed himself to be stupid, but since he thought he was in love, he tried to become eloquent.

"Athénaïs, let's gather red peonies for your blue opaline vase."

Athénaïs makes a bow and there is a fresh pealing of bells. Agénor feels he is losing his head. He would not have been surprised had it become detached from his shoulders and rolled along the fine gravel to the feet of his companion. He put his hands to his neck, doubtless to make sure that it was still firmly held down, and because Athénaïs was looking right at the whites of his eyes, he asked her, to conceal his confusion, if she wanted to become his wife.

A rose hid her mouth which fortunately served to conceal her smile. There was a yes, a yes all rounded out: the true 'yes' of happiness.

On the evening of their wedding, the breast of Athénaïs was discernable beneath the lace of her slip. Agénor mused about her ankles, her calves, the legs of his 'wife' – those legs he had never seen.

Ah, fashion! A noble boy had brought a virtuous young lady to the altar and he did not even know the form of the lower limbs of the one who would henceforth carry his name.

But why did Agénor, as Athénaïs slowly undressed, why did Agénor keep thinking about the story of the bell of St Gregorin? One night the clapper of the bell vanished, the devil alone knew how. The following morning, when he pulled the rope and heard not the slightest sound, the sacristan thought he had gone mad. He ran out into the country crying that he would be damned forever for having rung the angelus of silence.

The Angelus of silence, but the angelus of love, Athénaïs, with what tune, this evening, do we play?

The Angelus of love? Athénaïs laughed as her crinoline stirred and jingled. Agénor thought he had married a bell. His position as a husband, a power bestowed on him by Heaven, gave him the right to verify any suspicion, no matter how outlandish. His hand slipped under Athénaïs's dress to feel her legs. But the bride simpered and wanted to escape. He ran after her, grabbed her skirt and tore apart her underclothes. In the fracas, Athénaïs collapsed. What horror and damnation! Agénor finally understood the chiming and the reason for his discomfort and fear. Athénaïs had only one leg, a single peg in the middle of her body.

Could the young husband ever be consoled? Already his horses were saddled. A departure into the dust.

The inhabitants of the little village never knew why, during the fifty years she had been stranded among them, Athénaïs had always insisted on wearing a crinoline until a day came when she was almost a centenarian. A travelling circus passed through the village, in which a one-legged woman was one of the main attractions. Forgetful of her habitual reserve, Athénaïs pirouetted on the bridge and the effort caused her to fall into the river.

The peasants were flabbergasted and let the noble lady float on, her skirts blossoming up with a fine racket as she floated downstream.

With haggard eyes and making a noise that ceaselessly increased, she drifted towards the sea and at Le Havre she banged against the precious wood of a sailing ship and caused it to capsize and ran aground in the land of icebergs where, it was said, she was beatified by a Laplander archbishop who was also a dwarf.

(1926)

*****

originally published in *84*, special number, 1949
reprinted in Claude Courtot, *René Crevel* (1969) Paris:
Seghers

*****

RENÉ CREVEL: (Paris 1900–1935) A founder member of the French Surrealist Group, Crevel soon became distanced because of his contacts with the Parisian fashionable set, but then rejoined around 1928 and remained a key figure until his suicide when, suffering from tuberculosis and disappointed by the Communist Party's treatment of the surrealists, he signed himself off with a suicide note that simply read 'Disgusted'. Two of his novels, *Babylon* and *Difficult Death* have been translated into English but his most important works are his theoretical texts, gathered together in *L'Esprit contre la Raison*.

BENJAMIN PÉRET:

The Country of
Cocaigne

A crying child raised his head towards his father and when he saw the stars in his eyes asked him if happy days would soon come. The answer cheered him up. So he left his father, ran after a removal van and jumped up into the back. He made himself at home inside a wardrobe that was lying on its side and went to sleep.

When he woke the wardrobe had decayed and the movement his head made on awakening detached a large piece of wood which came crashing down on his stomach, breaking and scattering into small fragments on either side of him. He could get out of the van only with difficulty since everything it contained had succumbed to the same sad fate as the wardrobe.

When he reached the driver's seat he noticed that the van was perched on a mountain top with steep slopes on either side leading down into an immense plain where he could make out a few tiny things that moved imperceptibly about. For a long time he had known that toboggans existed. He slid down and a few moments later his head was inside the stomach of a cow which still continued chewing away. Suddenly an engine started up with a roar of thunder. Fear caused him to leap out from his shelter (at his age, too!) in time to see a large ditch opening up next to him. Into it flowed a pale pink boiling liquid which gave off a vapour that resembled water. What was strange was that there were creatures moving about in the liquid, and creatures that could not have been fish since they did not have scales and yet did have paws. Each one carried a little plaque on its back bearing various legends: *Knock before entering; Leave this place as you would like to have found it; Closed for stocktaking; Do what you must; Come what may; Laziness is not a good guide, etc. . .*" He was a bit surprised by this, perhaps with reason. For a long time he followed the bank along the ditch through a cultivated land in which solemn men dressed in braids welcomed him to the land. It was nightfall when he arrived at the side of a vast expanse of water and he had no doubt that he was at the seaside even though he was unable to see any waves. . .

"It's night," he told himself. "There are no waves at night."

He was just starting to fall asleep when two enormous monkeys as white as polar bears introduced themselves to him and cordially shook his hand. They told him they had known about him for some time.

This did not cause him any amazement as he knew that his father, the ambassador to Tokyo, had many friends.

"Do you want a cigar?" he asked amiably.

They accepted and all three of them set sail in a dinghy that came along at their feet.

After navigating for two days they disembarked on a coast bristling with green rocks in a landscape of strange copper coloured vegetation where the plants had leaves as soft as pomades. In this land there lived a multitude of camels as big as sheep and as cuddly as concierge's wool. Everywhere, as far as the eye could see, there were sewing machines, overcoats, blonde women who were naked and trembling with fright, and brown-haired little girls with impudent expressions who held their legs apart as if awaiting the male. There were also old women who cried silently into large silk handkerchiefs. Most especially there were perfumed arms that flew into the air on all sides like dead leaves and breasts that would fall on your head like apples.

The child contemplated this spectacle for a while. Then, taking hold of a breast, he ate it and felt himself becoming strong.

"I am a man," he said, and roared with laughter.

*****
published in Benjamin Péret, *Le Gigot, sa vie et son oeuvre*
(1957)
republished in BP: Oeuvres completès Vol 3 (1979 Eric
Losfeld)
French original © by Librairie José Corti
*****

BENJAMIN PÉRET (Rézé 1900 – Paris 1959) One of
the most uncompromising surrealists, Péret always lived in
accordance with his principles. As a Trotskyist, Péret fought
in the Spanish Civil War and in 1949 founded the 'Union
Ouvrière Internationale'. His distinctions were to hate
'priests, cops, Stalinists and business men' and his hobby
was insulting priests.

ROBERT DESNOS:

Universal Gravitation

One day when it was night a man who was sitting down standing up and lying down on a wooden stone was reading a newspaper which had not been printed by the light of an extinguished candle. The sun was shining in the night in which the thick, black clouds cast a transparent shadow on to the ground. Lightning furrowed the sky without it being possible to see it and the thunder rumbled silently. In the middle of a river, a man was drying his muscular, atrophied limbs. A male woman passing by on the bank in the middle of the stream spoke to him without saying a word: "Leave because it is too late not to stay. Breathe in the beautiful scent of the flowers which smell bad in the full nostrils of your blocked-up nose. Remain a virgin but hasten to father a family."

The man who was a woman spat out to fill his mouth. Dogs and horses sped through the air while the frogs and fishes drowned. A fisherman had a great catch of sparrows and bullfinches. The man who was a woman went together with the woman who was a man to the over-populated desert of large towns and thick forests. The way was littered with the corpses of the victims of nightingales while the lions came softly up to the sedentary travellers to lick their hands and neighed with pleasure when they were given bread, while the dogs miaoued with contentment when they found their oats and the ducks barked when they were offered joints of burnt red meat or an oyster bone by charity. Monkeys laid their eggs in mother-of-pearl caskets and obstetricians had great difficulty in bringing into the world little ostriches.

The man who was a woman was called Camille and the

woman who was a man Marcel or Marcelle. After walking for a long time they felt rested and bravely lay down together along the length of the road. Hercules and Henry III were killing each other in friendship from the heights of the Saint Germain-l'Auxerrois cellar. The Huguenots pursued the Catholics who followed them through the streets. Admiral de Coligny threw a whole family from the sixth floor of his mansion. At the same moment a flock of gazelles emerged from the opening of the stairs. Overwhelmed with terror, Hercules flew up to the bowels of the earth while Henry III stood on the bell tower to pray to Buddha and the angels so they would purify the earth. Meanwhile the man and the woman stopped beside the gas jet and quickly advanced along avenue de l'Opéra. They were completely naked beneath their heavy clothes. The crowd surged into the avenue, which was deserted. The applause was so loud that Camille and Marcel felt the need to go to sleep. A clock which had stopped was the only thing that made a noise with its ticktock. The moon cast the shadow of stars on the pavement which was cut up by a plough. A harvester cut down the wheat with a broad swing of the scythe as he enthusiastically attacked a haymaker who sowed rye-grass under his feet. Camille and Marcelle finally noticed a man who, as they approached, lifted up his skirt so as to improve his dance while his wife, with her hands in her trouser pockets, whistled a nice tune.

"Oh!" Camille asked Marcel. "Have you heard the smell of violets?"

and he replied by asking if she had seen the wonderful song.

And so Henry III, Hercules, Camille, Marcelle and the man and woman, the Catholic family, the harvester and the haymaker all sat down in a circle around the square table.

Glory be to God in Hell.

★★★★★

published in the edited collection *Robert Desnos* (L'Herne)
© Editions de l'Herne, 1987

★★★★★

ROBERT DESNOS (Paris 1900 – Terzin, Czechoslovakia 1945) Founder member of French surrealism who made decisive contribution to its early development, contributing the important novel *La Liberté ou l'amour!* and other texts of spontaneous bedazzlement. Deported by the Gestapo in 1943, he was to die soon after being liberated from Buchenwald.

JEAN FERRY:

Letter to an Unknown Person

We have just arrived in a rather strange land and I am not at all sure this letter will ever reach you. In actual fact I'm not even sure we have arrived because the earth still seems to be swaying under our feet even though we have disembarked from the ship. The 'Valdivia' herself vanished the moment I put my foot on the quay and I have no idea if I will ever see her again. There does not seem to be a Post Office on this island, any more than there are any inhabitants, so I do not know if it is possible to send this letter or how it would reach you, no more than I know who to send it to, but even so I hope you will one day receive it. And where are my travelling companions? I really don't know, but surely they can't just have vanished. There must be some trace of them somewhere, so I shall set off in search of them. I suppose I will find them but one never knows and for now I prefer to write this letter. After I have written it I will not have much else to do, for it seems that this is an island. I'm not sure about that, although when I arrived I did follow the coast and returned to my point of departure two days later. But yesterday there had been a high mountain with smooth slopes in the middle of the island, and yet today it no longer seems to be there.

What I particularly wanted to tell you was that you must never come to this country. People here suffer, you see, not from hunger, or thirst, and the houses are quite nice once you get used to them. No, what is really unpleasant is the mode of existence. I've never been able to cope with it. The solitude is too overbearing for my taste. Its not too bad during the day but at night. . . the sound of thousands of invisible breaths is astounding and, I don't mind telling you, frightening. It is difficult to explain, but you know what I mean. You must have experienced the sensation of stepping forward in the darkness, thinking that it is the last step on the stairs only to find that it isn't there. You are thrown momentarily into a state of complete disarray. Or when, in your bed, no matter how much care you take before falling asleep, your legs suddenly slacken and you fall you don't know where. Ah well, in this country it's always like that. Everything is made of the same material as that absent step. I tell you, it is impossible to get anywhere here and you must not come to this country.

I am only here myself through my own stupidity. No one warned me. The 'Valdivia' was en route to Melbourne. How could the captain have been so mistaken about it? But one night as the Southern Cross rocked in the sky, I was complaining to the chief-steward that we were wrong to let ourselves be taken in but he affirmed that the same thing happened every journey. And so here I am, completely alone, and I no longer desire anything, except that I have a strange feeling that it is absolutely essential for me to escape. But how? I shall certainly attend to the fact soon, and still have a few things to do, but tomorrow I shall go in search of the quay. Perhaps the 'Valdivia' will have returned. She must sometimes do so, since she has already been here once. I have rather lost count of the days, as there is no calender here, you know, and I have no wish to play Robinson Crusoe with a pole and notches. The only thing is I did not have all this white hair when I was on board the 'Valdivia'. I must start again tomorrow and go in search of the quay, I have waited for too long now.

During the day the streets are miserable and rainy, but that is not surprising since no one lives there. But at night, what a racket! Even without anyone being here, please note. I am a sober sort of person, and recognise that these houses have not been constructed by themselves. As they say, there must be a reason. But it is a terrible task, in this country where things do not happen as they do elsewhere. Since my arrival, I think I have been too busy to ask why and suspect that I shall never find out. It would be better to go back and look for the quayside.

Please understand, no one here wants to be disturbed. In fact I think that is why they never go outside. That seems simple enough, but how to explain it? Oh, they don't mean me any harm and if I stay here long enough no doubt I shall get to know them, but I always get the feeling that someone is there behind me, even though when I turn around no one is ever there. It gets on your nerves after a while. For instance, at this very moment one of them is looking over my shoulder as I write, but it is better not to turn around. I'll finish this letter tomorrow, for I cannot write while I am being watched. I'll go again to look for the quay. I am not unhappy, I assure you, and yet who would not like to see his best friend here? There are some people who would be happy on this island, but I am not one of them.

A little fantasy in life, okay, but when it comes to the point that you no longer know if the sun in the sky is that of midday or midnight, or when the fierce wind that blows over the plains wraps around your personality like the coloured bands around an American barber's pole, well, then, sir, I say, "Enough is enough!" Tomorrow, I have decided, I shall find the quay. My greatest fear is that the 'Valdivia' will return for me at the very moment I am not there and will depart without the crew having realised that I am here.

★★★★★

published in *Le méchanicien et autres contes* (1951) Paris: Gallimard
French original © Editions Gallimard

★★★★★

JEAN FERRY (Capens 1906 – Paris 1974) In 1930 Jean Ferry signed up as a radio operator on a steamer going around the world. This had a decisive effect on his sardonic view of the world, which he never appears to have quite convinced himself actually exists. He established contact with the surrealists through the agit-prop 'Groupe Octobre'. His passions were the cinema and the work of Raymond Roussel. He earned a living as a scriptwriter for directors as distinguished as Buñuel, Malle and Franju, although perhaps only his *Manon* (directed by Clouzot) contains a really personal edge. His work on Roussel, on the other hand, is magisterial, especially *Une Étude sur Raymond Roussel* (1953).

GEORGES LIMBOUR

The Hand Of Fatma

There are evenings when the sky has the colour and taste of ash. Like an undefined sadness, it has a softness of this infinitely fine dust – so much that one feels there could be none finer in the whole world – that suggests it is matter definitively consumed.

Has it given all its smoke and aroma? A female finger, dipped in a vase containing the remains of great passionate ardour descends from the sky and traces – very lightly – a sign on the brow.

O mockery of purple, braziers of blood, it was on just such an evening that I came to know the hand of Fatma.

I had been out in the fresh air and it had not yet got cold. Having spent a long time in open spaces, whether sea or desert, it is a luxury to be able to take refuge in towns with narrow streets which provide a fragile fortress against the assaults of the infinite. There is such a sense of security against the boundless there even if the murmur of the waves or the silence of the sands still pursue one through tortuous corridors. The winds, despite their subtle spirit, are themselves lost in the vestibules of this labyrinth and, unable to find a way through, whistle and turn in turbulence like demented dervishes. They will not break through the walls of this den in which life still pulsates in the shadow of humanity's black sun. Man feels ignominiously concealed there. The small crooked streets are like blindfolds which apply the night to eyes burned by wide-open spaces; the narrow streets resemble the thoughts of idiots and calm the anguish of those who take refuge there and the villages they form are compressed brains of cretins, insensitive to the light and in sympathy with what is subterranean. O, brain of the idiot of whom not one finger has followed the astonishing twists, and of which no hand has felt the weight; you are the twin brother of this village never conceived by an architect, never perceived by the clear vision of the sorcerer and was only contemplated, high in the sky, by the fleet eyes of the falcon.

For me who had carried the weight of the sun on my back for the whole day as a soldier carries his sack and, by the end of the afternoon, had felt it slowly slip, with its straps released from my loins, relieving itself of the objects one by one; gold and diamonds trickled down to my ankles from this split sack until the night fell, and I now wandered in streets which became ever more narrow, on a soft and pliant earth that was a sort of mould formed by the age-old decomposition of fruit peelings and dung scattered by the religious march of donkeys. A blue smoke filled the air: tobacco, incense, fires of straw and twilight mist.

On each side of the alleys, there were stalls in which there were neither cobblers, nor knife grinders, nor money changers nor usurers, but women similar to them, who also had inconsequential trades and little shops, women as sordid as them, insensitive and rapacious, and with souls long since tied to pawnbrokers.

From these stalls, where one gave oneself up to the dismembering of the human body, I heard the sounds of hammer and anvil, the rattling of chains, the sighs of the tortured, the blasts turning the embers red, the executioner's laughter (for you know how much the low voice of an old woman counting the stitches of wool can seem, in certain circumstances, to be orders to kill) and there above all of these shops hung a blood soaked sign: a red hand, the hand of a child that was neither male nor female and yet roused feelings of the most dejected and criminal love.

This open and extended hand was very often painted on a wall suggesting that a blood-stained criminal had fleetingly passed by.

It seemed that the criminal had become weaker as he continued down the street, for there were several stops and his hand was printed on the walls in so many striking places I called "stations". No doubt his hand itself must be bleeding for it had so much blood in reserve, capable of printing through the whole night along the length of the street, his suffering like a rotary printing press at night. As I walked swiftly along I thought I would catch him up. With what great thirst for his suffering would my eyes plunge into his eyes which have just known the last love, which has seen and desired death, and doubtless await it for themselves. In his expression I would see how he carried a horrible corpse. No, it will not be the cowardly fugitive one might expect, with the most hypocritical of shifty looks, the most cautious of steps, the most humble of smiles, but proud and with forehead already in the clouds above these accursed houses, lips forever purified and denying the kiss, already in a faraway country, scornfully leaving behind only a heap of flesh, one of those women he would not approach again in his life. I saw him as if coming out of a garden of olives, already betrayed by his crime, and pardoning him.

To meet up with him! He must have been stopped somewhere by the heavy pack saddle of a white donkey. As soon as I heard some cries, it was he! What were they doing to him? I dreamed of going to his aid. Had he fallen? Had he sought refuge in an old woman's dark house and had she, in her cowardice, alerted the crowd by her cries? He would have preferred to be stoned than have such a humiliating hiding-place.

There was no trace of his steps on the ground, his feet glided along rather than walked. Only his hand on the walls, marking his misery in the same way as insects or butterflies that stick to the walls to die.

By the time I had came to the boundary of the district my head was imbued with the smell of crime and the clamour of murder but I had encountered only dark and distracted faces which stared inquisitively at me, as though

I might myself have been the criminal. I compared my hands with those exhibited on the plaster and it was obvious that mine were longer and not as wide. But the hands of the people I encountered, the hands that I tried to detect in their sleeves where they were hiding as though ashamed of themselves and their fate, had the same form as the bloody imprint. The evidence suggested to me that I was cast adrift in a far away and hostile country in the midst of a barbarous tribe whose women wore the golden fetish on their chests, the sinister hand, like a miraculous sign of their power.

A palmist would have noticed it – though how could there be any among these brutes whose hands were without lines, polished by the rocks with which they stoned each other as brothers – these painted hands with palms as barren as a dead world, these were hands with no destiny. They belonged to the void, they were the hands of the inhuman night, impatient to seize a man and throw him down on to a bed without sheets from which the prostitute would toss him senseless into the large ditch which the body half filled.

I had been seeking you through part of the night, criminal, until I realised you did not exist, that you were only the phantom of a crowd fleeing it's ghastly cowardice.

Above the dismal shops, the hands opened and caused names to fall like dice: Zaire, Fatma, Olamém and the passer-by had only to collect the body.

I could feel those frightful hands pointing out my own hands, as if they were their enemies, that I hid in my pockets at the moment when a jawbone, erupting into an infernal laugh, opened wide under my eyes, with gold teeth that gleamed in the gloom like candelabra in a cathedral.

You speak of the hand of Fatma, my friends, but you do not know the terrible power of this hand, the hand of monsters that menace you and seduce you with their subterranean access, their metallic splintering, their inhuman grotesqueness of idols. It is the severed hand of a woman with the face of Isis, a tigress face completely devoured by leprosy to the extent that one might think that if one were to lie beside this idol and let one's living flesh mingle with its unreal matter, once the frontiers of horror have been crossed, one will pass from form to form beyond the human and from metamorphosis to metamorphosis to accomplish, in the anguish of an impossible return, the most terrible journey to the depths of darkness.

At the threshold of a shop, before a drawn curtain that hid her sanctuary, there stood a young idol, so proud and arrogant, with ankles, arms, neck and forehead calmly and fixedly bronzed, with eyes lengthened by make-up and spread like the wings of the bird of eternity, and with a face engraved with sacred signs and blue tattoos so that she appeared to be less of flesh than of wood, stone and metal.

At that moment the alley with its covering of waste seemed to me the way of Goddesses and Solar Myths. "Isis," I called out. "Isis in illuminated temples, at the threshold of deserts, in solitary places haunted by jackal, lion and falcon, you are less powerful and less dazzling than in these alleys which are your private abode, where you take your repast of men, goddesses who invite the Sun down to the carpet and curtains of your darkened lair."

Some of the women proffer their arms through the prison bars which prevented them from escaping. Others had silver rings on their ankles and wrists that secured them to their chapels.

And I saw lions lying at the feet of these whores.

*****

published in Georges Limbour *Soleil bas* (1972)
French original © Editions Gallimard, 1972
translated by Guy Flandre, Michael Richardson and Peter Wood

*****

GEORGES LIMBOUR (Courbevoie 1900 – Cadiz 1970) Traveller, sportsman and storyteller, although Limbour was a founder member of the French Surrealist Group group discipline was alien to his temperament. Frequent travels kept him at a distance from the group, but a scornful attitude towards Breton ensured his expulsion in 1929, accused of 'scepticism' and 'literary coquetterie'. His subsequent life proved how inaccurate were such accusations, since Limbour scattered his rich texts here and there with little concern for a literary reputation. His active life came to an end in 1970 when he drowned whilst deep-sea diving.

CAMILLE GOEMANS:

The Inimitable Bird

The inimitable bird was sustained by its own flight. With the imposing form of its head and limbs it resembled the toubek of Chile and the great toucan of Spain, but it was distinguished from them by an astonishing wingspan of spangled feathers, whose sparkling form resembles mica, and by the power of its song which, if we can believe the tales told by the nomadic populations which migrate through the glacial slopes, surpasses anything one can imagine. A great many legends circulate about this creature. But in the tales it is difficult to distinguish what results from impersonal observation, which is consequently impartial, in the accounts of those who have seen it pass overhead once or twice (for no one has ever seen it land) from the feelings of dread or admiration (often both) which surround it, familiar to those unstable lands which had more than all others been delivered up to the mysterious elements we have hunted from the territory of our civilisation, and whose complexity defies analysis. For the traveller, as he sees perils and natural difficulties increase, could not fail to be affected by such subjects of sudden and unreasoned fear and the abundance of others encountered on the way, which were divulged and communicated by the sentiments of the natives themselves before he could legitimately prepare himself against them, and which he could in fact only understand with the aid of signs.

We stirred ourselves into action at the first tidings we received that a shepherd had noticed traces of the flight of the inimitable bird several miles away from our camp. It was only as the sun was setting that we arrived at the place we had been told about, where we discovered, in the four hours it had taken the message to reach us, as henceforth others of its species would be honoured, as its equals are honoured, with the name *arrow*. In fact it is certain the traces remain visible only for a while and in a just a single place (generally marked by the ashes of a certain aromatic and little known fern), casting their eyes at the height and in the direction of the gaze determined by the height and direction of the gaze by which they had been detected.

A curtain of bronzed clouds rose across the horizon which, in this land, marks the passing of day into a nocturnal twilight whose brightness is barely tolerable for our occidental eyes, even though they are accustomed to bright electric lights invincibly, closing in the way certain varieties of flower close onto their fleshy prey, and all attempts to obtain at least a photographic image of the spectacle which, by definition, we were unable to see, remained unsuccessful since the films burned one after the other, and no professional trick was able to correct the defective means of mechanical investigation. It was thereby impossible for us to establish the presence of the inimitable bird's track, or of the bird itself, or to satisfy the disinterested curiosity which caused us to undergo so many dangers and which allowed us for close on a month to patiently accept the inconvenience of a stay in which each hour could, although we did not begrudge the fact, have been placed in the balance with several years of the greater certainties of a more normal existence.

*****

first published in Camille Goemans *Oeuvre 1922–1957*
(1970) Brussels: André de Ruche
French original © Editions Labor

*****

CAMILLE GOEMANS (Louvain 1900 – Brussells 1960) Founder of Belgian Surrealist Group, Goemans was the link between Brussells and Paris during the twenties since he worked at the galerie Jacques-Callot in Paris from 1926. He went on to establish his own gallery promoting surrealist painters before it was forced to close in 1930.

JOË BOUSQUET:

The Return

I.

It was as though her eyes sought out their secrets by entering my own. So young was she, our kisses opened directly onto fairytales she made up. But it is not to try to see her again that I have returned to this place.

Whenever I gazed upon her, or she turned her smile up to me, my soul seemed to hover in the space between us. The roses in the garden would float up out of their sleep, reflecting the horizons' unmade heart across my giddiness; and the furthermost silence brought back my dreams to life. The whole universe was placed between me and my heart. Happiness could gaze upon us, and yet our eyes had no way of bringing it any closer.

I was away for but a few months. The selfsame dance whose refrain is now on my lips comes back in every heart on a Sunday, ceaselessly offering up, between the wilting plane-trees, its mirror of pure water to the stars. Once music has recaptured the lost necklaces of every girl in love, once silence has crept back out of the silence, shall I find my way again without having to ask whom it is I have forgotten?

Already everything is so remote that her name alone encompasses my entire youth.

That name quivers in my voice, too trivial to forget, that child's name with its hint of silence, which stares deep into my heart, prompting recollection. . .

Until such time as the oars bury that song which mocks me with its tale of a final evening on the highway where our folk like to dance, the highway of farewells.

49

I was aware of an infinite depth about the way she spoke, as she counted off for me the dates of some distant year, without thinking, one arm about my neck; her poor face seemed to abstract itself from my wayward awareness, hiding away in my eyes as if to escape my icy heart. I would ask myself, what kind of shadow is it that seems to weep alongside those words she comes out with, whenever she stares at me? The spectre of my life! I watched in disgust as that spectre grew larger, edging up closer to me in its wildness. . .

In the villages they tend to stay up late dancing, on the feast day of the crazy. I recall that I used to slip away unnoticed, for I was already well lost before I actually left. That strange hour in which I pondered my rebellion has crept back tonight to make my voice embrace itself. A dense fog comes drifting through the fruit trees. The roses raise up the slumbers of the earth in their spiky veils. On this searing night of truth, I could hear my pain steal my life, which had hitherto lain safe in its enchanted depths, from me.

When I reached the end of a path chosen quite by chance, the first thing I noticed was that the wind had changed direction and was now sweeping what seemed like dead leaves from bygone years, piling them up at my feet. I bent down and touched the grass along the slopes. Taken aback by the whispering of familiar haunts, I suddenly imagined my body might be a cloak for their secret.

I think I must already have been singing. My voice stole back my soul from the gods. . . Oh, that sweet minute plucked from the past and secreted within the hour of my return! With each step, the paths that lay behind me had been closed off. My life turns into its own song, indistinguishable from the dusk. Death assigns us a name, surprised by our yearning for a pure space which has been betrayed: it is like a woman in love who steals away through the dementia of the rose-bushes.

The winds of time go begging, plundering. . . The soul of nightfall had merged into the indifference on the face of things. And there was I, staring at myself, all sense of direction lost... A man, a poor countenance in which everything disowns itself. The awkward mistruth of a shadow. I gazed upon the earth and saw that a body, in its tender faithlessness, had located it in the sky.

A splendid scarf of blood, looming above the abyss. Then came that moment when the evening star draws the pastures open. The desert of my gaze casts light across the slopes. Weightless, the night trembled amid the drifting reeds, cradling the vines at my feet and the almond trees across which rode the dark winds.

The branches, the pathway, like a young girl's fetching smile, tore the veil from my heart, unfurling the immensity in my eyes. Each leaf borne off by autumn attracted a look, a cry of pain, from the untamed air. I trod stealthily on, gradually more aware of the marvellous pain I was suffering.

II.

How quickly passers-by move on! There must be a celebration somewhere. No body troubles to look at my face. I feel as if the thoughts of other people were trying to seal up my eyes.

Now the night's breath responds to the sea, which I can scarcely hear from here, as it reminisces about its shipwrecks. In a song's fading, my name is erased, amid the blossoms of windswept beauties. Is it really the love in my eyes which restores to life the tamarisks, the rooftops, the roses, when everything on which I look escapes from me into my eyes? In vain the beauty of the sunset draws tenderness about itself... Its universe could only describe itself by casting me out of my dream; and I know there is no one waiting for me, anywhere. The whole secret of the path I am following lies in the things I leave behind me forever.

Through the deafness of the night, the village risks sending out the same covert flame. Each voice has lapsed into the all-encompassing silence: its astonishing sweetness persuades me I should return to the petalled shadows of the farmhouses; where branches bearing lovely smiles float back from afar to merge into my dreams; across the slopes whose secret my heart is learning by heart.

Across my dreamy legends, a fragile homeland reaches out to its exiled lilies. Skylines, shorelines, caresses, the countryside where I was born was fashioned by my heart and my eyes, as they swept across the fields, the daylight and all those hamlets, more mysterious still.

That murmuring in which the light hid from itself, those smells, that trickle of voices came drifting downwards from the sky, which my emotion saw in rainbow colours, tracing its salts in the cycle of its seasons. An immense body, encircling my delirium, a body made of wind and sunlight, crouching and stretching, encompassed the existence of the slightest human echo. I knew I could identify it in whatever direction I looked, since it would pluck the same fruit for my eyes from the least obvious horizons; and then a smile waylaid that nostalgia wherein my childhood races after me. As if taking its bearing from my own, a woman's life offered the promise of fresh spaces to my infinite desire never to die.

And once the sweet ray of light had split apart amid flashes of bright flesh, my eyes could trace the shadows of desire upon a hidden countenance.

The laughter of young girls was incapable of describing happiness.

Love lay over their beauty like a summer's dawn upon sleeping eyes. The dance, with all its reminiscences of love, had stored its silver heart among the stars.

Nights of fire where flowers would crowd in, bringing silence. Eyes which would invent the time of year, within that blinding purple clash of atmospheres in which life disputed its own rights ... When one is too close to daybreak, which erases all things, one has no idea how to wait, one doesn't even realise that one is waiting.

Hands blindly following their caresses! ... They con-

52

versed in low tones. Each name died away in my wayfarer's song, and the secret of that loveliest language of all was lost forever.

It is in my heart that oblivion holds sway over the eyes of those women who are no longer with us. I couldn't even work out how to ask which way to go.

III.

Why did life never identify its own reflection in my eyes? Everything on which I gazed had already abandoned me for good; thus it was that happiness passed me over, in songs, in farewells. . . It was the wind over the tombstones which nullified our words as we paused at the edge of everything, distanced even from ourselves, with the world opening its eyes anew in my dream.

Saddest of loves in which we were being dreamt by someone remote whom I could not trace and in whose shadow the memory of that evening comes back to me. Happiness has only ever been betrayed by its own shadow. . . Rocky hollow, thatched cottage or rat's nest, this is where you'll find bitterness, this is the summit at which the wanderer realises that what he has been seeking has meanwhile taken on the aspect of everything he has been trying to disown, and wonders if he might be on the verge of dying. Never again shall my sandals leave prints along the ruts. Never again shall children point me out in my black jacket or my corduroy trousers at the crossroads where I used to ask my way.

I cannot distinguish the road back from my own shadow. Oh, beauty of this evening which my heart makes even purer than the sky, where the stars pick out their partners, stealing me back from those who have given up waiting for me; its darkest song has reached its climax in my suffering.

. . .Wrapped within her smile, she brought me such bliss, and her child's gaiety was nourished by my life.

When her graceful eyes had reunited us in that great

flight of evening, the stammerings of love sought the shadows of our lips, as each avowal, exposing the nakedness of the soul, brought our thoughts closer to silence, expiring once it had voiced its secret.

Her smile was a naked dream. It was her purity that made my soul visible; while I could just make out a slight heartbeat, offering little resistance to me at the black core of the abyss and repeating, each time more softly, the name she had given me in the act of love.

Such at least are the thoughts in which a former life is laid bare, the gold gleaming at the bottom of the goblet too heavy to lift up. For in that time of youth, the dream of love would float on a sombre stream, which recollection has now drunk dry. How strange it all is! The trees of a separate highway trembled in the background of our impatience. Did her forehead bow down to obey the forehead of that evening which once more I see in my dreams? It was as though she had sought through me to be free of her own reality.

And her smile, telling me that space has been found anew.

. . . .

Her smile has chosen its giddy path within my eyes. And truly she is there. Her look draws out my secrets from within the mystery of the stars.

In that far place she had a name, Anne or Marion, I can no longer be sure. Was she pretty? Her features memorised my childhood, and made my whole life transparent.

That face wherein I felt invoked, I confess to myself in a low voice that it had circled about my entire existence.

Ah! Then my every thought was synonymous with her life. She was always daydreaming, and I recall how her slightest smile would cut short her gaze. An unreal sadness loomed over her beauty.

In a single smile, she would confide the secret of her tears to my loving gaze.

The whole miraculous structure of her life was founded upon my own.

I would stare at her as though through a glimmering dawn: it was the purity of my own life which I was drinking from her eyes.

Yet a mysterious gate lay open within her shadow; and all my flesh was aware of black pathways and hovels and the silence one observes when the dead are near.

In the half-dark where her memory pursued me, voices fell silent beneath the clouds at my heels; the same fire shines through everyone else's eyes, and they all seem to wait to hear love spoken.

It is beneath such candles that the song is taken up again: there was once a girl who danced so much she lost her heart. Her mouth was fed on smiles alone. . .

The loveliest of the stars has raised up the night so as to blind me with its infinite presence: my gaze is submerged, like a silver ring tossed into the flood of my heart.

IV.

These new silences run so deep that I know my being must have changed its secrets.

I have thrown away the tiny lamp which cast a shadow as long as my entire journey. What might I not rediscover if I am now to be lost?

A ringing sound rises up from the links of chains slipped by the night. Now other words, words of the tenderest kind, slip reluctantly down from hair that is loosed. A path is quickly beaten across the rubble of the prison.

The rose of risk blossoms within my flesh, unfettered from my shadow: a single life has enfolded each gaze and all the silence within its wings.

The world soars up anew, illumined in a silken giddiness, and only the sky remains to bear witness to its artifice. Harbouring deep colours, a hand, raised over the very air I am breathing, dies as it persuades me to stay alive.

This is surely no time to try to track myself down to the place where I am standing. So that I may be free of this body which the earth insists on taking back, the sky, the sky in all its lightness, has absorbed me within the sweetness of belief.

The bulrush of love might point towards a shadow, were it to move. Mistakenly, some absence or other reverberates in the hidden depths of my vague tenderness. . .

My gaze is reborn from its shadows and steals across the plane-trees, the balcony and the year's array of flowers, whose profound truth has found me out at last. The same solitary star exhausts itself to the east of every single thing. This is the land where everything depends upon my life, where the one thing to inhibit love would be an excess of love.

A new world, capable of surprising me, a world in which every being can know itself and find its apotheosis in my desires. . . Caught up in their own brightness, the silvery plane-trees become marvellous visions in the night. . . In all those places which once nourished my thoughts, I see tears welling up in colourless eyes as they dream about my life. . .

. . .She has no idea at all how to make herself known. The delicacy of her approach is enough to dispel all hint of a storm. The translucency of those glances which her presence sets alight for me is like a candle wherein life caresses its eyes and selects its zephyr, reviving all those beauties in which my naked soul revealed itself to chance. . .

. . .Kisses, pink and various, and then faces.

Here is the age old dream of a gaze in which the spirit can drink itself in, and, absolving the daylight from its allegiance to my shadows, carry off the arc of my madness towards an iris no one can foresee.

Something like trepidation tells me there must exist more light within the silence of things, within the fear of seeing my life's stagnancy disfigure those awakenings as they multiply about me;and I allow myself to be borne away on the winds towards those overflows where love tries to construct some sort of protection for itself. For in between my glances the winds traverse a landscape erased by the dazzling impulse of the flesh, across heather where I read the message of defenceless eyes.

Once there was a face in which the depths of my life were blown away, a face whose smile penetrated me deeper than my own dream.

Whereupon our eyes, true to their sky-blue hue, cast shadows across time.

Myosotis of the look, probing for sunlight in the crevices of time. Yes, I remember my youth. Inside my life, there was always a secondary life hidden away. A brother would peer into my happiness, with a benevolent eye.

His hands drew closer to my heart those unreal fields where love uncovers its chalice. He gazes on life, on the grass in the graveyards, on love as it fades. An hour's brightness floats between us, swollen like a tear about to fall.

The floodwater uncovers the heart of the last of the mermaids. In vain the wind invokes its departed spirits, predicting the death of all things that breathe and shine. My entire happiness is tied up inside my child's apron, and as I walk I shall turn to look back over my shadow's dream.

My cries are like the residue of blood that lingers in a deep wound. The sounds breathe, then die away. An enormous bowl of silence has been filled to the brim.

The world is like some alternative dream in which a heart falls apart; a dream in which the sky closes down its lid upon the secret of all the things we love. I can make out the tracks, the darkening mountainside, even the shape of bodies, as lovely as oblivion, that rivulet in which the blue sky looks for solace. And still that same solitary star exhausts itself to the east of every single thing. Upon the eroded cliffs where I come to my senses, my steps gather up the shadow as it pours down from the sky.

Tonight, the thoughts of the dead are turning back to the earth. I manage to open my eyes again without forfeiting my heart. The trees and the grass at dusk intoxicate my thoughts, inciting them to slip back into the shadow in its natural state.

My soul bares itself at the centre of this nocturnal landscape. Wretched spirit, in thrall to all those lightning flashes, the utter blackness of the sky has paid off your ransom tonight.

Listen, through the composure of the olive trees, a tiny river can be seen: everything it says is addressed to the stars. Through the lattices, the very roses intensify the darkness. If you, the living, were to weep, your tears would strip me of everything.

The necklaces of your eyes describe the distant outline of those windswept villages. Here, complaints may only be voiced in a low murmur. A sad brother would read out what happiness meant. His heart has taken on all my suffering. I would weep softly were he to speak to me about myself.

But it is she whom he best remembers. Ann, or Marion – I forget which name linked her to life on this earth, where her laughter drew together the crowns of all the gods I have ever worshipped. And now her face is heavy with my secret.

I gaze upon her and sense that my life now can go no further. A star shoots bleeding across the skyline, a companion to the black wind. Silence comes sweeping across everything.

*****

First published in *Chantiers* between January and
March 1928
reprinted in Joë Bousquet: *Oeuvre romanesque complète*,
Vol 1.
French original © Albin Michel, 1979
translated by Roger Cardinal
*****

JOË BOUSQUET (Narbonne 1897 – Carcassonne 1950)
Bousquet's life was changed when his spine was penetrated by a bullet in 1918, permanently paralysing him. He came into contact with the surrealists in 1924 and participated in their activities at a distance. Bedridden for the rest of his life, his home in Carcassonne became a place of pilgrimage. His work – novels, poetry, notebooks of musings and a vast correspondence – all serves as part of a quest to come to terms with the consequences of his debility and adds up to a profound exploration of human identity.

SALVADOR DALI:

Reverie

Port-Lligat, 17 October 1931, three in the afternoon

Lunch had just finished and I was about to lie down on a settee, something I was in the habit of doing for an hour and half each day. I will spend the rest of my afternoon working on a very long study of Böcklin which has preoccupied me for quite sometime.

I also want to use my rest period to consider a few things that seem so contradictory, for example and most especially – something particularly noticeable in the work of this painter – the antagonism between the sentiment of death and the complete absence of concern about spacial notions. I am sure to need to take notes during my siesta and so look for something to write on. This proves difficult, not only because of negligence and forgetfulness and so on, but also because I refuse to write (for reasons that have never been clear to me) on paper I have previously used for my notes. I therefore need a fresh notebook especially for the sort of intimations which form suggestions that are not fully thought-out, so as to prevent confusion. Finally I conclude that I will be able to remember everything in detail without taking notes, since I will begin writing immediately after my rest.

First of all I did everything necessary to ensure no interruptions. I gave instructions that I did not want to receive any messages. I went to the toilet and was then impatient to lie down on the settee. I then had a strange notion of the pleasure that awaited me in the bedroom, a notion somewhat different from the rather arduous idea about the contradictions I would have to overcome. As I rush into the bedroom experience a strong erection accompanied by feelings of great pleasure and amusement.

In my room I lay down on the settee. Immediately my erection gives way to a desire to urinate, only faint but still strong enough to make any consideration on the *frontality* of the 'Isle of the Dead' impossible. An absurd situation: that such a feeble wish to urinate could be so irritating, an absurdity so much the greater in that I had a capacity to retain urine for hours when I did not want to be disturbed or wanted to experience the pleasure of urinating profusely. I rejected the idea of getting up, but soon had to accept that there was no alternative and so make a concession and again go to urinate. Only four or five drops came out. I return to the settee, but immediately have to get up again to close the curtain and leave the room in half light. Again I lie down and feel a sense of dissatisfaction, as if something very important was lacking.

I did not have the least idea what it could be, which unsettled me to the extent that I would not be happy until I found out what it might be.

Suddenly, and without in any way forcing any associations, I recalled that, over dinner, I had mentally chosen (as I habitually did) a well-toasted crust of bread, and had taken it to the settee to carefully strip away its crumbs in such a way as to transform the crust into a sort of sludge. Then, even more carefully, I would have chewed it, pitted and compressed it with my teeth into infinite bits and powdered it down into a fine dough. Before swallowing it, working on it still more as I held it on both sides beneath my tongue, in this way experiencing its its faculty to adapt several consistencies in proportion to the amount of saliva. In this way I would be able to make the crust last longer.

As soon as I realised it was this bread I lacked, my unease vanished and I went to look for the crust, which had already been taken from the dining room and left in the kitchen.

I cut another slice, different from what I preferred, much smaller and not toasted, but I took it all the same because of its form, which was a husk. I returned to the settee, now with two crusts and this time nothing seemed to interfere with my deliberations.

I tried to keep my mind as clearly focused as possible on the famous painting of the 'Isle of the Dead'.

I now found it relatively easy to accept the complete lack of spacial difficulties in this painter's work, especially in the 'Isle of the Dead'.

My error was due to the limits I imposed, which had caused me to reduce specific problems to a question of perspective.

The same sense of frontality which had first disturbed me in respect of the painting, indicated an especially well-characterised spatially 'dominant' form.

It seemed essential for my study to be able to establish a system of relativity which would allow me to extinguish (if only fleetingly) the problems of perspective which I had long studied in the work of Vermeer Van Delft and G. de Chirico. I considered the analytical inadequacy of the evolution I perceived of an unconscious sentiment of melancholy in both painters, due to the difficulties of perspective combined with illumination. On this subject I thought concretely of Vermeer's painting 'The Letter'. It was impossible for me to visualise it completely with the lucidity I would have liked. This was due to the emotive significance that was going to arise, becoming extricated from the curtains, in the foreground (to the left) of the paintings in question.

I then felt my now flaccid penis rise up automatically, leaving the small crust I was still hollowing out on the settee. With one hand I played with the hairs above my testicles, while with the other I collected together some of the breadcrumbs taken from the crust. In spite of a few fruitless efforts to return to my thoughts, a completely involuntary reverie started. I located the curtain in Vermeer's painting in a dream of a few days previously. This curtain was identified by its form, place, and especially by its moral and affective connexion with the curtain in the dream which served to hide several small cows, in the depths of a very dark stable where, while lying in the excrement and rotting straw and exhilarated by the stink, I sodomised the woman I loved.

Here Begins the Reverie

I see myself as I now am but considerably older. I have, besides, allowed my beard to grow like that of the Count of Monte Cristo as I remember it in an old lithograph. Some friends had given me the use, for ten days, of a large farmhouse where I intended to finish my study of Böcklin, which would be one chapter in a vast work which I had for the moment entitled *Surrealist Painting Through the Ages*.

In ten days time I would return to Port-Lligat to meet the woman I love who was at present in Berlin, on the track of amorous adventures, as she had been in a previous reverie.

The farmhouse was called 'Windmill of the Tower' and I had stayed there for two months when I was ten years old, in the company of some close friends of my parents.

But the farmhouse in the reverie was slightly different. It seemed to have aged extraordinarily and, here and there, had the feel of ruins. The pool in the garden had become about twenty times bigger. I no longer felt satisfied with its actual location in the garden, surrounded by enormous oaks that hid the sky from view, and so I transported the pond to the rear part of the house where it could be seen from the dining room, along with Böcklinesque sky of clouds and storm, that I recalled having contemplated from this room, which dominated a vast and expansive horizon. The location of the pool had also changed, since I remembered it as being viewed lengthways while in my fantasy it was placed transversally. I saw myself from behind, in the dining room, finishing off my light refreshment of crust and chocolate. I was dressed in clothes of black velvet similar to those worn by the friend who owned the farmhouse when I stayed there as a child with the addition of an extremely prim little cape of white thread pinned to my shoulder by three small safety-pins. With the remains of the crust in my hand I very slowly descended the main stairway of the house which opened onto the courtyard.

The stairs were half in darkness, due to the pre-twilight hour which was accentuated by heavy clouds. As I went down, almost imperceptibly, I could hear the sound of very fine rain. I thought: "What's the point of going down if it's raining." But I continued and found myself in an entrance full of dry leaves emitting a heavy odour of decay which, mingled with a smell of animal excrement that came from the courtyard, caused me a very sweet confusion that allowed my mind to wander.

I emerged from this euphoric state with a very active erotic emotion.

This was due to the fact that my glance encountered the half-open stable door I recognised, without the slightest doubt, as being that of the dream.

But this emotion was accentuated in an extraordinary way, since I noticed the well known presence of the swaying tips of cypress trees which, immediately beyond the stable, in reality separated the court from the meadow in which, in my reverie, I had invented a vast pond.

The emotion caused by the cypress tops resulted in the instantaneous association with another group of cypresses situated in a public square near Figueras called the 'Fountain of the Log'.

In the centre of this group of very old cypress trees thickly planted in a circle had, in the midst of stone seats which had become very drab through wear, there flowed a ferruginous fountain. A small aluminium glass was attached to a small chain. The foliage of the cypresses began almost at ground level and the summits were held together by iron links that formed a dome that served to enclose the fountain within the cypress trees. Inside was absolute shadow, a freshness greatly appreciated by my family. On warm spring evenings, after a Sunday walk, drinks were taken there once we had rested on the fresh and coarse seats. I was only allowed to go near the water after having eaten my bread and chocolate. The fountain was even more rigorously forbidden, except during the hottest time of the year, for when autumn came it became so humid as to be dangerous. As my reverie continued it seemed indispensable to substitute the cypress grove behind the wall of the courtyard with the Fountain of the Log. In the almost complete darkness of the night which had fallen very quickly I saw the extremities of the cypress from 'behind the courtyard wall' come closer together and form a single thick black flame. From the moment I made out the odour of the courtyard to the present I had undertaken the following automatic acts: several times I placed the breadcrumbs, which I had accumulated for a while, into my nostrils. I slowly took them out with my fingers, experiencing some difficulty, as though it was a question of the dirt in my nose. Sometimes it was enough merely to breath out. This was especially pleasant and gave the illusion that it was the dirtiness of my nose, an illusion almost always directly proportional to the greatest lapse of time between the introduction of bread into my nose and its expulsion.

The process of expulsion by breathing was not without annoyance. The ball of bread fell all over the place and as I tried to find it in the folds of my clothes or on the settee this sometimes served to unsettle and almost interrupt my reverie, particularly when (as happened frequently) the bread crumbs fell under my body in such a way that forced me to find it again by arching my body. So I had to get up from the settee. I pressed my body up by my head and feet to allow me to feel all over the settee and finally I found the ball. The closer it was to my feet, the more difficult it was to recover it again through such contortions and a few times, after laborious efforts, I was forced to sit up as I searched round my body, lifting my buttocks in case the ball had fallen directly beneath where I sat. I raised my buttocks in a rather inexplicable way, so that the operation was always done abruptly with some jerks which rarely gave me time to recapture the ball.

I was obliged to perform these jerks several times with the fear that, with each jump, the springs would cause the ball to fall off the settee. Each time this risk caused me to shake with a very perceptible fear, localised in the heart.

Sometimes, as the ball emerged from my nose, I was able to hold it between my nose and upper lip as I projected warm breath from my nostrils, in a way that rendered the ball very warm, and caused it to ooze and slightly soften.

I tried to do all this with one hand (the left) while with my right hand I manipulated my penis which had become considerably harder, although it had still not become erect.

At the precise moment I had the representation (otherwise of an extraordinary visual clarity) of the aluminium mug attached by a chain, I took the ball precipitously from my left nostril and introduced it, with the greatest possible care, beneath my foreskin which my fingers pulled back as I experienced a slight erection which immediately ceased.

Continuation of the Reverie

The same day I encountered the stable from the dream in the farmhouse courtyard, as I took a coffee with a glass of cognac after the evening meal, I conceived a project, in the form of a reverie, which would be realised in my general reverie. I will briefly set down the elements of the sub-reverie. Since it was extremely long and complex this would seem more appropriate than a detailed exposition. I will merely note the general and indispensable details as related to the more general reverie which would be difficult to follow without some of these details. Basically it was a matter of enacting, in dream, an act of sodomy in the stable I identified with the dream. But this time, instead of the woman I loved, an eleven year old girl, Dulita (someone I had known five years before) would be substituted. This girl had a very pale and anaemic face with vibrant but sad and distant eyes, which distinctly contrasted with a body exceptionally well-developed for her age, with a bearing and lethargic gestures I found very alluring.

In order to realise the fantasy of Dulita's sodomisation, in the stable, I needed to invent several stories to establish. the conditions of the dream, for verisimilitude was indispensable to my reverie's unfolding. This is how I proceeded. Dulita's mother, herself a strikingly beautiful woman of around forty, a widow always dressed in black, had fallen madly in love with me and agreed, through her masochism, to my fantasy of sodomising her daughter, and was even ready to help with her complete ardour and devotion.

So I sent Matilda, Dulita's mother, to Figueras to negotiate with Gallo, an old and incredibly unprincipled and experienced prostitute I had known some time before, who I felt was indispensable for Dulita's coming initiation.

Once Matilda, Dulita and La Gallo had moved into the farmhouse, it would be formally forbidden for them to speak to me, or even to communicate with me whether by action or writing. I wanted Dulita to believe I was deaf and dumb, a great scholar whose health would be endangered by the least importunate gesture. Each evening, after the meal, the table was cleared and coffee and cognac served. It was the only meal, in fact the only time of the day, I would spend with Dulita and the two women as, for the rest of the day, I would remain in my room working on my study of Böcklin and would take my other meals there.

It was at this time of the evening, in complete silence and contemplation, that I would transmit, in writing, my requirements relating to the fantasy down to the tiniest detail.

Gallo would be first to receive my orders and the whole responsibility for the execution of all my directives (exact to the point of mania) would lie with her, and she would in turn explain them to Matilda if necessary. But it would be up to her to communicate any details she thought were indispensable.

For the five days Dulita must suspect nothing and would even be fortified with pious readings of extreme chasteness and treated with kindness and love as if she was preparing for her first communion which would in fact take place very soon. On the fifth day, two hours before sunset,

Dulita would be taken to the fountain of the cypress grove. She would be given bread and chocolate and La Gallo, helped by Matilda, would then initiate Dulita in the grossest and most brutal way. She would be aided by a plentiful supply of pornographic cards which I would carefully choose beforehand.

The same evening Dulita would learn everything from La Gallo and her mother: that I was not a deaf-mute, and that in three days time I would sodomise her in the filth of the cow shed. For the next three days she must behave as though she knew nothing about it. It would be absolutely forbidden for her to make the slightest allusion to it (that is, Dulita would know that I knew that she knew). Until we entered the shed the charade of mutism would continue and usual appearances be maintained.

To realise the programme of fantasies as I experienced them in my general reverie, one of the essential conditions consisted in the ineluctable necessity of my witnessing Dulita's initiation, at the fountain of the cypress, through the dining room window, something which in fact seemed impracticable for a purely physical reason: the cypress trees completely surrounded the fountain. So it appeared I would be unable to see Dulita's initiation which could only occur at the fountain. Suppose a small entrance was created through which they would have to bend as they passed through? But then a new and particularly exciting fantasy brought a solution to the problem. A fire, caused by an enormous pile of dry leaves not being fully extinguished, had burned away part of the cypress area in front of the fountain, leaving it open, but in such a way that a charred branch would still provide a slight and almost non-existent obstacle to contemplation of the scene with Dulita.

Otherwise, the same fire had burned away all the surrounding shrubs and densely mingled trees.

Because of this on the day her mother and La Gallo would force her through this location to the fountain Dulita would have to get dirty and blacken her white pinafore and her legs. The idea of Dulita getting dirty then became indispensable and would complete to perfection the ensuing fantasy. I would see Dulita reach the fountain with feet dirtied by the pestilential mud mingled with decomposed moss in which the paving around the fountain was enveloped, for whenever the pipe blocked up with leaves it caused frequent floods, particularly in the autumn. Although it was enclosed the dry leaves, scattered by the squalls of stormy days, still entered. But the fountain in the cypress grove which I could see thanks to the fire was still not visible from the dining room. It was hidden by part of the wall that continued from the stable.

Displacing the fountain to bring it again within my visual field seemed to me an unsatisfactory solution that would destroy the coherence of my reverie. Instead I noticed quite clearly that the fire that burned the cypress had also destroyed the separating wall and in so doing allowed 'immediate communication between the stable and the fountain in the cypress grove'.

The desolate and ruined aspect of the area surrounding the fountain was intensified by a pile of calcinated stones from the wall which added an ambience perfectly in accord with my plans. With a strange emotion mingled with anguish and pleasure I suddenly realised that the disappearance of the wall would, towards the end of the afternoon, allow the shadows of the cypress trees to slowly extend the length of the courtyard which had previously been completely in shadow. The sun would reach the first steps of the stairs to the entrance which at that time of the year would be covered with dry leaves.

Thus the sun, in the moment preceding its setting, would penetrate, in a cadmium line, into the first floor room, with its shutters half-closed and furniture under dust covers on a floor covered with corn left to dry, and would for a few minutes illuminate, in all its bedazzlement, the extremity of the finger of the statue in greenish marble – its arms raised and with hair masking its face and one hand – and which had, with the pond, been removed from the group of the fountain.

In spite of the disappearance of the wall which had hidden the fountain in the cypress grove, it remained impossible to see it from the dining room, for it was hidden, far to the left, by the window.

After several unsatisfactory fancies which nevertheless led me gradually to the solution, I conceived the idea of seeing Dulita's initiation through a reflection in the large mirror in her own room, which adjoined the dining room. Thus I could observe everything from my own chair, with the advantage of a certain complication and vagueness of images that was totally desirable and had already been discerned from the light and incomplete charring of the cypress. Thus, thanks to the great distance separating me from the scene, the images would come to me in a state of imprecision which would be particulary unsettling.

I could now see, with clearness and absolute precision, the next phase the reverie would follow.

It was the evening of Dulita's initiation, on Halloween. Dinner was over and we had risen from the table, on which there remained only three cups of coffee, three liqueur glasses and a bottle of cognac. Dulita was to my left, facing the half-open door of her bedroom. She occupied the place I had during my childhood stay at the farmhouse. Like me, in a different period, she was preparing for her exams. She was sitting in front of her books with an open pencil box in which I saw a rubber with the design of a lion on it. The ambience is exactly that of my first stay at the farmhouse. Gallo took the place of the owner, smoking in silence as she read the newspaper. Matilda took the wife's place and was knitting. That evening the silence was greater and the atmosphere stifling. Finally I did something that imitated a habit the owner used to have towards me: I soaked a piece of sugar in my cognac and put out a hand towards Dulita. With her hand still over her notebook, Dulita noticed my action and reached forward to take the piece of sugar between her teeth. This was the signal to go to bed. I finished the cognac with a very slow mouthful. Behind Dulita's head, through the half-open door of her room, in the mirror, the black cypresses of the fountain rustled.

It was the solemn afternoon of an insipid All Soul's Day. I got ready to watch Dulita's initiation.

I placed Dulita's everyday slippers on the dining room table. I took my prick out of my trousers and covered it with dirty rags. With my eyes fixed on the area around the fountain as it was reflected in the mirror, I saw Dulita between the two women, dressed in a white and very short and tight skirt with new canvas shoes. Gallo was dressed in a very brightly coloured and luminous cotton dress and Matilda in black. I ran to the window in Dulita's room, since I wanted to see all the details of their passage towards the fountain through the singed bushes. They advanced very slowly and with difficulty as they tried to avoid the large charred branches, but Gallo and Matilda pushed Dulita into the dirtiest places as though in jest. At each step, the sometimes thorny and coarse shrubs caught Dulita's legs and buttocks and left her with long black marks. Sometimes they stopped to see how they might best advance. Gallo spanked Dulita on the pretext of dusting off the stains, but with such violence and savagery that she pretended was only fun.

Dulita tried to run away after Gallo knocked her against a wall covered with burned ivy. Dulita ran straight ahead, without heeding where she was going, through the shrubs that grazed her and drew blood. She ran on towards the fountain whereupon she slipped on the moss covering the paving and fell down. She had been spattered everywhere and was very dirty. She smiled for a pardon and wiped herself with a handkerchief, arranged her hair, pulled up her stockings, as she held her skirt pinned in her teeth revealing her dirty thighs.

Gallo and Matilda arrived a few moments later. Gallo was all sweetness and kissed Dulita on the brow. Matilda cut some bread and kept the crust for Dulita who was now sitting between the two women. At that moment, the scene conveyed a great sense of transcendence and solemnity.

Dulita now combed her hair with a very red celluloid comb which gleamed and flashed in the declining sunlight. The shadow of the farmhouse advanced towards the fountain and allowed the whole foreground of burned shrubs to reach the three figures in shadow.

Dulita ate (a mouthful of chocolate, a mouthful of bread) with great deliberation. She rocked her right leg which was near Gallo.[1]

I thought the sun, at that moment, illuminated the finger of the statue in the room on the first floor and the corn on the ground became, for a moment, fire-coloured. I saw a fleeting image of myself sodomising Dulita, as we lay on the corn in the same room. This vision would motivate a new element in the central reverie, to which I returned with the image of Dulita wiping away the breadcrumbs from her skirt and leaning over to drink some water.

From this moment, Dulita's gestures as she cleaned the aluminium goblet at the end of the chain and threw the water three times across the exact and relative positions of Gallo and Matilda, the illumination of the buttocks were perceptible beneath the transparency of Dulita's clothes as she bent forward and, on her knees, etc. . . all this, as I said, took on a lucidity and an exacerbated, half-hallucinatory, visual concretisation. The time during which she *emptied the glass three consecutive times*[2] produced a clear and exact illusion of *déja vu* which coincided with a very strong

[1] At this moment I experienced an erection and masturbated by rubbing my penis against my stomach. I took out the piece of bread from my penis which fell to the ground and rolled away. This distracted me for a moment as I hesitated about whether to recover it. I do not remember what point the reverie had reached. I felt a profound anguish which vanished with the image of Dulita swinging her legs. I pursued the reverie with my hand held motionless behind my buttocks. This position was very uncomfortable and caused cramp in my arms. I remained still until ten minutes after the end of the reverie.

[2] I later tried to masturbate with the representation of this image but, as ejaculation approached, the image was transformed into that of the woman I love, crouching near a rabbit hutch.

erection. The moment Dulita wiped the glass, before drinking, was almost unbearable. It also had the greatest visual power in the whole reverie. Afterwards I also saw in a very confused way Dulita, who I had not seen drink, wipe her mouth with her hand. Gallo, using all her charm, compelled Dulita to sit down again between herself and Matilda. I thought this would be the beginning of the initiation. The shadow of the farmhouse reached Dulita's knees.[3] I waited incredibly tensely for Gallo's starting signal. Gallo placed the album of pornographic photographs on her knees. Matilda caressed Dulita's head and Dulita leaned over the album and tried to open it, but Gallo held back her hand and, as she did so, looked into her face and put her finger to her lips as a sign of silence and reflection.

Then Gallo raised her head and I saw the survival of her great beauty. I was very moved when Gallo slowly opened the album. I could not stand it any longer and found myself going back to the dining-room table with eyes closed and my mind filled with the last image.

As I sat on the chair I occupied each evening at supper time, I continued to think about the scene of the fountain as reflected in the mirror, and masturbated gently with the linen wrapped around my prick. I now saw them at the fountain, smaller and further away. Their faces and expressions were vague and offered me an almost complete border for my fantasies.

I observed nothing particular about the group. Dulita showed no reaction. She had a very low and still face, a mixture of shame and concern. From time to time, Gallo turned the page and murmured things very close to the girl's inclined face which was concealed by Dulita's hair. In

[3] At this moment I uncovered my penis, took out the ball of bread, which I had for a long time kept under the foreskin, and put it between my nose and upper lip to smell it. It was very warm and had a light odour of semen. I put it back in the place from which I had taken it with the hope that the longer it was left there the stronger it would smell.

a confused way I saw the group descend towards the courtyard, for darkness had come very soon after the sun had set. I hurriedly placed an ear of corn on the chair on which Dulita would have to sit for the next three days without mentioning the fact. On third day, the eve of the reverie's 'manifest' act, everything was removed from the table.

Three coffees and cognac were brought. The same profound silence prevailed as on the other evenings. I felt very emotional and was unable to speak clearly.

Dulita fidgeted imperceptibly with the ear of corn. The details I gave for the next day were short and to the point. Finally, as on the other nights, I offered Dulita the sugar cube soaked with cognac. She stood still a moment before taking it with her teeth. I saw her look through tears, while a large drop was born from my orifice.

Next day was Sunday. We took advantage of the fact that at four o'clock everyone went to the village. I awaited a sign from Matilda in the meadow and raced, covered only in my burnous, into the room with the ears of corn on the first floor. There I found Dulita, Gallo and Matilda all stark naked. Dulita masturbated me very clumsily, but it still excited me a great deal. The three women went across the courtyard towards the stable. Meanwhile I ran to the fountain in the cypress grove and sat on the bank of moistened stone and took my penis with all my might between two hands, then went to the stable where Dulita and the two women were lying naked in the filth and rotting straw. I took off my burnous and threw myself on Dulita, but Matilda and Gallo immediately vanished and Dulita was transformed into the woman I love, so ending the reverie with the same images I had experienced in the memory of the dream.

So the reverie came to an end, and I just realised that I have for some time been in the process of analyzing in an objective way the reverie which I have just experienced and which I now annotate with the greatest scrupulousness.

*****
first published in *Le Surréalisme au service de la Révolution*
issue no 4 (1933)
reprinted in Salvador Dali, *Oui* Vol 1 (1971)
French original © Editions Denoël
*****

SALVADOR DALI (Figueras 1904–1989) The writings of surrealism's greatest celebrity deserve to be better known than they are, often being both dazzling and penetrating and of equal importance to his paintings.

PIERRE UNIK

Long Live The Bride!

"Long live the bride!" shouted a bricklayer in overalls. Everyone looked round. A large black car passed by on the boulevard. It drew up outside a urinal. Out stepped the bridegroom and groomsmen, all with flowers in their buttonholes and bright pink cheeks. They formed a queue outside the urinal, each waiting in his turn. A priest appeared. The bride looked around for some iron to touch. The priest stopped at the urinal, and jostled those in front of him to let him go first. The chauffeur jumped from his seat and rushed off. A moment later he was back with a policeman. The officer summoned the priest, who in the meantime had been grabbed by the ears by two of the groomsmen, and politely made it plain that it was indecent to enter a urinal wearing a dress. The priest conceded the point with a gesture of resignation and the officer left.

The priest, noticing a man passing by, ran up to him and greeted him in a low voice. After a short conversation they seemed to have come to an agreement: the priest gave the man twenty pence which the latter held between his teeth as he took off his jacket, trousers and waistcoat, leaving only his shirt. The priest took off his cassock and put on the man's clothes. The man was trying to work out how to put on the cassock when the policeman noticed him from afar. Seeing him dressed in nothing but a shirt the representative of Authority summoned a colleague and together they chased the man, who had still not managed to don the priest's cassock. When he saw the officers, he dropped the cassock and ran off in his shirt-tails hotly pursued by the two officers. So the priest was in civ-

76

vies, but still had his cassock over his arm. The bride
had got out of the car to touch the plaque in the cleft in a
tree, believing it to be iron. The priest, burdened by the
cassock and unable to hold himself in any longer, without
realising what he was doing, threw the cassock over the
bride and dashed into the urinal. At the same moment the
bridegroom came out. Immediately he noticed a priest.
When he saw that the latter had the face of his future wife,
he was gripped with terror and ran off, shouting "They've
changed my wife into a priest." It so happened that on the
opposite side of the street was a gun shop. He promptly
bought a revolver, and returned to the urinal. The chauffeur was hooting to try to get everyone back into the car.
Wild with rage, the bridegroom drew the pistol and fired
a shot at the bride-priest who collapsed, before blowing
out his brains as he cried, with a theatrical gesture:
"Fatality!". But while he had been buying the gun, the
man in shirt-tails, having succeeded in dodging the officers,
had returned just as the priest came out of the urinal with a
look of relief on his face. The priest recovered his cassock
from the stupefied bride and the urinal was empty, as all
the men from the wedding party had now relieved themselves.

So what had happened was that the man in shirt-tails
and the priest, having gone in to recover their respective
clothes, were now standing outside the urinal. It was at this
very moment that the bridegroom had returned with his
revolver. Having taken him from a distance to be his bride
turned into a priest he had fired at the latter. But he had
actually killed the priest.

With the husband dead, the wedding ceremony had
been rather undermined. The parents wondered what to
do. They could hardly remain there and send away the
guests: it would have defied common sense. The chauffeur,
who had been contracted for several hours, would be
furious; the guests were already in the mood for fun and
were especially looking forward to the dancing and dining.
They would be very annoyed when they learned the

truth. And then the dinner had already been ordered, a room booked for the whole evening. So, what could be done? It was hardly possible to continue without a bridegroom. The man who had taken the priest's clothes was still there. Couldn't he take the place of the bridegroom? He hesitated, but both the father of the deceased and the father of the bride, not to mention the chauffeur, encouraged him. Well! He consented to become the husband. He entered the urinal and exchanged his clothes for those of the dead groom. By now the police officers had returned shamefacedly, pitifully empty-handed. They did not recognise the man now he was dressed.

Everyone got back into the car.

The car drove off.

The wedding got underway.

A passer-by called out: "Long live the bride!"

★★★★★

published in *La Révolution Surréaliste* no 6 (1926)

★★★★★

PIERRE UNIK (1910–1945?) One of the more militant of the communist sympathizers in the Surrealist Group, Unik wrote the screenplay for Buñuel's *Las Hurdes*. Arrested by the nazis, he is known to have escaped from Auschwitz, but nothing further was ever heard about him.

Honeymoon

I had fallen asleep amongst the twenty breasts, twenty mouths, twenty genitalia, twenty thighs, twenty tongues and twenty eyes of one woman. That's what made my awakening all the more agonizing, all the more harrowing, for I lay crucified on my own double bed, which had been stood on end before a large glazed balcony that opened onto a desolate street. Beyond the balcony, which doubled as my display cabinet, day was breaking. I was completely naked. I felt cold and ashamed that someone might see me from the street. A pair of delicate, female hands bloomed above my feet like two white spikes and, though it was doubtless those same hands that were nailing me to the wooden bedframe, I consoled myself with the thought that they were perhaps merely trying to remove the nails. The shame of my nakedness filled me once more with anxiety. I invented a prayer for that moment, a prayer full of tenderness, in which jumbled memories of words from a book on charitable works, learned by heart as a child, mingled with lines by Paul Claudel and fragments from my second epistolary.

When my tender prayer was over, an army of green-winged flies, field snails, cockroaches, toads and small white mice began to crawl up my legs until my whole body was covered with their filth. Behold the suit reserved for me! The flies boiled about my head in a hostile swarm. A hideous fluttering crept over my belly and my arms, my face and my armpits and even over my two profusely bleeding hands each fixed to the bed by a broad-bladed knife. My vision grew clouded and I felt that at any moment I might faint. The source of my greatest suffering, however, was not that but the decapitated head of a dark-haired woman, who was watching me with pleading eyes from one corner of the balcony, as if her fate depended entirely on me. That horribly pale face, resting on a small bedside table, was lit by the tenuous first light of morning and from it flowed a slender thread of blood that had already formed into a large puddle on the floor of the balcony. At last, the head spoke, and the voice of María Ana broke like dawn upon the oppressive night of the bedroom.

"Now, my poor deceived husband, my poor pale-faced cuckold, now I can tell you how I hate you. Never again will you touch my breasts, breasts that are now caressed by the hands of angels. My sex now wanders the bordellos of Mediterranean ports frequented by bold, young sailors, and my feet run after unbound arms and virgin lips. All that remains for you is this decapitated head, these timid eyes and this perennially jeering mouth. And this great puddle of my own blood dripping onto the pavement of a dawn street and onto the neat white uniforms of the first schoolgirls to appear. It is the clock of your crucifixion, your bloody clepsydra. When the last drop of my blood falls, your dream will end. . ."

Then bells, which I knew to be far off, began to sound directly above my head, an impatient, monotonous booming. From the street came the smell of incense together with a murmur of prayers, the footsteps of a procession and a rustle of petticoats. Behind me, someone uttered a heartrending cry that eclipsed all the other noises.

I saw that the night table was collapsing as if beneath a great weight and that María Ana's head was rolling to the floor, dragging with it as it fell four plump candles I hadn't noticed until then. Floating in the sky, which was just beginning to turn pink, was a large, oblong cross about which flew several silent crows, like a sinister flock of winged coffins.

★★★★★

published in Agustín Espinosa, *Crimen* (1934)
translated from the Spanish by Margaret Jull Costa

★★★★★

AGUSTÍN ESPINOSA (Puerta de la Cruz, 1897 – Teneriffe 1939) Founder member of the Surrealist Group in the Canary Islands, he organised the important 'Exposición colectiva de arte surrealista' in 1935. At the opening he translated the address by André Breton into Spanish in a rather idiosyncratic way. According to one commentator, "Breton said one thing in French, and Agustín said the opposite in Spanish!"

PAUL NOUGÉ:

The Gallant Hot Shot

During a trip, as the car passed through the woods, the driver stopped near a rifle range and said that a round of shooting would be a good way to kill some time. And he gallantly offered his hand to his dear wife, to that mysterious woman to whom he owed so many pleasures not to mention, perhaps, the greatest part of his talent.

Several of his shots were a long way off target. One even hit the ceiling. As his charming wife was giggling away he suddenly turned to her: "Look," he said, "You see that doll, down there on the right, with its nose in the air and a rather haughty look. My dear angel, it's the very image of you." He closed his eyes and pulled the trigger. The doll was decapitated.

He then leaned towards his dear wife and tenderly kissed her hand as he said: "Ah, my dear angel, once again I have you to thank again for my skill."

And as the weather was fine, they continued their trip.

★★★★★
published in *L'Experience continue*, 1981.
French original © Editions l'Age d'Homme, 1981.
★★★★★
PAUL NOUGÉ (Brussels 1895 – Brussels 1967) Main theorist of the Belgian Surrealist Group and one of the most provocative figures in surrealism. Neither his important theoretical texts nor his highly original poetry are as known as they should be.

GILBERT LÉLY:

Arden

A forest in Hungary. Inert, as multicoloured as autumn, wild cockerels stood deep in the dead leaves. *You.* That much was certain. Oh, the laughter of security after the barbarity of days. I had no memory of the past (the insults of a coachman). At almost every step you stopped and wildly offered me your mouth. The forest, in its October, seemed to me to be a projection of our love. Certainly I possessed the notion of my happiness, but sometimes felt a vague horror that at the slightest modification of our affective economy the forest would dissolve and give way to another milieu that would conform to the new movements of our soul. The light did not move: it was always five in the afternoon in autumn. On a path, to the west, passionate cavalcades were obedient to the rhythm of Chopin's second scherzo. Olive-green horses, mounted by ladies and by pages in black, scraped the ground in rhythm, following the most impetuous gallop with the most measured steps, and sometimes danced on the spot as they reared up in comical glory. We stepped out from the leaves to admire this spectacle, and, our feet fitted out with new slippers, penetrated pleasantly into the pure and slippery clay of the slope. *Your eyes had an unknown frankness.* Each gesture of your hands caused the transparent vegetation of joy to be born in hoops in the air. And you loved me, you loved me; chéri, you said, but in a particular way, changing the closed é into an open è and separating the syllables: chè-ri, and in such a languid way. Your kisses slipped into my throat and penetrated into my veins, like stems in vertiginous growth, daughters of the stones and water. *You will do justice to me.* Suddenly your body was spread out on a flower-bed of plants whose form I could barely make out, but which I knew to be hemlock and your body turned over and seemed to offer me the whole of its former sweetness. Your eyes closed in a mechanical way, like those of a doll when it is placed on its back. I was held back by a strange doubt. . . It was then that the pacifying decor of the forest dissolved. The shadows exiled us to the far north of Europe in a solitude crossed by polar breath, announcing the first ice-packs. You lay, pale and still open, near a copse of leprous trees, where some of the engravings that once adorned our bedroom were hanging. I recoiled with fright and disgust, because you had become a dead woman that no one had the right to touch and because I recognised that your body had not turned over particularly for me, not for me, Arden, your lover, but for the nameless man, the companion of your stroll who, just now, you nourished with kisses. *You did not recognise me. . .* When you stood erect, bizarrely magnified, on all sides from the ground a sort of circular architraved colonnades which barely came up to our ankles rose up. Without examining more closely these witnesses of a civilisation as advanced as that of moles, like phantoms we began to plunder the tiny architecture which had the resistant feel of stone and yet would still collapse into ash under the point of our canes, like the still entire calcinated lumps of coal one crushes in winter dawns as one clears away the remains from the cold fireplace.

*****

published in Gilbert Lély: *Oeuvres poétiques*
French original © Editions de la Différence, 1977

*****

GILBERT LÉLY (Paris 1904–) Along with Maurice Heine, Lély was a pioneer of the study of the work of the Marquis de Sade. His poems and tales have their own perverse grandeur, especially the texts of *Ma Civilisation*, an important collection.

FERNAND DUMONT:

The Region Of The Heart

I cast the dice on one of my final poetic possibilities: that fortuitous (but nevertheless certain) encounter with a woman not yet seen, but whose perfume accumulates on the horizon like a storm cloud.

In the infinite maze of possibilities it was a conjecture similar to that which certain games of chance offer, in which it is impossible to escape the consequences of a decision taken for it is true that circumstances never offer their possibilities again.

One morning there was a dawn such as I had not seen for a long time (for sleep completely occupied me with the hope of deciphering the confused message of dreams and discovering the signs which would have directed me along the road of the eventual at whose end the unhoped for encounter would occur). This dawn entered into my room and softly woke me up as it held its fragile beams of dim blue light above my tired eyelids. When I opened my eyes, I could see that it was still draped in a sumptuous cloak of mist. It spoke a few words I did not really understand but from which I deduced that it was essential to leave without wasting a moment. It then vanished and gave way to one of those unforgettable April mornings which seem to belie in the most formal way possible the misery of the world.

Without hesitation, I decided to leave the same day for the land of forests older than man's memory where I had spent several holidays. It was early evening when I arrived and the following morning headed off to a valley completely off the beaten track. I particularly remembered that it always seemed that beyond the high wooded slope which I had never crossed there must be an extensive region in which chance and illusion could be encountered at each step. With beating heart I ascended slowly ready at each moment to turn and contemplate in all its grandeur a landscape which must have remained the same for centuries when my attention was drawn to the fact that beyond the still bare branches was a large clearing silhouetted against the clear sky. A few yards still separated me from the summit of the hill. Although out of breath, I cleared it in bounds but could not contain myself: more than a thousand yards down below was the sea. To left and right high wooded mountains formed an immense gulf in the form of a horseshoe whose extremities were lost in the mist and at my feet, on a very small island, rose a castle.

All around me was silence. The air was quite different from what I was accustomed to breathe. It was appreciably lighter, more transparent, and everything seemed so barely real that I pinched myself to ensure that I was not in the throes of an illusion.

Prompted by irresistible curiosity, I descended. The most contradictory feelings assailed me, but I did not waste a moment and by following a barely perceptible footpath along the ledge soon reached the point of the sea at which the castle appeared from behind the trees. I went down to the deserted shore to look closer. Its mass of grey stone was bathed in sea, light and silence. I had lost myself in hypotheses when a small boat I had not seen leave the castle approached, splitting the still waters. The oarsman signalled for me to embark and beneath the postern I was welcomed by a man who, if appearances were to be believed, was the lord himself. The strange thing was that I understood his words perfectly and as I was about to apologise for my ignorance of his language, I realised that I could speak it with the greatest of ease. I had the presence of mind to tell him that I had got lost and asked for shelter. I needed to be careful to allow him to speak and guess from his words what I was doing and not awaken his contempt by asking questions that would make it obvious I was merely living through an extraordinary adventure.

He was a very tall and handsome man of about forty. His countenance and the words he used suggested a man of uncommon intelligence and I soon learned that I was in the presence of a man who had an extensive knowledge of the problems I had vainly sought, until now, to clarify.

He summoned his servants to show me to one of the rooms prepared for travellers. As I passed through a maze of corridors and stairs. I noticed that I was in a castle which, if one could judge by certain architectural details, must date from the fourteenth century, but which nevertheless had none of the melancholy one generally associates with buildings of this period. I knew not what to believe and, as I dressed, I delivered myself up to the wildest suppositions.

The most important thing was to reveal nothing and, no matter what happened, not to lose my composure.

In the great hall I found myself in the presence of a crowd of people and understandably felt too intimidated to talk as much as I might have liked. The lord took me round, introducing me under the name I invented in the heat of the moment when I arrived. There were around fifty men and women each of whom seemed to be more strangely beautiful than the others. They were cultured beings and I then learned that they were all devoted to a singular work which I will speak about later.

Already conversations had developed here and there as I tried to hide as best I could my stupefaction and ignorance that youth alone could excuse when, with a sense of amazement, I noticed a splendid woman I immediately recognised enter the room. There was no possibility of error, this was certainly the person I must encounter, the one I had sought for such a longtime. I was so stupefied I was unable to find a single word to say when she was presented to me by the lord, who was her father, under the name of Nebuleuse. I felt it even more in that she too seemed to hide a great emotion as she looked at me and as I looked at her, both of us all eyes, and in her looks a dark light which emanated only when one is placed by chance in the presence of a being who is immediately recognised through irreplaceable necessity.

By chance or by design her father left us alone and, as we sat conversing on a stone seat, in the alcove window which opened onto the sea. I was still unable to find words to break the silence. We looked into the distance and looked stealthily at each other, as happens in such circumstances, we encountered each other's glances and immediately I felt it would be useless to speak for we had already signed a pact which would connect us forever.

That was as far as we got. People were moving towards the table and I was seated between two guests from whom I learned that the next day would be devoted to a study in clairvoyant manifestations, a subject about which I knew nothing. During the meal it was clear that no one had the slightest interest in my presence and I was surprised that I found everything that was happening perfectly natural, to the extent that my previous life seemed an insignificant long ago memory, which is perhaps what happens whenever we undergo strongly emotional experiences.

During the evening, groups formed and I again found myself with the lord and his daughter. The conversation touched upon the most diverse subjects and I had to be careful not to reveal who I really was. This was made easier for me by the fact that all I needed to do was listen to a sort of inner voice which told me what to say as I needed to explain my origins and reasons for coming. From the almost imperceptible signs Nebuleuse made to me, I understood that I must not make the slightest allusion to the secret pact we had signed in that single glance, and the evening ended without complications. I retired for the evening fairly early, on the pretext of tiredness, and spent the night going over the events of the day point by point and wondering how I managed to find myself alone again with this woman who henceforth would be for me the most entrancing in the world. Although I was exhausted, when dawn again entered my room it found me still awake and this time was able to express its joy at finding me here and cryptically let me know I was on the point of obtaining what I always desired. I barely had time to get drowsy. Already assorted sounds of morning recalled me to reality.

The day was devoted to experiments in collective clairvoyance.

We assembled on the top of the keep with a view over the sea. Soon there was not the least wrinkle, the slightest shudder, and then, when it was as uniform as the balustrade of marble on which we were leaning, it all became slowly, very slowly, transparent, so much so that after a while the bed of sand and rock which extended from the shelter to the depths became as clearly visible as if the sea had completely retreated. After this, a being who was tall and who we had at first taken for a rock higher than the others, began to walk. He constantly bent down to gather the debris we could not see clearly since it was too far away and piled it up in the middle of a large bank of fine sand. Then he set fire to it and continued his comings and goings as if his mission was to clear the ground of the considerable debris strewn around. As we continued to watch we realised that this debris was nothing but lost illusions that had disintegrated in the depths of the gulf like so much crude jetsam.

At one moment he came forward from a large galley half submerged in the sand with its double row of oars, and when he leaned toward it, he saw that it was in fact a decrepit cathedral. He threw the debris on the building and soon a thick smoky cloud escaped. With a gesture he broke the buttresses. Immediately cries rose from inside and hundreds of people ran out and danced around, taking each other by the hand as though they wanted to celebrate their liberation.

However, the fire of illusions was finally consumed. The giant retrieved some of the firebrands and threw them on the building from which a thick cloud of smoke came.

Then the cloud rose from the seabed as the sea slowly lost its transparency so that it appeared to float over it, but at the same time a phenomenon similar to what happens when a luminous beam of light is projected that is presented at first as a confused image in which one can distinguish nothing, the cloud became distinct imperceptibly under our eyes and as the sea regained its usual aspect the cloud appeared as no more than a large island that the currents carried into the wide-open sea.

During the whole time I took advantage of the general inattention to have a long hushed conversation with Nebuleuse.

That night, by means of the instructions she gave me, I was able to find her room.

It was completely hung with shadow and thus its dimensions varied considerably in accordance with the intensity of light. When a small night lamp alone illuminated our love-making, it became a very small circular room which silently passed through nights humming with stars.

It was in this room that I experienced the most unimaginable nights of my youth. Nebuleuse was more beautiful than daybreak, stranger than the unseen, she was born from the wake left by the tail of a comet in a polar mist. She was never similar to herself as much that it was impossible to reach this sad region of lassitude with her. We could love each other indefinitely, and each time I took her in my arms, the most complicated problems became crystal clear.

During the day, I mingled with these extraordinary beings who had all become masters in the art of realising their thoughts. While here the most skilful have difficulty communicating through an always imperfect language, which continually leads to all kinds of misunderstanding, the castle inhabitants had for a long time learned how to make the internal reality of their mind immediately visible for everyone.

As one might imagine, it is difficult for me to explain this clearly since, to do so, I need to use language itself, but

I nevertheless believe I am able to give a feeble idea of the means of communication practised at the castle.

Everything suggests to me that it was only an unmeasured amplification of the poetic step which, as we know, consists of creating images. But if poets' images remain purely verbal, the images used at the castle were crystallised for others in the same way as dream images for the sleeper. They were confounded with reality to such a point that, for example, when a character at the castle told a story as I am doing at the moment, those within the same domain would have the perfect illusion that they themselves lived it. They would see, hear, touch, feel; they would be hungry and thirsty and they would love and LIVE.

It will thus be understood that, in such conditions, the chance of interpretive errors ceased to exist and knowledge could be taken collectively to the most distant limits.

Time passed, devoted to love and wonders.

Already autumn lengthened the shadow of the mountains over the gulf.

No one seemed to suspect our rendezvous in the little room of shadow and life seemed something infinite when in the course of a night close to the equinox I could not resist – I still don't know why – the desire to confess to Nebuleuse who I was and explain to her the details of my adventure. She listened to me with deep sadness and, when I had finished, gave me a little file which she pleaded I must look after and show to no one in the world. We separated with the feeling that something between us had changed.

The following day the lord asked me if I did not wish to be shown around the castle. In truth I had never dreamt of it and accepted more through politeness than desire. He took me everywhere and explained with admirable minutiae the details about this building conceived so as to give maximum comfort and security. Nothing here could give more than a feeble idea of such an ingenious adjustment to the necessities of life.

He showed me rooms completely hung with dreams where one could, if one was not careful, die without even realising. He took me to the room of shadow, which was, during the day, out of proportion and unrecognisable. I followed him into the depths. He opened a heavy slab of stone which he operated by means of an odd system of counterweights and asked me to descend with him into a room whose floor was strewn with wonderful fishes. In response to my surprise he explained that the room had been constructed in such a way that at high tide the sea entered. The fishes were attracted by bait fixed to the walls and came into the room through the high window and were then trapped when the tide fell below the window-ledge. Along the ground, against the wall, from one place to another, narrow openings had been made. The servants would collect the produce of the previous tide and put down fresh bait. As he spoke the lord followed the servants through the opening but when I tried to go after him the trap slammed shut before me.

At first I thought it was just a fault of the trap, or a joke in bad taste, since I had no reason to think otherwise. I examined the still moist room which, as I said, had only one window by which daylight entered and which was fortified with solid bars, the threshold of which was level with my shoulders. Outside the beach extended toward the sun, which was so bright I could barely look at it.

I waited for a considerable time, convinced that at any moment the trap would open.

Finally I lost patience and called out.

I listened for a long time but heard only the murmur of the waves. In a few moments the sea would rise. I cried out again, cried with all my strength. Already the sea was beginning to enter surreptitiously through the openings.

I took refuge on the stairs, which was only temporary since I would soon be drowned in this cave with no exit.

Suddenly I recalled Nebuleuse's gift: the little file. In my confusion I had forgotten all about it. There was not a minute to lose: the sea had already reached the threshold of the window. Fortunately night was falling.

I threw myself on the bars like a madman and managed, I don't know by what miracle, to file away the weakest part very quickly. I worked out that complete darkness would fall as the sea reached the top of the window.

As I held on to the bars, I waited for the extreme limit, torn between terror at the thought of the trap opening and fear of being seen in the castle if I left before it was completely dark.

Finally I decided to leave. I was so stiff with cold I found it extremely difficult to swim. I made my way round the castle as quietly as possible as I brushed against the walls and finally reached the place where, when I arrived, I noticed a boat had been moored. It was still there. With the file, which I had kept with me by chance, I cut the cable and used the oar to push myself towards the open sea. It took the energy of despair not to give up, but I was still under the shock of the nightmare when I managed to put enough distance between myself and the castle, and so could feel safe.

Finally I abandoned the struggle and fell asleep.

I was awakened by a light shock: it was the dawn which had leapt into the boat and forced my eyes wide open so I could peer through its clothes of mist to the high buildings around a discernible beach. It kept me company until I reached the shore and I could see it had grown much older. It vanished the moment I landed. The embankment was still deserted. I was in rags and had no money.

I went into the first hotel I came to and quickly explained that I had escaped from a shipwreck. I refused to give my identity and telephoned home. I thought I was in the sway of new wonders when the telephone was answered by Nebuleuse herself. She apologised for the surprise and told me that she had been waiting for me with impatience and confided that she was not used to the stuffy air of our times. I asked her to send the necessary money by telegraph so that I could buy some presentable clothes and pay the hotel and train fare and assured her I would be at her side that very evening. I was wild with joy.

I cheerfully told the police, who had been called by the hotel owner, that I came from X. . . where I had been on holiday, that I had left the previous evening in an open boat and had intended to take a short journey but had been carried away by the tide.

That afternoon an express took me back to town. During the journey my joy faded a little, as flowers become weary after a day of too much sun. Still, I ran straight from the station to my house.

An unknown servant opened the door. With three bounds I was in my room.

It was empty.

I saw on my table, at the foot of a large white sheet of paper, a small signature fading away.

I barely had time to decipher it. It was wiped away under my powerless stare and I slowly saw appear, like a print submerged in the developer, the portrait of the one I had lost.

It is in a tint pale like certain immemorial legends. The whole of her face expressed such an irremediable melancholy and in her eyes there still burns the reflection of the fire of lost illusions.

I only have to glance at it to be absolutely sure about certain things.

Her right hand is held over the region of the heart and her left hand, index finger extended, indicates a secret place in the research of which I have sworn to devote my life.

29-30 August 1934

★★★★★

originally published in 1939 (editions du Groupe Surréaliste en Hainaut)

republished in *La Région du coeur* (1985) Brussels: Labor
French original © Editions Labor, 1985

★★★★★

FERNAND DUMONT (Mons 1906 – Belsen 1945) In everyday life a lawyer called Demoustier, Dumont was otherwise a jazz trumpeter who founded the Hainaut Surrealist Group with Achille Chavée. Secretary of the Committee of vigilance of anti-fascist intellectuals, he was arrested by the nazis in 1943 and died in Belsen. His *Dialectique du hasard au service du désir* (1942, published in 1979) is a brilliant exploration of the relation of desire and chance in everyday life.

JINDŘICH ŠTYRSKÝ:

Emilie Comes To Me In My Dream

Emilie is quietly erased from my days, my evenings and my dreams. Even her white dress had darkened in my memory. I became increasingly less flustered thinking about the mysterious imprint of teeth I discovered one night on her lower stomach. Vanished were the last hypocrisies that stood in the way of foreseen emotion. Left forever, the whole choir of young girls that smiled vaguely, impassive and indifferent, evoking the memories of their hearts, torn from passions and deceitful humility. Now I had finally freed myself from this face I had sculpted as a child in the snow, the face of a woman lost through the availability of her belly.

I see Emilie cast in bronze. Men of marble are no longer troubled by fleas. The small heart shape of the upper lip recalls ancient enthronements, while the lower lip, used as it was to being licked, caused me to think of the foliage of bordellos. I slowly walked beneath her, with my head in her skirt hem. From close up I studied the hairs on her calves, thoroughly crushed by her fretted stockings, trying to imagine how a comb would be needed to groom her hair. I learned to love the smell of her sex, at once wash house and mouse hole, a pin cushion lost in the flower bed of lilies of the valley.

I became prey to the phenomenon of crossfade. When I looked at Clara, I invariably saw her with Emilie's features. When Emilie wanted to sin her sex recalled the hay loft and the spice shop. Clara herself had the feel of a herbarium. My hand wandered under her skirt, grazing her stocking tops and the clips of her suspenders to caress the inside of her thighs. They are hot, humid and delightful. Emilie brings me a cup of tea. She wears blue slippers. I will never be completely happy. I suffer from the sighs of women, from the contortions of eyes open at the moment of orgasm.

Emilie never sought to enter the world of my poetry. She observed my garden from beyond the enclosure, so ordinary and natural fruits seemed to me terrible fruits of a prehistoric paradise. As I waited, I mechanically took the one hundred steps on the footpath, like an idiot, like an exhausted dog dragging his muzzle into the grass to outwit death and flee his destiny. I struggled like a madman to revive the moment somewhere in the south, when the shadow once lay in a particular town square. Emilie, supported by the enclosure, passes hastily through life. I see her quite clearly: each morning she rises with dishevelled hair, goes to the toilet, urinates, sometimes she even has a shit, then bathes with tar soap. With her scented genitals she hurries to join the living, to cause her feeling of crossroads to evaporate.

What sublime joy when Emilie laughed! Her mouth seemed hollow and arid. But when you approached this upper hollow of sensual pleasure with your head you heard something rustle inside and when, at your encounter, she opened her lips, red flesh surged forth from between her teeth. Old age likes to haggle with time; only in the arms of pleasure does morality sleep in peace. And Emilie's eyes, which she never closed at the moment of supreme pleasure, took on such a sweet expression that she seemed not to be of this world, and it appeared that she was ashamed of what passed her lips.

In places where I seek my youth, I find the buckles of golden hairs carefully conserved. Life consists in a ceaseless killing of time. Each day death corrodes what we call living, and life ceaselessly swallows our desire for the void. The image of the kiss vanishes even before the lips join, every portrait turns pale before one has the chance to look at it. Finally, a maggot transpierces even this woman's heart and laughs in its hollow. Afterwards, who will be able to assert that you really existed? I saw you in the company of a young naked girl, beautiful and marvellously white. Then this young girl raised her arms and her palms were darkened with soot. She left the imprint of one of her hands between your breasts, while she covered my eyes with the other in such a way that I perceived you as through torn lace. You were naked, clothed only in an unbuttoned cloak. In that precious moment I saw your whole life: you looked like a bounteous plant quickly rising into flower. Two shoots appeared in the ground and dissolved into one at the very place you started to fade away, but at the same time the body you thrust forward, with navel, breasts and head and from which come two pretty buds. However at that moment the lower part of your body collapsed and shrivelled. I writhed in front of you as I touched the hem of your cloak, groaning with a love I had never known. I do not know to whom the shadow I called Emilie belonged. We are welded together forever, inseparably, and yet we are turned back to back.

This woman is my coffin. As she walks she hides me within her features. And so, when I curse her, I consign myself to hell and love to fall asleep with an impression of her hand on my phallus.

On the 1st May you will go to the cemetery where, in alley no 10, you will find a woman sitting on a tomb. She will be expecting you, and she will read the cards for you. You will then seek the explanation on the walls of the boarding-school. But the girls' heads in the windows will take on the look of buttocks-buds and asses-tulips, trembling as the lorries pass in front of the building. So they do not fall into the street, you will feel intense fear, a fear close to the pleasure you felt in your childhood at the first convulsive stiffening of the phallus and to the horror you felt when your sister taught you to masturbate with a little *alabaster hand*.

From whom do you still expect consolation? Emilie is

98

torn apart, the wind having dispersed her image, fragment by fragment, over your unknown places. You can no longer recover your tranquillity by her intermediary. For a long time you had forgotten how to cry through moments of separation.

The filament was sleeping and somewhere behind a thicket you were expected by a woman cut out of raw meat. Will you feed her with ice?

Lightly dressed, Clara always sat on the divan and waited to be undressed. One day she took the revolver from my night table, aimed at the painting and fired. The cardinal raised his hand to his chest and fell to the ground. I felt sorry for him and when I later visited suburban bordellos and paid the whores for their experience, I was always conscious of the fact that I was buying myself a fragment of eternity. Once a man has tasted the saltiness of Cecile's sex he would sell everything, his jewels, his friends and his morality, just to feed the monster hidden under the pink tutu. We never know how to distinguish the first moments, when women only play with us, from those when they become desperate. One night I woke just before dawn. It was the hour the petals fall during bird songs. By my side slept Martha, who held all the ways of loving in reserve, hyena of Corinth with uncovered sex opening up towards dawn. She caught my glance filled with disgust and I knew with certainty she wished this terrible nausea on me with all her heart. I saw her sex swell and flow from her belly. I saw it endlessly grow bigger, leave the bed and extend over the floor, invading the whole room like lava. I immediately fled the house, racing away like a madman. I stopped in a deserted town square. When I looked back, Martha's sex gushed forth from my window, looking like a monumental tear of unnatural colour. A bird arrived, pecking at my seed. I threw a stone at it. "Be happy, you can renew yourself ceaselessly," a passer-by said. "Your wife is now giving you a boy."

Each day two beetles had a midday meeting behind the sky-blue foundations of the Virgin of Lourdes. I entered into the catacombs quite innocently. A row of cubed closets aroused my curiosity. Secured by their legs and with heads lowered, young men hung in the crowns of olive trees where their pretty buckled heads, bent to the rose, were grilled in the flames of little fires. In another room I saw a swarm of naked beauties mingled together to form a solid mass, a sort of Apocalyptic Monster. Their sexes opened mechanically, some to the void, others swallowing their own saliva. I noticed in particular one whose lips were contracted in silence, like a mouth that would like to speak, or like a man with petrified tongue trying to say cock-a-doodle-doo. Another smiled like a rosebud; I can still recognise it today amid a thousand specimens preserved in formyl. It was the sex of my deceased Clara, who had been buried without having been bathed in mentholated water, something she loved so much. With a desolate feeling I took out my prick and shoved it, indifferent and without thinking, inside the solid mass, telling myself that death always knew how to connect vice with misfortune.

Then I placed an aquarium in my window. In it I kept a vulva with golden hair and a superb replica phallus with a blue eye and delicate veins up to the temple. In time, though, I threw away everything I loved. Broken cups, wigs, Barbara's slippers, flasks, shadows, fag-ends, sardine tins, together with all my correspondence and used preservatives. This world had seen the birth of several strange animals. I considered I was a creator. Rightly so. Later, when I sealed my box, I observed with satisfaction the decay of my dreams, until the day when the partition was covered with mould and no one could ever see anything. However, I did have the certainty that inside everything I loved in the world would continue to exist.

But it is still necessary to nourish my eyes. It was swallowed voraciously and brutally. And at night, in my sleep, they digest it. Emilie spread the scandal far and wide, encouraging everyone she encountered to desire it and think about her hairy crater.

I again recalled a childhood story. It dated from the time I was expelled from school. Everyone despised me. I no longer had any friends but my sister. I visited her secretly at night in our hiding place where we lay together arm in arm, with legs enlaced, and imagined, at the end of a long and persistent reverie, the state of torpor into which those who vacillated beside *dishonour* fell. One night we heard silent steps. My sister made a sign to me to hide behind a sofa. It was father who entered and he closed the door of the room carefully and, without saying a single word, lay down next to my sister. At last I was able to witness how it was done, the thing they call love.

The beauty of Emilie was destined not to wither but to decay.

*****

published in 'Emilie prichází ke mne ve snu' (Prague 1933)
translated by Andrew Lass and Michael Richardson

*****

JINDŘICH ŠTYRSKÝ (Prague 1899 – Prague 1942) A restless spirit with a bundle of creative energy, Štyrský was the most productive of the early Czech surrealists. His paintings, collages, photographs, theatre designs and writings are all of the highest quality and represent one of the outstanding achievements in surrealism.

ANDREAS EMBIRIKOS:

King Kong

for Yorgos Makris

Sleep would not come and I had gone out into the streets of Paris, where I was living in those years (between 1920 and 1930). It was the time when, after midnight, began the reign in Europe of the music of the Negroes.

Sleep would not come and I had gone out into the streets. It was the time when I would thrill to the joy of Picasso, bathed – no, baptised in the shimmering radiance of the spirit of André Breton.

Sleep would not come and I had gone out into the streets, filled that night with ennui, because I had not found the company I craved.

The sounds of day had long faded away and I trod the macadam, reluctant to return home, because my flat smelt musty and it was hot indoors, stiflingly hot and dusty.

Inhaling deeply, I took no notice of where I was going and went forward, saying over and over again like a charm, the words of André Breton: "*Lâchez tout, partez sur les routes. . .*" with the hope in my heart that, perhaps, at long last, with the aid of chance, I would happen upon something pleasant, and all the while my mind was ablaze with the (to me) astonishing figure of André Breton.

Borne thus from Montparnasse and led almost mechanically by my footsteps I arrived finally in the streets of Montmartre (there, in the rue Fontaine, lived Breton), filled with the ennui I mentioned before, and continued to walk idly among the alleys that surround the Place Blanche, as well as that square with the multi-coloured neon lights, whose name is Place Pigalle.

Above me the stars panted in the sky and the night was magic, filled with stars, filled with the joy of the Cosmos.

Around me rose the houses – remnants from the age of Haussmann and other periods, and among them many buildings from the time of Baudelaire, of Paul Verlaine , of Jules Laforgue and of Rimbaud, and in their midst, by God, the souls of these poets can often still be seen to wander today, crowned with haloes and clearly visible, utterly alive.

"Lâchez tout, partez sur les routes. . ." I kept saying over and over again and went forward, lightening the burden of my ennui and anguish.

"Lâchez tout, partez sur les routes. . ." and from the corners of the alleys and the doorways of old buildings came whispers of feigned desire: *"Venez faire l'amour, chéri. . . Pour une moment. . . Pour toute la nuit. . . Pour une branlette. . . Pour une sucette. . . Laissez-moi faire et vous verrez les anges. . . Venez, monsieur. . . Venez!. . ."*

"Lâchez tout, partez sur les routes. . ." I kept saying to myself, and went forward, while further off, here and there, with their short capes folded and thrown carefully over their shoulders, policemen slowly paced, and now and then, their bicycle chains humming in a quiet free-wheel and always in twos, always paired, slowly passed in the night, astride their machines, the law enforcers of Paris, the *agents-cyclistes.* And each time, I thought I would hear burst out from chests dressed in dark shirts, or in tight vests, I thought I would hear burst out, projected passionately upon the night, a sudden cry, blazing like a knife-slash:

"Mort, mort aux vaches!"

All of a sudden, the small street that was dimly lit, everywhere else, by sparse streetlights and, at the point that I had reached, vividly by the sign for some basement cabaret with a first-rate negro band, and while I was passing in front of a cinema that had closed its doors some hours before, I hear issuing from the cabaret the long drawn-out, yearning notes of saxophones and a man's voice – which from its accent must belong to a negro singer – crooning:

I'm singing the blues of the world
just singing a song
just singing a song.

It was a marvellous voice – a little hoarse – a voice that issued from the soul of the universe. At once I stopped and listened, at the same time staring with astonishment at the placard outside the adjacent cinema.

The coloured advertising poster depicted a giant gorilla, much taller than the big trees that were shown surrounding it. In its left hand, the great beast was holding, and looking tenderly upon, a small, tiny, terrified woman, who fitted easily into the span of its hand. Struck diagonally across the placard was the inscription, in red letters: "Coming next week" and next to it, in the middle of the picture, in huge black letters on the upper half of the placard, had been printed the title of the film:

KING KONG

The nostalgic song continued. Finally applause and shouts were heard in the basement. Then, abruptly, like a tempest breaking out and in an instant swelling to its climax, there broke upon the night a burning music, vividly alive, hotter than the desert khamsin, with words that sounded like inarticulate cries mingled with the bellowing, the heavy breathing of wild beasts furiously in rut.

The negroes were now playing a dance tune, with drums, cymbals and rattles, a dance that could easily be heard outside in the street, a dance that swept everything before it, and brought to the place where I was standing the corybantic surge of deepest Africa, with fast throbbing pulses and frenetic, orgiastic leaping.

Then something incredible happened and continued for some time. From the outside world began to pour within me, like a great river, the almighty lord, he of the basement cabaret, he of the caves of Creation, ruler of absolute 'being', king of life's instincts; from the outside world began to pour within me, swelling, gushing and yelling, the full rhythm of the 'id'.

All at once, every trace of ennui, of melancholy within me was dispersed and I felt a boundless happiness, as though I were not a single individual, but a whole Edenic people. It was as though a great earthquake shook me to the foundations and all of a sudden it seemed to me that there, before me, the asphalt of the street burst open, and in my presence spouted forth, like a giant geyser, warm, from the depths of the earth, from the depths of creation, viscous and white, the spermatic fluid of the panting world.

The music, the song and the frenetic dance continued. The street, where I was standing, became with every moment endless, wide open, a temple filled with the sound *tam-tam*. All I remember is the pitch of the voices, the timbre and the fervour, with which the negroes vented their passion, a passion that made the entire surrounding space shake and tremble, like a place of mysteries, like a sacred place. But the sense and the tune of that song remained indelible in my memory, in the same way as, even when we no longer remember the words, the sense remains of the pronouncement of an oracle, or a special poem, or an initiation, especially when one or other of them encapsulates the flash of archangels' wings, or, like the clash of heavenly arms, the crash of thunderbolts.

Yes, the music, the song and the dance continued. The emotion that held me in its grip was such that although I wanted to run to that cabaret and take part myself in the frenzy of the dancers, for a space I was incapable of movement. In my throat I felt a great lump, as though a sob were rising from my inmost being and I stood rooted to the spot, facing the entrance to the basement dive on the side of the cinema, staring in amazement at the giant gorilla of the placard, staring (O Kenya! Ruanda-Urundi! Uganda! Zululand!) staring at the black king.

Then something unbelievable happened once again. From the entrance to the cinema and while the voices from the cabaret could still be heard, easily demolishing the building, as though in response to the voices of the negroes, like a great brother to them, or like a Messiah coming forth from the groves of Eden, with terrifying grunts burst forth the great gorilla ape, King Kong, with his sexual organ at the ready, quivering fully erect and twitching in the air, its crimson head indescribably pulsating.

The gorilla was fantastically large – like a seven storey-building. The head was a massive cliff; the legs the colossal trunks of baobab-trees and the hairy, broad chest a thick Sargasso sea. With his right hand, which every so often brushed the street, leaving only the negroes' cabaret untouched, he threw down or just lightly swept aside (but with the deafening crashes of wholesale destruction) stone, concrete, and wooden beams, as though the time had come and Armageddon had broken out, and all the while (miracle of miracles) in his left hand, setting her free from the plot of the film and the bonds of daily servitude, in his fist he held a white, blonde woman of ravishing beauty, who was lifesize, but appeared in that gigantic palm quite small, tiny, like a plaything of a woman, a toy for very small children. The teeth and face of the giant gorilla bore an expression of ferocity out of this world, but his eyes were full of tenderness and the great ape, emitting grunts highly charged with desire, took especial care, as he traversed the wreckage, not to let the tiny woman fall from his grasp and in falling break her ribs.

It was a staggering sight. No sooner did Kong appear than the few pedestrians in the street scattered in panic, emitting farts and exuding in great profusion the shit of their holy terror, here and there, far from the triumphant gorilla, and among them 5 whores, 2 pimps, various characters of the night and there even went, pedalling with all the strength of their legs, fleeing at top speed on their gleaming bicycles, their hearts in their mouths, went fleeing helter-skelter, paired even in flight, two *agents-cyclistes*.

But I stood my ground, shaken and vibrating like a chord stretched to the limit, with the certainty that at last a great good had come upon the world. The place of the boredom and ennui in my soul was taken by a great enthusiasm. A holy tremor shook me and my soul was in ecstasy. Finally the lump in my throat dissolved and what had been on the way to becoming a sob became a howl of triumph, and, as I saw the black giant going forward, his footstep slow, hieratic on the macadam in front of me, as I watched the white woman in his fist, as I saw him go forward in triumph and desire, I shook all inertia from me and running after the passionately grunting king, as he receded at the far end of the street, and while from the basement dive came sounds and speech of the jungle, mingled with the sounds and speech of heaven (Tam-tam!. . . Hallel-u-jah!. . . Tam-tam!. . . Hallel-u-jah!. . . Gong-gong!. . .) I ran after the beast blazing like a forest, I ran after him with joy, crying out, shouting aloud with all the strength of my lungs, as though in my soul a great gong were beating, I ran after the gorilla, shouting at the top of my voice:

"Hail, Messiah (Hallel-u-jah!.. Hallel-u-jah!. . .) Hail, Adam risen from the dead! (Tam-tam!. . . Tam-tam!. . .) Hail, Phallus and Navel of the Earth! (Tam-tam!. . . Gong! . . . Gong!. . .) Hail o great genius of the Universe! Hail, o hail the deliverer — Hallel-u-jah! — King Kong!"

Glyfada, August 1964

*****

first published in *Oktana* (1980)
Greek original © Virika Embirikou and Leonidas Embirikos
translated by Roderick Beaton

*****

ANDREAS EMBIRIKOS (Athens, 1901– Athens, 1975) Animator of Greek surrealism, Embirikos formed the Greek Society of Psychoanalysis with Marie Bonaparte, using techniques that seem to have influenced or anticipated Lacan. During the war, as a Trotskyist sympathiser, he was held hostage by Stalinist guerrillas, an experience that had a deep impact on him. The colonels' coup in 1967 ended his career and left him in despair. The posthumous publication in 1990 of the first two volumes of his scandalous erotic prose epic *The Great Eastern* established him as one of the most important and controversial Greek writers of the century. His collection of tales entitled *Grapta* was published in English by Alan Ross under the title *Amour, amour*.

MARY LOW & JUAN BREÁ:

An Evening At Home

Fred Lobster was strolling about in his house, inspecting everything in his usual way. He was very wealthy – nobody knew the source of these riches – and lived in a large, overbearing mansion downtown. He was a tall, saturnine man, slightly stooped, with a somewhat expressionless face.

However, like most of us, Lobster was more than his appearance. His chief characteristic was that he carried everything to its ultimate end. This could be seen in his furniture. The legs on his tables and chairs were made to look like real legs – human legs, booted or shoed. Those of the dining-room table were female: pale and shapely, dressed in fine black stockings with pink garters just above the knee, and high-heeled shoes. And the tablecloths were all frilled and looked like petticoats. The bureau legs, in the study, were less frivolous: masculine, they wore trousers and natty shoes.

All the arms of the chairs ended in hands with flexed fingers. Some wore rings; others had watches on the wrist. (Lobster used to go around every day to make sure the watches were keeping good time.) And then there were telephones shaped like ears.

Some of the windows in the bathrooms had faces painted on them, slyly peering in. Other windows presented immense eyes. It was a disquieting house: one could never feel alone.

Lobster liked this haunting: he had been heard to speak to the faces at the windows. He also used to pat the hands on the chairs and flick the garters on the table-legs. It amused him; he would give one of his hollow laughs.

This evening he was awaiting a guest: Elsa, a rather thick girl, like a Thursday. He had invited her to dinner and some horizontal fun afterwards. As he waited, he arranged the table himself – he never had servants in the house on evenings like this. It was a cold meal, colourfully set out: sea-food on green plates, salad on blue, while the sauces were trapped in little jars like clasped fists.

When Elsa arrived, he took off her coat lovingly, kissed her under the ear, and offered her some drink in a glass like a flower. She sat on the sofa – which was a huge, non-committal beast, headless but hairy, with clawed paws – and chatted brightly. Lobster did his best, but he was not very good at conversation. To help himself he had a basket handy, filled with expressive masks. They were all different. From time to time, he put one briefly on, according to circumstances: sad, merry, reflexive. His eyes looked intently at her through the slits.

After dinner, there was some gallant handy-pandy, and finally Lobster felt emboldened enough to invite Elsa into his bedroom – to show her not his etchings, but his collection of glass eyes. They always had an erotic effect.

His bedroom was curious. It exactly resembled a sleeping-car on one of the old luxury-trains. The bunk was made up, and above it a painted landscape was made to slide continuously past the window. There was a vague chuffing sound, as of a steam engine. As soon as Lobster got Elsa onto the bunk – and this he managed quite quickly – he set going a mechanism which joggled the bunk like the motion of a train. It was very conducive to love-making. The two of them churned and heaved away to the movement of the train, until at last Elsa began to groan very loudly and clutch very hard. Lobster felt that his moment had come, too. Quickly he reached up and touched a switch. As the 'train' ground to a halt, a sepulchral voice boomed out:

"Chicago. Ten minutes."

They had both arrived – in more senses than one.

JUAN BREÁ (Havana 1905–Havana 1941) Founder of Cuban Trotskyism, Breá was a globe trotting surrealist who took a key role in the 1933 Cuban Revolution and fought in the Spanish Civil War (his account, with Mary Low, of the early months of the fight for the Republic (*Red Spanish Notebook*, 1937) is recognised as a classic). Made an active contribution to surrealism in France, Romania and Czechoslovakia. Published, also with Mary Low, a theoretical text on surrealism, *La Verdad Contemporanica* (1943) and a volume of poems, *La Saison des flutes* (1938).

MARY LOW: (1912) Born in England of Australian parents, Mary Low's childhood was spent travelling all over Europe. In 1933 she met Juan Breá, and shared his life until his untimely death. Activist in the Fourth International, she played a prominent part, with her second husband Armando Machado, in the Cuban Revolution of 1959. In 1964 settled in Miami. Is also a leading expert on Julius Caesar (about whom she has written an historical novel, *In Caesar's Shadow* (1975). Apart from works written in collaboration with Juan Breá, she has also published several volumes of her own poetry.

LUIS BUÑUEL:

Cavalleria Rusticana

In the middle of the unfinished afternoon, with no landscape or distant moon, a withered tree clenched its imploring branches, stretching them toward the inflexible mirror of the sky which went on reproducing to infinity that atrocious gesture.

On the intact cord of the horizon, three motionless shepherds, without conscience or crook, made an enigmatic vignette on the incredible late afternoon.

Why do the two subtle oars of afternoon – light and shadow – not furrow breezes nor stylise forms?

Desolation was sobbing brokenly, and in the farthest corner of the sky a star breathed out its last sigh.

Not a house, not a flight, not a stream.

We were three siblings. He, she and I.

$$HE = SHE$$
$$SHE = I$$
$$HE = I$$

We were three twins. Beneath our roof no crystal kisses ever flourished on our brows. It is sad and humiliating to speak about it, but we were three parthenogenetic twins.

This is what happened one afternoon, or rather *that* unfinished afternoon with no landscape or distant moon.

For a long time until she almost lost sight of it, my sister, leaning out of the long gothic window, the one solitary light of the dwelling, had been saying goodbye to it with the gentle caress of her handkerchief. Then she had sat down by the fireside and spinning there had diluted the hours with her glances, always with a murmur of streams, always virgins, as befitted her maidenly condition.

112

Nevertheless, from her heart there weighed the black presentiment of the afternoon, with the monotonous and inflexible swing of the pendulum.

Suddenly the garden barked. Someone was walking along the avenue.

Ah! At last.

He returned. It was six and somewhat of time. But he returned without *her*. Where had he left her? What did he do with her chaste joy? In what gloomy minute had she joined herself forever to the hermetic hair-raising afternoon, as irremediable as the past?

Aghast, holding my breath, I saw him enter without asking him about it. In his eyes the last death rattle of day was still trembling.

My brother dropped his old Arab rifle in a corner and began to sob by the fire.

What anguish, my God!

"Brother, is it possible that you, her, *our sister*?"

Without emitting a cry, he was twisting about with grief. Copious tears rolled down his face, but before falling to the ground they congealed on his cheeks, his chest. They were burning tears, tears of wax, and repentance live as a flame, trembled above his head. Already the whole of him was melting like a thick candle.

Bound, elbow to elbow, darkness and night entered the dwelling.

★★★★★

published in English in *Arsenal: Surrealist Subversion* no 4 (1988)

translated from the Spanish by Mary Low Machado

★★★★★

LUIS BUÑUEL (Calanda 1899 – Mexico 1983) Surrealism's greatest film maker was also, much as he might deny it, an accomplished storyteller. Joined the group after Breton attended a screening of *Un Chien andalou* with the intention of demonstrating against the work of someone he had heard was an imposter, but instead he ended up by applauding.

MARCEL MARIËN:

The Oedipal Drip

There were five of them in the bedroom, all completely bored. The dead man was lying on the bed dressed in black as if mourning his own demise. His old and crotchety elder sister, Aunt Adolphine was there, and two cousins, Guillaume and Gaston, whose existence had almost been forgotten, together with Sylvestre, the deceased's only child, and his wife Marguerite. They had been there for hours, with nothing to do, saying nothing, except for a few furtive words demanded by the circumstances and muffled expressions of apology. When night came, Marguerite showed her aunt and cousins to their room in which they would rest until the following day, when the burial would take place.

Sylvestre remained to watch over the body alone as he had expressly requested. At first, and for a long time, he did not think about anything. Now and again he would glance up to look at the distended and livid face of the dead man illuminated by the lampshade on the bedside table. Sylvestre watched with dry eyes, less pained than bored at being forced to undertake such a thankless, if inevitable, task. In fact he no more liked than disliked his father; he was simply 'someone else' and he felt neither sympathy nor contempt for him.

He needed to get up and go to the adjoining bathroom. It was not necessary to turn the light on, since, with the door ajar, the table lamp was sufficient to illuminate the way. He washed his hands and suddenly, as he turned off the tap, felt a surge of anger. It was something that was so much stronger in that it rose from the depths of the past and concerned a childhood memory he had completely forgotten until that moment.

He must have been ten years old when his father, over several weeks, persistently scolded him for not properly turning off the kitchen tap. In actual fact, the rubber seal had worn out and it was necessary to turn the tap very tightly to completely turn off the flow of water. The child's hands were too weak to be able to completely prevent the discharge. And each time the father angrily reprimanded him.

Not very long after, the family moved to a house where the taps fortunately could be turned off without difficulty. The incident was forgotten and Sylvestre had thought no more about it until that moment that ought properly to be qualified as posthumous.

He glanced at his father, whom he could see exactly profiled from where he stood and, without being able to stop himself, with a mechanical but spontaneous gesture he opened the tap just enough so that it rhythmically drip-dropped with a second between each drip.

He returned to his place by the side of the bed and carefully examined his father's face for the whole night, not withdrawing his gaze for a moment. Finally, as day was about to break and the light appeared in the chinks in the shutters, it seemed to him that, the harder the drip of water hit the bottom of the sink, the more the anger of long ago was slowly rekindled in the dead man's face, augmented by a vague distress at his powerlessness to make the slightest complaint about it.

★★★★★

published in *Figures de poupe* (Jean-Claude Simoën)
French original © Marcel Mariën, 1979

★★★★★

MARCEL MARIËN: (Antwerp, 1920) born of a Walloon father and Flemish mother (or vice versa), joined the Belgian Surrealist Group in 1937 and has been one of the mainstays of Belgian surrealism. Storyteller, collagist, object-maker. His memoirs, *Le Radeau de la mémoire* caused a scandal on publication in 1983.

MICHEL FARDOULIS-LAGRANGE:

The Tasks And The Days

1.

The sky appeared above a relief of men and beasts.

It was the warmth that brought Sebastian into the land of the living. His body had conserved all the night's virulence and, since his return, the sun had become red and the forests had flared up.

Joy took possession of organic functions and restored them to full clarity –
then, as clouds gathered round the sun, half the earth was lost and the shipwrecked of the light clung motionless to the raft.

It was the start of winter and the snow had hardened to block all exits from the farm.

A flock of sheep passed, day and night, in the same rhythm. He advanced across the traces of the dark evolution of the season. The two brothers wondered when the wave would come to a halt and who would be bold enough to seize their wool, negotiate the rotation of the earth and unite with vaster physical factors.

So began the third long day. Since their departure from the Jardin des Plantes, Barnau and Sebastian had calculated the newly-born time as it spread across the three days. The first was that of dead Horatius, the second that of the lightning of his substance, the third will be inert, and transcendence will be mingled with the combat of the elements.

The donkey's head came up behind the window pane and also incarnated the memory of a fine day in the midst of winter.

It was an interruption into our vital itinerary, a cry of amazement.

Eugenie saw it and considered it was a foretaste of an innocuous period before the darkness

The fool, under the gleams of the animal, was expected; he put on his own skin. Large bumble bees buzzed around his head. He chased them away with an almost human gesture which is not in the nature of donkeys.

With his laughter, a child can cover these two frontiers; let us go and descend together to the depths of instinct.

The donkey recalled the heroic anabase, the brass medals ornamenting his forehead,

what a radiant ascent, as much so as the expressions and hands of those who followed him are miserable!

The fool watched the donkey and the latter returned the look with the same stubbornness and finally fell asleep, they felt they were separated from the one body, one slept while the other woke.

Which of the two projects the innocence of its image?

The head took on specific proportions, the eye was swollen;

it was a glass eye, in the cavity of which there was fixed a lifeless swarming.

We turned towards the lacy and bright grimace, mingled with the procreative act.

We tickled the head with golden wands and further hollowed out the dead eye.

The stomach was shaken by a delicate and devoted hand.

Everything became delight. When the donkey lowered his head, a ray was seen in the middle of his skull, above the warm matter.

And he scented himself as he promenaded his genetic habits.

Our psychology is like the first circulation of blood in the foetus.

Madness was depth itself, intangible as regulations existing in an extinguished and paradisal moment.

The effort necessary to press the grapes is superhuman, the juice is condensed.

We take the head by the ears, the spike trails along the ground.

Each time the head moves the spike wags like a tail.

We have provoked the cacophony of tumbling weights and mutilated bodies, but the coherence of discourse never reaches the beauty of this wide brow, nor the tenderness of the mouth, which seems delivered, for it is beaten to death. "Isn't it, speechless child?"

The eye is a necropolis of ants and insect skeletons, constituting a composition;
death goes back for several years, but it has passed beyond a superior degree of desiccation and the vision is pleasant.

There is also a swarm of living insects which descends the forehead and sticks to the mouth and the heart. . .

Once, the donkey carried a burden of branches. It came before the fire, corpulent, with its glorious bundle. It suddenly came to a halt in the midst of the party, spreading its legs and releasing its smoking water.

The children dispersed laughingly, then formed a tighter circle around him, jolted by the cries of the fire!

Life, at present, attracted by a familiar voice, descends into the valley.

Barnou believes in totemism, and that is what differentiates him from the antediluvian state of his brother. The latter has taken the animal as he was, without cerebral revelry, and gone to sleep with him; his lucid hours have enveloped the embalmed head.

That evening, the marmot passed by, donned his hat, and called over the donkey.

Marie returned to the farm with a body bearing the trace of hooves; she was pregnant with Sebastian.

The donkey had departed. We had heard footsteps resounding through the nocturnal softening of plants and quenching themselves in calm waters.

Life then became transparent,
the racial values of reality degenerated into madness.

When we later descended into the abyss, near to the bank, we discovered the donkey's remains.

Its hoof formed knots in the middle of the currents of water.

We recalled the age of flocks that passed through the olden days and were suddenly convulsed in the decors.

The perspective was supported by a rhythm of Ionic columns,
through which,
diabolical
reincarnated children,
the HORATII,
cavorted and laughed.

2.

The moments were idle.

Marie was becoming heavy and Barnau went to work in the woods to pick up the threads of his life again.

The imprint of his curbed emotion was not slow to take shape. He had thoroughly excavated the farm, and collected rotten wood and old, light wood. From the hay, colourful, fragrant mists came out to meet him at set times, punctuating the various stages of his unique dream.

They were the girls of the farm who had once travelled by train, who had darkened with melancholy and grown up in the saraband. One-eyed sorceresses of vaginal obscurity, they took apart the frames of skeletons and disentangled the movement.

At night they vanished, leaving their nuptial traces on the ground.

Barnau could not start straight away since the shadows had returned to place themselves between his desire and his work. The whole of nature was then seen in flames, illuminating a new origin of fecundation which abolished the contact of beings.

Eugenie fell ill and Marie had furuncles on her arms, which were caused by her pregnancy.

Barnau was entrusted with the day to day tasks. One might have said that circumstances conspired against his need for evacuation, for to animate the woods with his own breath was an organic need.

Marie's furuncles were a hotbed of infection. They spread in the air and the blood. The purulence reached Barnau's hands which trembled at contact with the piece of wood. They painfully squashed the idea of perfection. Henceforth there was a sickness at the heart of any concept of eternity or exuberance.

Sebastian came silently to work at Barnou's side. There was an elemental struggle. Sebastian watched for the members that would come out of the woods, his mind secreted. In the intimacy of matter the yellowing eggs of the insect were to be found.

Barnou wiped them but they still remained incrusted; gradually the woods became a field of hatching in exuberance. It was still-born chaos of stagnant mud, uniform time. The waves collapsed against the wooden dams. The seeds wanted to dissolve in the initial foam, although the torrents carried them along. Barnou worked for a long time. The sleeper was lying over the solidified waves, everywhere there were graduations of the rotundity of his body.

(HE FELL, WOUNDING HIS EXTREMITIES)

His arms were foreshortened by the sea climbing up to his elbows and no depth is greater than those sounded by these arms. They triumphed over all resistance and palpated the constellations. Long hair covered the limbs of this still slight adolescent. He made a gesture of defiance towards multiple and perceptible nature. Once two oranges slipped from the table. The fool took one of them and bit into it. The other one rolled away and stopped, tremblingly, at the edge of unknown places. When it stopped moving, a flame sprang forth as a sign of alliance with universal breath which caused the trajectory of the orange to reverse, leave a luminous fluid and proceed beyond the sleeper, prolonging his existence into infinity. It stuck to the hair and the wave which surrounded his body. It penetrated his sleep and all the tributaries of life were thrown into musical notion.

When the fool bit into the orange, he was astonished that his brother had not instantly been seized by the purity of the fall and circulation. The colour was suspended, audaciously, and the orange, as it shook, consumed itself in erotic delirium.

The wave still kept its independence, receded; it caused the blossoming over the cross-currents and seaweed of the sleeper.

The sea shared the adolescent desire. Its depths were sweet, its sponges, elementary and neuropathological, slipped down to regions participating in sleep. Duration was filled with gigantic and microscopic shadows married together in light.

The first wave repelled the floating orange. Agitation reigned among the organisms lost in the foam and creation hesitated.

It was an intermediary state before the transgression of the birth of form.

The prototypes asserted their authority and threw discord into the most remote parts of being remaining in control. The wave drowned morbid plants and scourged the sleeper's body. A wide-open breath rose and spread, provoking the orchestrated flight of seagulls around their prey. The orange went off to recapture the purity of its image.

Sometimes the water, sometimes the air, sometimes the fool hastened towards time,
and, in that moment, the man displayed his round and tortured face for the first time.

Seaweed formed the sheath of the sleeper, fading into the polar night. The wave rose, slipped under his body and reached its highest point a little further on, marking an ideal difference in the order of substance.

The adolescent loved sleep because it engendered the static concept that the dream explored: movement is merely an illusion.

The two dishes of the scales became level –
chaos is a door open to the fixity of light.

The team of horses which, once upon a time, disturbed the night –
phantasmagoric, gleaming in the visual development of myth, inflated in inertia.

The whinnying and the uproar and the precocious spasms of madness, are congealed memories.

Barnou's work enlarged the internal dimensions of being, just at the integral hour of creation.

The whole grew by the mutual sympathy of its parts.

The fool is merely an apparent puzzle, an accident quickly expelled by the norm. He has bitten into the orange in the belief that he would explode the agreements of immobility and reach the face of the sleeper by the sparks and wake him up.

He wished for a renewal of consciousness that emanated from tortured flesh.

The flames of evening danced on the sleeper's face.

They came from far away, through the ebb and flow of the sea,
they penetrated the future, instituted the march of time,
they came close to the absolute without touching it since they were powerless,
like the bird which skims over a graduation of colours without being able to combine with them.

While working Barnou was shaken in his habits and used artifice on the attraction and repulsion of his senses. At times he neutralised himself and his work, all alone, was gnawed away by events. An enormous machine suddenly displaced him, pulled him back towards new and super-natural traces.

The landscape was covered in mist. The periodic old age of fairies reached incoherence. They no longer symbolised the rotation of the ages, but something which went beyond visible entities.

If Barnou left the house and went out among the tree trunks, the true belief he might offer himself, no matter how great and diffuse, could never mingle in the ageing flow of the girls in the train. At the end there was perhaps a flowery sexuality which destroyed ordinary measures.

Certain photos hidden at the bottom of drawers have the same spirituality, the same melancholic eventuality. However, transcendence is a witticism lacking an image, a motionless old age, installed in a series of accidental causes, a fever of incomplete forms.

The strength of nature in its symbolism is greater than that of man.

Pushed forward by jealousy, the fool wanted to remove all originality from the piece of wood. His ecstasy jaculated on the waves while the adolescent protected the contours of the universe. A centrifugal force and a centripetal force, reflected on one another, commonly believed in the last spaces in which their magic would take on grandeur.

There followed a third force, a subjected one: Eugenie, with an infantile and stupid smile, had been seized with terror in the face of the decline.

To the fireball as it faded into the distance on its extra-terrestrial journey, she conveyed the tenderness of her expression.

It was necessary for someone to remain fixed to his place to give a human meaning to enchantment. It was Eugenie! Afterwards came Marie, poisoned by the spasm of love. She believed in her own female destiny, immutable in the face of great speeds, leaning as she was over the washing machine and following the motion of the spontaneous bubbles of water!

The things she had loved continued to get bigger in reciprocity and to bathe in marshy waters.

Sometimes a stem rose and illustrated the pattern of sickness with its tumours. It grew very fast.

It raised the woman's spirits and her belief in reverie.

Each new sensation was unexpected and illuminated the organs. Everything was reconciled and returned to origins; three-dimensionality was reflected in the internal state of meditation.

At any moment reversibility could surge forth and be consumed; it was loveless.

To endure, it must be surrounded with the amazement of the soul.

This is the meaning of the adolescent's coupling, lying alongside the first homogeneous laws.

The need for miracle caused sympathy to rise up from a rich spring.

In the enchantment a violin shared in the adolescence of the world, with its burst arteries, flooding Marie's starry clothes with music.

In the infernal trench arms were extended: each morning's forward march of the universe. . .

One day Marie slit the throat of the pig in the courtyard.

Barnou heard the cries of the beast as he was administering the last duties for the care of the sleeper. His work was interrupted by the torrent of blood.

The beast resisted as he cried out with a raucous and hard voice. The spasm had been quick, it had offset the technique of instinct and had thrown him into the shadows. The carnage declined and the groaning stopped.

The pig was soon dissected and its blood filled the bucket in the bottom of which a patch of sky was reflected darkly. It had surrendered to the vortex of life and his breathing.

He went off, plump and pink, falling on his side and blinded by the jolt of renunciation. He had embraced the hope of rising as a vapour above the bucket, above his body, and vanishing.

The sleeper's journey ended there. The happy times of his sleep had been disturbed, awakening was effected in the midst of the stormy sea.

For one last time he went to perform the final leap, through such mechanical gestures, nature is impoverished and the richest forms degenerate through repetition. The elements have undergone the blood-letting of time and act only out of a sense of necessity.

The child had died,
but he could still fall artificially from the carriage door.
Having lost his autonomy; an alien, withered hand, will push him outside.

It is the end.

The sleeper turns somersaults in the flames of the fireplace. Grains of light hover around his body and around his ultimate freedom.

★★★★★
originally published in *Sebastien, l'enfant et l'orange* (1943)
French original © Le Castor Astral, 1986
★★★★★

MICHEL FARDOULIS-LAGRANGE (Cannes, 1909) During the war, as the leader of a communist cell, he was sentenced to death by the nazis. After the war he edited the journal *Troisième convoi* (1945–51) on the fringes of surrealism; he was a close friend of Georges Bataille (the subject of his book *GB, ou un ami présomptueux*, 1968). Fardoulis-Lagrange is a major writer whose work raises important philosophical issues on the nature of time and creation.

GISÈLE PRASSINOS:

The King's Ostlers

Any minute the train would be coming to look for us.

The station was dark on the platform as little streams ran between the paving slabs. We were the 'King's Ostlers'. We were forced to walk in a file with hands behind our backs and successively fold and unfold a long band that was inflated with air like a rubber tyre. If ever our fingers stopped working an iron bar would come down to beat them and make them start working again. We could no longer catch breath between the folding and unfolding either. If, as we went about our task, our tired hands allowed the beginning of the roll to slip so that the whole band escaped into daylight, we would be whipped and forcibly held where the train would pass from one moment to the next.

Soon the train entered the station.

I noticed my friend busily climbing a ladder in order to escape through one of the broken panes in the hangar.

He was dressed in green: a shirt of well-tailored velvet and with musketeer's boots. His freshly cut hair, Joan of Arc style, rose graciously with each effort he made. His eyes ran with tears and he scanned the air with despair. His hands, moistened with work and tears, could barely grasp the side of the ladder for fear it was in danger of disintegrating. His bands of material, fixed to the back of his waist, hung down below his feet. He seemed paralysed, aged, and worn out. He had asked me to choose when we were presented to the king and I started to cry as I thought he was slinking off without saying goodbye.

My comrades had been given a rest and walked in groups along the platform and mingled their bands of bright colours which still bore the marks of being rolled up, like so many admirable tails dragging the whole of their length into the dust and little streams.

My friend had not yet got to the end. His tears had started to cover the wall and his soaking clothes had lost their freshness. His appearance had also been reduced. His boots sometimes faltered as if he had become blind.

The train whistled and smoke rose high in the air and hid the sight of my friend. By now my comrades were sitting comfortably in their compartments and chatting as they cleaned their bands for the next day. We were at Angers. The excursion would be going to Chartres where the king awaited us.

Soon the locomotive was set in motion with little jerks and hundreds of handkerchiefs leapt to the windows while I stayed on the bench.

For a moment smoke filled the whole station. I closed my eyes to avoid the fall of ash and dust. . .

When I opened them again the station had cleared and its little streams gleamed between the burning stones.

My friend was stretched out bleeding at my feet, still grasping the broken pieces of the ladder in his dislocated hands. His beautiful and tearful eyes no longer moved. His black hair, now as long as mine, covered the whole of his greenish nudity.

★★★★★

first published in Gisèle Prassinos *Les Mots endormis* (1967)
Flammarion
reprinted in Gisèle Prassinos, *Trouver sans chercher* (1976)
French original © Éditions Flammarion, 1976

★★★★★

GISÈLE PRASSINOS (Istanbul 1920) The entry of Gisèle Prassinos into the Surrealist circle at the age of 14 has gained a legendary status. Born into what had been a wealthy and cultured Greek family which was forced to move to France to avoid persecution during hostilities between Greece and Turkey when Gisèle was only two (her father had to sell his library of 100,000 books to pay for the journey), she grew up in a difficult but stimulating environment that is reflected in her work. Aside from her novels, stories and poems, she also creates objects, particularly in fabric, and has translated Kazantzakis into French.

LÉO MALET:

Simple Tale

On 15th July 1927, around four in the afternoon, a well-dressed man, accompanied by a woman, consulted the metro map at Place Daumesnil. It is perhaps necessary to mention in passing that the map at Daumesnil station is to be found in a casket of red velvet abandoned to the south wind. At quarter past five the Chief of Police of the 12th district saw the man we have just mentioned enter his office. Sitting himself comfortably in an armchair, the man proceeded to take a revolver out of his pocket and hold it within reach of his hand. Still without saying a word, he placed under the eyes of the policeman a faded photograph showing a bouquet of roses. Beside the bouquet was an ink-well which held a carnation rather than a pen-holder or stopper. Everything lay on a wicker chair. As the civil servant seemed to understand less and less, the gentleman passed a pair of gloves in front of his eyes, as conjurers do. At six the evening papers, printed on a single page, announced in bold letters that a map of the metro had vanished. What I am recounting here is not some boring tale, but the greatest poetic revelation of the century. Anyone initiated into it knows as much. So I make these disclosures, several years – is it ten? twenty? – after the event for the benefit of the profane. It would be a waste of time for you to look it up in the papers of the time. I destroyed them all. Bouquets of flowers, bouquets of revolvers, bouquets of inkwells, bouquets of chairs. A tobacco pouch that explodes. A search of the anarchists' place was made and ten thousand tons of dynamite seized. The investigation was at a standstill. It was then that the news came. What news: the Commissioner of Police received in his personal correspondence a lovely female heart that could tell the future. Both capital and capitalists were uneasy. On the park benches, in the avenues and boulevards, lovers were turned away. On the walls of Paris one could read large posters that proclaimed the following:

REMEMBER 1912
BE ON YOUR GUARD AGAINST THE TRAGIC
BANDITS
COEUR AND BROWNING

For it had been in 1912 that an automobile that changed colours like the approach of love, driven by a dozen suicidal goblins, stopped on rue Ordener in an orchestration of gunfire. And the bank messengers, their boats shipwrecked, shed blood everywhere. My part in the affair is well known. My mistress was executed on Boulevard Arago. That was when we took our hammers down to Avenue de l'Opéra to deal with the jewellers' shops and distributed pearls and razors to the crowd. Then we all made off, still in the car with changing colours. Nothing more was heard about us until the day when silver coins fell from the sky and were transformed as they touched the ground into copper and nickel. At night, Paris became a river of diamonds. The Seine which, in the serials, was overwhelmed with corpses, now bore untold riches in comparison with which sexual organs resemble beggars. The car, yellow, red, green, grey – I no longer know what – appeared for the last time. Jumping over the parapet of the Pont au Change it vanished, drunk with pride and joy, in pursuit of Death.

★★★★★
published in Léo Malet, *Poèmes Surréalistes*
French original © Editions de la Butte aux cailles, 1983
★★★★★

LÉO MALET (Montpellier 1909) From the age of sixteen led a vagabond existence as a singer in a Montmartre club. During the thirties lived on his wits until he was able to put his experiences to use in creating the character of

Nestor Burma and becoming one of France's leading thriller writers. Some of his books have recently been published in English for the first time.

LEONORA CARRINGTON:

The Royal Summons

I had received a royal summons to pay a call on the sovereigns of my country.

The invitation was made of lace, framing embossed letters of gold. There were also roses and swallows.

I went to fetch my car, but my chauffeur, who has no practical sense at all, had just buried it.

"I did it to grow mushrooms," he told me. "There's no better way of growing mushrooms."

"Brady," I said to him, "you're a complete idiot. You have ruined my car."

So, since my car was indeed completely out of action, I was obliged to hire a horse and cart.

When I arrived at the palace, I was told by an impassive servant, dressed in red and gold, "The queen went mad yesterday. She's in her bath."

"How terrible," I exclaimed. "How did it happen?"

"It's the heat."

"May I see her all the same?" I didn't like the idea of my long journey being wasted.

"Yes," the servant replied. "You may see her anyway."

We passed down corridors decorated in imitation marble, admirably done, through rooms with Greek bas-reliefs and Medici ceilings and wax fruit everywhere.

The queen was in her bath when I went in; I noticed that she was bathing in goat's milk.

"Come on in," she said. "You see I use only live sponges. It's healthier."

The sponges were swimming about all over the place in the milk, and she had trouble catching them. A servant, armed with long-handled tongs, helped her from time to time.

"I'll soon be through with my bath," the Queen said. "I have a proposal to put to you. I would like you to see the government instead of me today, I'm too tired myself. They're all idiots, so you won't find it difficult."

"All right," I said.

The government chamber was at the other end of the palace. The ministers were sitting at a long and very shiny table.

As the representative of the Queen, I sat in the seat at the end. The Prime Minister rose and struck the table with a gavel. The table broke in two. Some servants came in with another table. The Prime Minister swapped the first gavel for another, made of rubber. He struck the table again and began to speak. "Madame Deputy of the Queen, ministers, friends. Our dearly beloved sovereign went mad yesterday, and so we need another. But first we must assassinate the old queen."

The ministers murmured amongst themselves for a while. Presently, the oldest minister rose to his feet and addressed the assembly. "That being the case, we must forthwith make a plan. Not only must we make a plan, but we must come to a decision. We must choose who is to be the assassin."

All hands were immediately raised. I didn't quite know what to do as the deputy of Her Majesty.

Perplexed, the Prime Minister looked over all the company.

"We can't all do it," he said. "But I've got a very good idea. We'll play a game of draughts, and the winner has the right to assassinate the queen." He turned to me and asked, "Do you play Miss?"

I was filled with embarrassment. I had no desire to assassinate the Queen, and I foresaw that serious consequences might follow. On the other hand I never had been any good at all at draughts. So I saw no danger, and accepted.

"I don't mind," I said.

"So, it's understood," said the Prime Minister. "This is

what the winner will do: take the queen for a stroll in the royal Menagerie. When you reach the lions (second cage on the left), push her in. I shall tell the keeper not to feed the lions until tomorrow.

The Queen called me to her office. She was watering the flowers woven in the carpet.

"Well, did it go alright?" she asked.

"Yes, it went very well," I answered, confused.

"Would you like some soup?"

"You're too kind," I said.

"It's mock beef tea. I make it myself," the Queen said. "There's nothing in it but potatoes."

While we were eating the broth, an orchestra played popular and classical tunes. The queen loved music to distraction.

The meal over, the Queen left to have a rest. I for my part went to join in the game of draughts on the terrace. I was nervous, but I've inherited sporting instincts from my father. I had given my word to be there and so there I would be.

The enormous terrace looked impressive. In front of the garden, darkened by the twilight and the cypress trees, the ministers were assembled. There were twenty little tables. Each had two chairs, with thin, fragile legs. When he saw me arrive, the Prime Minister called out, "Take your places," and everybody rushed to the tables and began to play ferociously.

We played all night without stopping. The only sounds that interrupted the game were an occasional furious bellow from one minister or another. Towards dawn, the blast of a trumpet abruptly called an end to the game. A voice, coming from I don't know where, cried, "She has won. She is the only person who didn't cheat."

I was rooted to the ground with horror.

"Who? Me?" I said.

"Yes, you," the voice replied, and I noticed that it was the tallest cypress speaking.

I'm going to escape, I thought and began to run in the direction of the avenue. But the cypress tore itself out of the earth by the roots, scattering dirt in all directions, and began to follow me. It's so much larger than me, I thought and stopped. The cypress stopped too. All its branches were shaking horribly – it was probably quite a while since it had last run.

"I accept," I said, and the cypress returned slowly to its hole.

I found the Queen lying in her great bed.

"I want to invite you to come for a stroll in the menagerie," I said, feeling pretty uncomfortable.

"But it's still too early," she replied. "It isn't five o'clock yet. I never get up before ten."

"It's lovely out," I added.

"Oh, all right, if you insist."

We went down into the silent garden. Dawn is the time when nothing breathes, the hour of silence. Everything is transfixed, only the light moves. I sang a bit to cheer myself up. I was chilled to the bone. The Queen, in the meantime, was telling me that she fed all the horses on jam.

"It stops them from being vicious," she said.

She ought to have given the lions some jam, I thought to myself.

A long avenue, lined on both sides with fruit trees led to the menagerie. From time to time a heavy fruit fell to the ground, Plop.

"Head colds are easily cured, if one just has the confidence," the Queen said. "I myself always take morsels marinated in olive oil. I put them in my nose. Next day the cold's gone. Or else, treated in the same way, cold noodles in liver juice, preferably calves' liver. It's a miracle how it dispels the heaviness in one's head."

She'll never have a head cold again, I thought.

"But bronchitis is more complicated. I nearly saved my poor husband from his last attack of bronchitis by knitting him a waistcoat. But it wasn't altogether successful."

We were drawing closer and closer to the menagerie. I could already hear the animals stirring in their morning slumbers. I would have liked to turn back, but I was afraid of the cypress and what it might be able to do with its hairy black branches. The more strongly I smelled the lion, the more loudly I sang, to give myself courage.

★★★★★

published in *The House of Fear* (1988) New York: E.P. Dutton. London: Virago
© Leonora Carrington 1988
translated by Katharine Talbot and Marina Warner

★★★★★

LEONORA CARRINGTON (Clayton Green, Lancashire, 1917) the daughter of a textile tycoon, Leonora Carrington came into contact with the surrealists when she met Max Ernst in 1936. Her paintings and stories have established her in the front rank of surrealist artists.

BENJAMIN PÉRET:

A Story Celebrating The Blue And White

That spring morning, a young woman, who might have been a princess, wandered down the Champs-Elysées dragging a wheelbarrow full of apples behind her. When she reached the Rond-Point she burst out laughing and said: "There's something in the air."

As if to prove her right, a Remington typewriter fell, or rather was placed, at her feet and began to function as though someone was actually tapping the keys.

The young woman, Madame de Freycinet (she was in fact the wife of a former minister), was a little taken aback. Nevertheless she continued on her way. But she had hardly gone a hundred yards when a lyrebird flew down from a lamp post and landed on the apples. At the same time, the paving-stones rose up to reveal an enormous pipe. From the pipe came a one-eyed negress who called out, "Captain!... Captain!"

Madame de Freycinet stood to attention and gave a military salute, saying: "My child, you are certainly a credit to the nation."

She handed over the lyrebird which, furious at having to leave the wheelbarrow, yelped until it ran out of breath. The negress in turn gave a military salute and, slicing the toes off her right foot, put them in place of the lyrebird which, having finally calmed down, had jumped on to her head.

This was not to be the end of Mme de Freycinet's adventures, though. When she reached the Select Bar she stopped for a moment to get her breath because, curious to relate, ever since the negress had placed her toes in the wheelbarrow its weight secmed to have doubled.

She muttered to herself: "What weather! It is so marvellously warm and yet all the clocks say its seven o'clock, even though I left the Place de la Concorde at midday. It's just not possible!"

She had hardly formulated this thought than the Select Bar advanced towards her and gobbled her up like an animal. At the same moment a fully decorated general fell from a first floor window with arms outstretched. He was only a yard from the ground when he straightened himself up and, propelled by a considerable force ascended vertically into the air, before vanishing in the direction of the Place de l'Étoile.

It would be twelve years before they would find him again near the North Pole. He would be called 'The Nation'.

*****

originally published in Benjamin Péret, *Le Gigot, sa vie et son oeuvre* (1957)
included in Benjamin Péret, *Oeuvres complètes* Tome 3
Eric Losfeld (1979)
French original © Librairie José Corti

*****
BENJAMIN PÉRET: (See page 33)

MAURICE BLANCHARD:

Ode To Stalin

"Does he shit then, the beloved Gobalmightyarsehole? Does he really shit?

"Yes, HE does shit."

"No, I refuse to believe it! Something like that could change the face of the earth! Surely it cannot be real shit that HE shits, our brilliantfatherofthepeople, the Beloved Gobalmightyarsehole? No it must be real Russian leather he shits! Tell a white lie! Have pity on we of little faith!"

"No, HE really does shit shit."

"But it's not possible! Surely his arsehole is made of platinum? Isn't his arsehole bunged up with a finely cut emerald as big as my head?"

"No, HE has a greenish arsehole in fact, around which extend divine haemorroids that hang down in latrine juice and sway back and forth when HE makes the effort to force HIS dung as he growls and grimaces and ooh, ooh, ooh!

"But still HE must have a golden prick, our Beloved sixthhighestoftheglobe? You can't say he does it like everyone else! The Olympian Zeus had one but it was not functional, like a poetic image of the moon in the style of Aragon. But HE, the Grandbrilliantbeloved Gobalmightyarsehole, HE! He has to inseminate the Party's hysterical women every morning over breakfast."

"No, HE always gets hoodwinked, Alleluia!"

"Liar! Scumbag! Our need to believe is so great that in that case everything would have to be started all over again!"

"Not at all, you just need to eat it, HIS shit!"

(1947)

139

*****
first published in Maurice Blanchard, *Nous autres sans patrie*
(1947)
French original © Isabelle Blanchard
*****

MAURICE BLANCHARD (Montdidier 1890 – Toulon 1960) From a working class background, Maurice Blanchard became a metal worker, before a distinguished war record (he was one of France's first fighter pilots) led to the chance to be an aeronautical engineer. He received several awards for the prototypes he developed and was the inventor of a sea plane. A chance discovery of a volume of poetry by Paul Éluard secured his allegiance to surrealism and he became, although little recognised outside surrealist circles, one of its greatest lyric voices. He translated Shakespeare's Sonnets into French.

The Dictator

The dictator wandered distractedly through the meadows. Without thinking about it he gathered clover with
three-leaves and, still without thinking about it, whether
by using his spit, by a discreet stitch or by expert dissimula-
tion, created a four-leafed clover.

Following the thread of the footpath he was already
within the shadow of the tower. From on high the tower
quivered, blindly, in the green meadow. It was an ivory
tower. The crackling of hay was brought on the limpid air
as the clouds and summer winds tore at the snow column.
It was there that the dictator, now just fine dust in the
distance, would soon speak to several million men, women
and babies.

The orator soon entered into the immense circle of his
listeners: the babies, although used to this density of social
atmosphere, were ill at ease and cried like lambs going to
the slaughter. Almost all the children played familiarly
with the monstrous fire-crackers and it was a marvel not to
see them fly off into fragments, them and their packet of
powder. The adolescents, on the other hand, were already
responsible and carried large banners. Most of the men and
women lay on the ground and silently gathered blades of
grass which they chewed as they dreamed. Everyone
moved around the itinerant stalls through an inextricable
disorder of electric cables that fed the myriad of loudspeakers buried in the grass, hidden beneath small columns or
even held by inert sentries.

Suddenly the dictator felt cramped by this crowd that
was at once rowdy, because of the children, and yet
meditative among its adults. An underground tram system

soon brought him to the foot of the tower. He entered through the dark square of the monumental door into the cylindrical ivory building and felt tiny compared to the height of the tower in the atmospheric immensity.

Everything had been calculated by the most careful engineers so that his first words burst out of the loud-speakers at the precise moment that, as the day came to an end, the moon appeared in the notch formed by two enormous elephant tusks, raised like two antennae in front of the last balcony of the tower. This meant they would illuminate the dictator in all his majesty and the tower would have, especially from the distance, in the elegance of the ivory, the allure of a genuinely blazing mirror in the middle of the interminable grassland or rather in the midst of a sea of human beings.

As the moon came to rest docilely in the notch of ivory for the dictator, the crowd immediately fell silent. The adults even stopped their ruminating meditation and the children stopped howling and bawling.

How solemn this moment was when land, moon and elephant encountered each other in the sky! A poetic moment for the whole people! This is how Brocelte, the succinct historian, reported the reason for such expressive veneration. After having recounted a few illustrious facts about Queen Etha, he said, verbatim:

"*. . .It was during a terrible epidemic that a shepherd named Edoré asked one fine day to speak with the queen. He had crossed the Elédan, the Tamir and the Eredan on foot and was dropping with fatigue as soon as he had formulated his desire. Queen Etha had a premonition of the importance of such an extraordinary journey, and wanted to see the still unconscious traveller. He was lying on a divan near the window through which the surge of moon rays entered the room. No sooner had she entered the room than the queen noticed something wondrous about the sleeper's posture. His hand was bathed in the light of the star even though the rest of his body remained in shadow. This hand pointed to the only object in the room which was also subject to the same* *pre-eminent luminosity: an ebony elephant which had been brought back to the country by one of the queen's ancestors after a journey to who knows where. Queen Etha, whose sagacity was more than substantiated by preceding events recognised a celestial sign in the way the object had been denoted by the moon and the sleeping hand. As soon as he awoke, the sleeper would, in his turn, confirm the queen's belief. In his dream he had in fact seen a monstrous moon rolling over the world. This moon, which was like an immense spherical egg of protoplasmic light, had imprisoned a gigantic elephant. The dreamer had also seen the whole people prostrate over the course of the lowering star, waving latania leaves and so giving grace to the imprisoning moon and imprisoned elephant.*

"In fact the object of the shepherd's visit was an idle request. Yet he had been the unconscious messenger of the destiny of our people because the very wise Queen Etha, who understood the occult message, instructed the doctors of the realm to make potions from latania leaves and the powder of elephant bones. In less than a week, thanks to this miraculous remedy, the terrible epidemic had vanished from the whole realm."

The dictator knew that the witnesses of the tragic image, exhumed as it was from the depths of millenary memory, would be overcome with tumult. In fact it had been a genuine hysteria which set in motion the first retrospective apparition of moon and ivory. Afterwards the dictator used the precious conjuncture with great care and only at the most audaciously political shifts.

This was probably one of those shifts.

Whatever the case, at the point we have reached in our story, the loudspeakers did not function properly and burst forth in a fury of cackling words. The frightened children rose and there was a unanimous clamour of cries and gnashing of teeth. There was a vertiginous gap of silence, as the loudspeakers sputtered to clear the line for the near yet distant voice of the dictator.

They were at the end of the DECENNIAL PSYCHO-LOGICAL PLAN. The Revolution had caused so many

143

profound changes in the national mentality that the dictator wanted to underline the meaning of what had been done and what remained to be done in respect of what the bill-boards called the "conquest of auto-psychic man".

This formula had initially only been a publicity stunt, except to a small group of scholars, but which had to be taken seriously when the old traditional mentality was manifestly seen to suddenly change. These changes were not simply the result of advertising: all at once men were imbued with new ideas and feelings.

One day as they travelled on their way some men encountered boundary marks in the form of a centaur and considered the problem of friendship in a different way. On another occasion, they learned that the daisies, which had grown thickly and tightly together, covered the country in a continuous white cloak: the people were summoned, on such a day, to live for a few moments entirely surrounded by a surprising floral sea. Later it was recognised that man in that country had taken a further step towards love. What nevertheless remained most noticeable, and came to the attention of everyone, was what had preceded this new filial love which had so astonished the stranger.

So it was that one evening, throughout the country, the inhabitants were awakened by a music that each had forgotten but still retained an unforgettable nostalgia. It was a tune of an unprecedented sweetness and majesty. It was literally a celestial music, for it came, but how, from heaven. Everyone ran to their windows:

By an unknown use of light and colour there was painted in the sky a scene of such tragic density. What people saw was a cottage whose straw was so veracious its palpitations could be seen in the breeze. By the open door a pale woman was seen, dressed in an interminable white chemise and standing in the middle of the room, anxious and still. On a wretched bed a sleeping child, who, was in the throes of an uneasy nightmare.

144

The woman watched the road that rose to the cottage. Along this road came an old man bathed in the light of a crescent moon, limping with a wooden leg and his head covered with straw.

All the inhabitants of the country, each one at his window let us repeat, saw the same pathetic apparition. Struck by the equal beauty of the music and the scene, the adult even woke up the baby without fear of causing a seizure. It was some time later that all the children began to love their parents, as they had never done before, with a love devoid of all hypocritical convention.

For all these reasons they awaited the dictator's speech with impatience.

These are some of his words (his speech lasted for several hours) and it is said his twenty million listeners were hypnotised by moon and elephant. It is true that by the end of the speech a certain lack of attention was apparent and the engineer-psychologists were reduced to projecting, just above the tower's balcony, a gigantic four-leafed clover with the green luminosity of poppy into the sky. We would also add that the babies were far from being the least attentive). So these, as we say, are a few of the dictator's words that evening:

"As soon as our revolution has delivered you from the anguish provoked by what I call 'the dialectical apparition of precarious sustenance' (does not this single word characterise the sordid aspect of man's life, from antiquity to the thunderclap of my insurrection?) – it put on its most beautiful skates and passed over our meadows with the speed of the spirit since it was spirit itself. None resisted its blue eyes that brought both love and death. That was the time I decreed, obedient to its look of snow, the metamorphosis of man. It was no longer a question, my people, of giving you a life of luxury and comfort – such would have been an easily attainable and puerile game – but of creating a new man or rather, more precisely – a man. A man who would be prepared to bear on his own shoulders the weight of his depths, on whom there would be a complicitous look of friendship and

who would assume all the risks of his condition, someone who would hurl himself like a sling on the brow of love and the unknown.

I immediately undertook this task with the help of the engineers of the College of Psychology. I am not in the habit of offering facile rewards. Nevertheless I can say that the results surpassed my most optimistic hopes.

Already you are the envy of your neighbours, who hate you with an intensity that can only be explained by dissemblance. You have yourselves taken part, amazed by your own metamorphoses. We have already changed our most basic instincts: today you recognise that your relation to flowers, for instance, is not merely idyllic and urbane but often mortal? This year the violets have provoked many murders: the rose of Bengal decimates our armies. Egoism, at least as it was known before our revolution, monopolistic and stupid, has soon been liquidated. Today, in this country, egoism serves merely to diminish identity, and prevents us from taking ourselves for our neighbours.

We have caused all the idiotic forms of fear to vanish. Now the seductive forms of this emotion can see the light of day.

Fear of midday is mysterious and passionate. I have been told – forgive me for going into details – about the case of a child subject to a completely new interesting fear: he is afraid of not being lost. In the nation I believe this child will be recognised as a man of the first rank. He is already assured of wondrous adventures. But it is perhaps in the domain of love that the changes have been most marked. The unity of lovers was, until the past few days, only metaphorical. But it has now become acquired fact since, as you have noticed, not without a little amazement I would wager, that if one lover dies in our country it inevitably means the death of the other.

I have delivered your soul from digestive needs. You are ready for adventure. I am the first leader of real men. This is why my government is, as it must be, psychological.

Here and now my engineers and myself have inoculated you with the microbe of uselessness. This constitutes new meaning for you. Certainly not what ridiculous societies still call common

*sense, a name which is accurate, being the sense of the vulgar —
but the common sense of poetry.*

*I do not want to reveal all my secrets. I will speak only later
about the causes and modalities of those changes for which you
have been the unconscious theatre — if such an affirmation proves
necessary. Have no illusions. You are on a tightrope and down
below the stupidity of your traditions still exercise a seductive
attraction for you.*

*But you can have confidence in us, in my engineers and
myself. I tell you this: now everything is possible. Your metamorphosis is unlimited. Let those of you who are already tired of
renewing themselves, which means they are tired of living, let
them have the courage to hang themselves on the lamp-posts. At
least they will amuse the birds. I WANT TO SHOW MY
PEOPLE THE WAYS OF COMETS. EVERY DAY
MUST BE A NEW DAY FOR YOU."*

(These last words were underlined with an increase of
luminosity on the ivory notch of the entire balcony and to
the dictator, far away, a sparkling atom.

It appeared that some of the engineer-physicians concentrated the rays of the moon, by means of immense invisible
lenses in a distant place, and directed them precisely by
turntables on the summit of the tower which became
quasi-atmospheric in the celestial conflagration.)

The dictator added: *"You will be the conquistadors of the
modern age. Not at all like those whose naive idea was sail and
wind and unrestrained accumulation of gems, under the ridiculous
symbol of the death's head. But similar to you alone: the wind of
our sail is human fury, our gems are those of ardent memory. We
sail under the sign of the trembling clover."*

In the sky the clover was accentuated by the fluorescent
light that was, one might say, hypnotic. The dictator, as he
descended in the lift, crumpled between his fingers a natural
four-leafed clover he had gathered in one of the gardens
hanging from the ivory tower.

*****
first published in *Tropiques* no 6–7 (February 1943)
reprinted in René Ménil: *Tracées*
French original © Robert Laffont, 1982
*****

RENÉ MÉNIL: (Fort de France, 1904) Organiser, with Jules Monnerot and Étienne Léro, of the group *Légitime Défense*, organised by students from Martinique, which was to have led to the formation of an Antilles Surrealist Group, but was more significant as the first genuine manifestation of black consciousness among the French colonial intellectuals. With Aimé and Suzanne Césaire founded *Tropiques* (1941–45), one of the most important surrealist journals. An incisive critic, most of René Ménil's articles, tales and poems were scattered in various journals until he brought together a collection of his work under the title, *Tracées* (1981).

FRANCOIS VALORBE:

In The Town Of Eps

The despotism of the ruling family takes several strange forms in Eps. Particularly arbitrary is the fact that official cars are invisible to pedestrians. Invisible but not entirely inaudible: one can hear the light humming of their powerful engines which serves to warn people of the danger. This is not great when uniformed motorcyclists precede the cars to clear the street, even if it is peculiar to see them formed in front of an empty space of a hundred or so metres. Even then people have to take great care and it is odd to see the anxious faces of passers-by as they try to ascertain, by sound or by current of air, whether or not their masters' cortège has passed. As normal traffic circulation resumes, so the end of the alert is indicated. If things were always like that it would not have be too bad. The problem is that most of the time these ladies and gentlemen go on their jaunts unescorted and just for the hell of it, so it is said. And the pedestrians are always in the wrong. To be able to cross the road with confidence at any time one needs to have good hearing since the royal cars, or more precisely their drivers, are less concerned about the 'riff-raff' – to use their own phrase – than with the stains caused by their remains, which severely stained the tyres. On the other hand their bumpers are equipped with atomic, or atomising, qualities. In this way the injured pedestrian is vaporised and simply disappears into thin air, thus allowing the princely vehicle to continue on its way in tranquillity.

Among the pedestrians of Eps, people are divided into the prudent and the fatalists. Although it could be shown from the annual statistics prepared by the prudent that the fatalists suffered most in the hecatomb, the latter still perished in the comfort of knowing they had lived and died free from anxiety.

✮✮✮✮✮

published in François Valorbe, *Le Chimère vierge* (1957)
Paris: Losfeld
French original © Eric Losfeld

✮✮✮✮✮

GEORGES HENEIN:

The Dictator's Philosophical Stroll

An extraordinary sweet taste of defeat permeated the evening air.

History is dotted with initiatives and resignations in equal proportion. Sometimes such events occur against all expectation and without being announced while other times nothing happens worth more than a shrug of the shoulders. It is only then that the hierarchical distance artificially maintained between the actions of the dictator and the free and easy movements of fashion models sinks into the mist of a smile. For this is also the hour to smile at the bitterness of the past. To organise destiny, embellish a window display, lose a fortune as one gains a wife, all such infinitives finally become of equal value as soon as one extracts from destiny, from the window display, from fortune, from the woman, the exorbitant importance one had attached to them. Everything becomes a means of exchange when the evening air abdicates and the sweetness of defeat renders the last twitch of the raison d'état importunate.

In the gardens it had started to turn grey-blue and as it spread out the town once again discovered the soothing dimensions of laziness. Nonetheless, the dictator's telephone was afflicted with a persistent ringing that was imperative and excessive. If life had been following its usual course it would have been answered. But now the only possible response to life was a shrug of the shoulders – significant for those who seized their opportunities and absurd for those who were serious unto death. Life was now simply part of the dictator's indifference and had the same colour as the gardens at that moment.

The last filaments of power were exhausted in vain appeals to the telephone, which deliberately refused to answer. The dictator thought about something else. The dictator did not think about anything at all.

He used a red pen to mark a map of the world in the nervous way of gamblers at their limit and whose fate is resolved by the absurd. The dictator decided to go out. For a long time he took in with a look of farewell and horror the many papers of all sizes and handwriting that he left as they were on his desk. Almost all were marked 'Confidential'. They were police reports, or reports from ambassadors, confessions, prophesies, messages conceived in the outmoded style in use in chancelleries and, something quite out of place in this world of heartless documents with nothing human about them, there was an anonymous letter, a threatening letter framed with the traditional cross-bones and as ever signed, with some variants: a lover of freedom! If the letter had been more heinous due to a signature and address, the dictator might have been tempted to prepare its author for the feeling of personal triumph he would feel the next morning when he saw the headlines of the first morning newspapers, the enormous capital letters over eight columns of the first poster put up, the new workers' voice, powerful once again and spreading the news from district to district, and undermining the repose of the old respectable houses of tyranny.

But still, what a sense of disappointment there would be if, behind this romanticism of lyrical menaces and badly assembled bones, there was merely the restless brow of some embittered, mediocre and persecuted bureaucrat. . .

Giving way to a residual theatrical impulse the dictator went to the window and flung open the shutters, in the hope that a gust of wind from outside would disperse and carry away forever the official memos that cluttered his desk. But the evening air was calm and nothing stirred. . .

The dictator had reached the most seething if not most secret parts of the city. Descending by means of the celebrated secret door dear to good adventure stories, he knew how to keep his bodyguards at a distance and, having no need of an itinerary, pretended to have lost his way and stared boldly at the women and grinned darkly in hairdressers' mirrors. He took pleasure from the way in which the foyers of cinemas gave a résumé of the week's news, displayed in trivial signs which caused him some mirth. He was the man who inaugurates, harangues, inspects, causes the wrinkles of his forehead to dramatically move, who appears to weigh the flowers presented to him, while, in the shadows, the spectators seek their neighbour's mouth with the prospect it offered of a facile thrill, as facile as what happens on the screen the moment the bandits go too far.

Light begins to circulate in the veins of the shivering neon signs. Above the roofs, a whole advertising anatomy reacts tremblingly and lends the city a tumultuous outline in whose light initiates alone are able to recognise the sites of their desires. Each, more or less consciously, seeks a sign addressed to himself alone. And the dictator vainly questioned this sky at the mercy of a short-circuit, this insubstantial sky which responded simply with the words CADUM, CADUM... On the ground, bordering the footpaths at long intervals, men with sandwich boards encouraged new vices as they offered passers-by a minute of love, standing-up, anywhere, anytime.

The dictator had rarely walked anywhere in his life. But each time he did so he discovered a special interest. He tried to draw a meaning from each exterior wall, to draw out a lesson, an argument that would be favourable to his power: was the wall going to be pulled down, or would it be reinforced? On this evening's aimless walk he no longer had any reason to interpret stones, physiognomies and demeanour in his favour, and it was this, of all the things that happened, that most bewildered him. Caught in the stream of crowds, at the mercy of the city, he allowed himself to be drawn towards the gardens. To those gardens where it was no longer grey-blue, but where love frolics had become more distinct, and where promises were gathered in corners of lips.

And suddenly the dictator realised that the only thing he knew about the gardens up till then was the annual budget for their maintenance. The whole of this flowerbed of murmurs and yearnings had remained unknown to him. Or perhaps he had preferred to repress the memory of it. . .

But as the knockout blow of defeat had not propelled him into acts of despair, so he had not abandoned himself to the ineffectual, to the exasperating nostalgia of force, and the elementary enclosure of the gardens did not tempt him towards open displays, to become an anonymous man in the arms of an anonymous woman.

On the other hand what did tempt him at that precise moment was the desire, as he passed from avenue to avenue, to completely re-absorb himself in essential and connecting formulas, to turn to abstraction in the way certain acids turn violet and certain expressions to madness, to see everything through the white vapour of mental laboratories – was to cross the equator of human trajectories again, passing from action to idea. Not far away voices penetrated the night, limpidly speaking about the ideal conditions for the exercise of power. The dictator convinced himself he was finally able to make contact with this hermetic space, something so common among clandestine lovers of power, among those who fashion a whole empire in their own image but are prevented from translating their ambition into anything but sociological postulates. Who would ever venture to count such hard and isolated men, who, in each age under each sun, govern only in dream and command in silence?

He had almost been one in the faded days of his twenty years. He might have remained so. Everything had been determined once and for all by a chance occurrence, almost under protest. Without warning he had become mingled in a political demonstration. Pushed forward by the surge of the crowd and under threat of the police batons, he had merely taken the head of a group of demonstrators, without knowing anything of the issues at stake, and responded to the repression, brilliantly co-ordinating their actions to put a stop to the violence. Next day his name and picture were in all the papers. Important people took his hand and thanked him for his actions at a critical moment. A dazzling star, not the subject of a few abstract meditations, was raised in the sky and bore his name alone.

And now, on this evening, to return, without more delay, to the old props and greet the old chimeras! Neither tiredness nor disappointments were invoked. That was too easy in his profession... He had bobbed about enough in a pool of regrets, marinated long enough in equivocations of deferred justifications.

This moment was the limit of a career he had for a long time found monotonous. The dictator felt jealous of true failures. Of those who never undertake anything, of those who, by some mysterious reflex, even if only an unfortunate obstacle, always stopped short on the threshold of the action towards which their desire unfolded.

The dictator's jealousy was interrupted by the same diaphanous voice, rising above the thickets with disarming affirmations: a man of action is not really the opposite of a pure thinker; nor really from someone who just split hairs. It was possible to take pleasure in the effort hair made to exist when one had just created baldness.

The dictator tried to discover who the voice belonged to. But a group of statues barred the path. The significance of these statues was lost, but their gestures continued to cradle the pallor of adolescents who had come to entertain them with their first conflicts. Here a queen, there an infanta, are invited to curse with the tips of their fingers both the paternal roof and the hideous consequences of poverty.

The dictator walked on more slowly. He hesitated. He no longer knew whether to compromise with the statues or intervene in the very theoretical discussion which seemed to pursue him at a few yards distance.

In every statue there is a conspirator on the lookout. But

do not trust too much these reckonings without precise pay-offs. In themselves they seem harmless enough, then one day the statue hoists itself up, completely bronzed with the new sun and with a smile that no one has ever seen before. His machinations had come to fruition somewhere in the world, very nearby or very far away, without needing any other announcement.

It was this smile the dictator sought. This triumph would place the extent of his defeat in proportion. Show yourself to the Gentleman, heralds who announce calm skies after the storm! The time had come for statues and abstractions to cease playing hide and seek. And you, beautiful unknown lady of stone, turn over your palm so that each of us may lean over its line of serenity. . .

A voice rose from the neighbouring thicket: "I do not believe in dictators who end up badly. A dictator is either so feeble that he adapts to the conditions of his defeat or so intelligent that he spends the rest of his life drawing diagrams to explain his defeat. In both cases his spare time is reckoned. And his little hands mock all the perfumes of Arabia. . ."

Someone approached the dictator with measured step and made a gesture for him to light his cigarette. The dictator took out a lighter whose flame revealed an indistinct landscape suddenly drawn out of the darkness. On the thin fringes of flame, as they rub their eyes, reefs of a more provisional world collide with the least recognisable forms. In this cruel triangle of light the dictator's nose was outlined with untimely harshness.

Nothing so far has been said about the dictator's physique, which was slowly in the process of coming apart. Some of the faces pulled in the hairdressers' windows offered a clue to it. These were faces of circumstance. Think about a clown rejected by his circus and forgotten by the public. That was when the real facial contortions began, which concerned him alone. At that point all his seriousness in the face of life took the form of face-pulling and corrupted even the taste of bread and any possible friendship. The dictator's nose choked up the garden. The whole of the flame of the lighter concentrated around its edges. This nose did not breathe. In the centre of a face whose insignificance was ready to affirm itself to any flame one wished, this nose that resembled that of a master of ceremonies in a deserted place, remained solemn and numb to feeling. It had the sort of look that would ridiculously attract photographers and sculptors. To some it would say, "Am I worthy enough?" To others: "Am I Greek enough?"

The dictator fell into a sort of panic. Why had this ridiculous passer-by felt the need for a cigarette and asked him for a light? This Nose was a provocation to dictatorship.

The unknown man had already thanked him twice, but the dictator still did not extinguish the flame. The dictator recognised it was necessary to go through a series of facial contortions before liquidating what remained of the nose on his face. What would he do tomorrow when he woke up in a grubby hotel? It was not insignificant when one began to see again in a completely abstract way, to once again cross the equator. In any case to return into the authenticating garden. There were voids to be filled unconditionally in the misty circle directed by leaves, statues and fountains. This was how large distinctive tables were raised in coastal houses for late travellers who are known to prevail over the storm in spite of everything. . .

The stranger was more and more troubled by the double fixity of flame and dictator and felt obliged to offer a cigarette. He received no response. Finally, with a lethargic gesture, the flame went out. The dictator relaxed. He was now able to let himself to speak without fanfares to a man whose identity he did not know and whose features he could not make out. He did not ask for much. He would be satisfied with a place to spend the night. The stranger was rather at a loss. He had come from across the frontier and knew nothing about a town which he still found hard to grasp and would not yield to his sense of being a stranger in a strange land. And both remained there, stupidly set like stakes, determined to discover a direction under fragments of old memories and recommendations, speaking only sluggishly with short and incomplete sentences.

Pink proficiency of the debauched, bloody proficiency of malefactors, useless proficiency of the end of day as if proficiency was able to resolve no matter what. As if proficiency could be believed. The curtains of fashion houses are perpetually drawn over the most inflamed eyes of the world and the divans of beauty parlours sometimes initiate the strange howls of torture.

Gradually the man with the cigarette persuaded the dictator to follow him to the Hotel Terminus, where he had stayed since the previous evening. Hotel Terminus, was this not in fact the ideal address, where in the ebb and flow of the rapids in which one no longer hopes for anything in particular, it was possible to call out the most incredible name to the night porter without a second thought? It was true that, since the evening, a sense of identity was no longer an attraction in itself. When the dictator and the stranger exchanged names as they left the garden, the dictator was able to use his real name without the other showing the least spark of curiosity.

So they exchanged stories. Their misfortunes and gossip. The dictator was plied with questions. With his back to the wall, one could say there is no way out for him. After all, who are you, Sir, to come to dream with me in Hotel Terminus whose rooms smell both of the train and the dungeon? For myself, my poverty has led me for thousands of miles before I asked you for a light. And you?

The dictator pretended to be one of those ruined business-men who are picked up on park benches at meal times. Because of his cash-flow, the finance companies stopped all his credit. "They sent me to the wall", he groaned, the dictator, business-man... "All because of a little delay, they sent me to the wall...."

They arrived at the door of the Hotel Terminus. In the

bright light they looked at each other fixedly. They entered and went to their rooms, with no hint of somnambulism in their step. Two turns of the key and they placed the eardrum of their dreams against the rapid charms of the beyond – you know it! The appeal of whatever happens when you are not there. . .

Tomorrow it would be a holiday in town and garden. . .

*****

published in Georges Henein: *Notes sur une pays inutile* (1982)

French original © Le Tout sur le Tout, 1982

*****

GEORGES HENEIN (Cairo 1914 – Paris 1973) Key figure in Egyptian surrealism, which he discovered while studying in Paris in 1934. Separated from Breton in 1947, having accused the latter of recuperating surrealism in its pre-war form. He was forced to leave Egypt in 1959 after crackdown on the press by Nasser and thereafter lived in exile in Rome and Paris. Henein's reflections, as a 'stroller between two worlds', on the relationship between European and Oriental culture are of capital importance.

MARCEL LECOMTE:

The White Scarf

A few days had passed. One evening Ilien entered a high street cinema. He had arrived in the middle of the screening and wanted to wait for the first part of the film when an actor, who had made a strong impression on him when he first saw him on the screen, would be featured.

He first had to watch the weekly news. After a few scenes showing important events from abroad, there was an item about the dictator of the country returning from some promenade, passing through one of the streets around his Residence.

First he saw the passers-by stop, lining-up along the pavement ready to applaud and give an ovation as announcements of the arrival spread.

The cameraman tracked in to the dictator. Everyone now had their backs to the pavement. Nevertheless, Ilien noticed one person remain just where he was, with his back turned to the crowd even when the cortège passed in the midst of public enthusiasm. Ilien was astonished to realise that it was the man in the light grey suit, who was absorbed in contemplation of a shop window that contained a carefully thought out display of handkerchiefs, shawls and scarves.

Then, one evening the following week Ilien walked though the corridors of a house in which he had been invited to a grand ball.

For several hours he had taken a full part in the rather drunken merriment, which was a little perilous and at times noisy as it reached its height, but now, as he wandered through the abnormally vast building, it was reduced to a feeble echo of the dancing, songs and music until he found himself walking along in a profound silence.

All the same he interrupted his walk when he saw his reflection in a mirror through an open door. He noticed that his shirt collar and tie had been disarranged by the motions of the dance and entered a room furnished with a divan, table and a few chairs.

To the left, at the point where the mirror came to an end, was an exit whose door was only half-open and revealed a corridor which turned away at an angle and was lit only by the light of the room.

He had barely finished the complex knot of his tie than he found that as he looked at himself in the mirror he was being spied on through the door by which he came in.

He turned and saw, half-hidden by the wall, a young woman who seemed content to maintain for a moment longer her bizarre and impressive posture.

Finally she approached him with the most natural air in the world. She was dressed in black and, suddenly raising her veil of black lace, touched his arm and told him to sit down. He obeyed. This person's expression, which was especially sharp, impressed him. Without any preliminaries she asked him to look at the five photographic portraits of women on the wall and say which of them most affected him.

Every time Ilien was placed in the presence of a young woman, something very special and distinct always happened.

In the depths of his mind there remained the image of a particularly rare type of woman, whose appearance alone sufficed to cause him a sense of rapture that had no ulterior motive. He had already encountered this several times and always consequently compared it with the aspect of such a woman that he had been able to observe over a period of time.

And then this woman who had made her entrance in such a strange way, although not fully resembling this type, nevertheless she retained certain vague echoes of it, as did the five portraits on the wall. From that moment Ilien felt a certain irritation, a consciousness of pain.

161

A little while later the young woman herself sat down on a chair to Ilien's left but shifted the chair so that she was soon perpendicular to her partner while, for almost the whole time Ilien appeared to be casually observing the photographs, the unknown woman glanced from him to the portraits on the wall.

She seemed to find the test she had so oddly set fascinating.

At the very moment Ilien was about to say that the five portraits were those of the same woman and that the variations in hairstyle, expression and lighting given by the photographer had transformed her aspect to such an extent that one might well hesitate for some time before it was possible to recognise all in all a malicious trap and that the portrait which nevertheless seemed to affect him most of all was. . . As he turned to face his companion the latter rose and burst out laughing, fleeing towards the open door through which she had earlier spied on him. Ilien wanted to follow her but remained sitting in obedience to the imperious sign she made before vanishing.

It was some time before she returned bearing in her elegant arms a large silver tray with two glasses of champagne, but she had barely crossed the threshold than Ilien heard her cry out with amazement, a cry of distress that strangely upset the mood as he noticed that the young woman's eyes stared over his head towards the furthest part of the room.

Ilien rose hastily and turned to see, without his having heard him, the man in the light-grey suit, coming towards him from the corridor, his face solemn and his expression particularly tense, and now fixed in the posture of someone caught by surprise holding a white scarf in his upraised arms.

Ilien could not help immediately thinking of the engraving about which he used to ponder in a book that had belonged to his father. It had obsessed him throughout his childhood. In it was represented, according to the legend, a prince in a room of his palace who was oblivious to the fact that he was about to be strangled by a conspirator's silk handkerchief. The scene was imbued with a powerful impression of internal pathos and external calm, deprived of all passionate exhibition, which filled him with the sense of something hidden which he was unable to understand.

And Ilien felt as if he had been snatched from the real world and thrown into something that had become an implacable adventure. He grasped his revolver and advanced on the man but doubtless was not quick enough, since the light immediately went out and the sound of the tray falling and the breaking of glass was heard while Ilien recovered soon enough to race into the corridor in pursuit, firing several shots as he did so.

For two or three minutes he heard the sound one would associate with fleeing steps echoing in the distance, although less hurried than might have been expected and even though he was unable to catch up he did not stop the pursuit, looking to the right, to the left, in front and sometimes behind him, progressively switching on the electricity, which the other had turned off, as he did so.

Finally Ilien completely lost his way in the labyrinth of corridors and rooms. His face was red, he was out of breath, and supported himself on the staircase bannister.

He stood still for a moment, as the extraordinary animation of the pursuit was followed by complete silence, and stared at the stairs and at a door facing him, considering them insistently; each thing, every one a mysterious sign which seemed to be in the process of dismissing him from life, from this life of his, which he distinctly felt had thereby become entrusted to them, whose presence he had thus come to see as being somehow obligatory. They appeared to be of a singular density.

Having reached the upper floors he noticed that the party continued unabated.

When he entered the great hall, the orchestra was playing a tune which had become the popular hit of the day and a circle of dancers had formed which turned around and around the room, here and there bumping into the spectators.

One could not have failed to appreciate that the confusion was constantly on the increase.

As for the host, he seemed to want to show an example by his excess, as he lay inert on a sofa, body and face adorned, covered with paper streamers and delivered up to the care of two or three ladies.

Ilien judged he would not be in the mood to hear about the new attempt on his life but he did find the young woman and learned that she was a friend of the host, and lived in the house. He had entered her room by chance and she, having succumbed to the highly-charged atmosphere of the joyous night, had been unable to resist the temptation to tease him.

Cutting short her questions, he made a telephone call to Mac Joyce, a young detective with a particular interest in this case. He arrived without delay and together they examined the house, revolvers in hand, accompanied by the young woman, but they were unable to find anything untoward except for a chair knocked over by Ilien himself during the pursuit.

★★★★★
originally published in Marcel Lecomte *L'Homme au complet gris clair* (1931)
reprinted in ML: *Oeuvres* (1980)
French original © Jacques Antoine, 1980
★★★★★

MARCEL LECOMTE (Brussells 1900 – Brussells 1966) A founder member of the Belgian Surrealist Group, Lecomte soon took a position on its margins. An interest in gnosticism and Catharism and medieval magic gave his work a different focus from that of other Brussells surrealists, especially Nougé and Magritte, whose attitude he considered to be over-intellectual, and he was closer to the French surrealists, and particularly to Joë Bousquet. He was drawn to the inherent strangeness of even the most banal events, and this is one of the main themes of his stories.

LISE DEHARME:

The Wind

People are not as wary of the wind as they should be. God only knows all the things the wind has stolen and keeps hidden in secret underground stores somewhere near the Fountain of Medals in the vast heathland in the province of Les Landes. The wind is an ogre. If it is so strong it is because it gobbles up adolescents seasoned with mustard from Old Man River. It has more banknotes and cheques than the world's biggest bank and it has taken so many leaves from the trees and shoots from the plants that it could recreate the whole of nature anywhere in the heavens it chose. That would be the end for us and for all others.

With all the hair it has torn from ladies heads it subsidises thousands of hairdressers and displaces flowers, denudes forests and heads, and causes floods and baldness.

If the wind is a haberdasher, it also collects ships, since it has a fantastic fleet ranging from small paper boats to the best armed battleships, ancient schooners lost in the mists of time and ghost ships that have fallen from the skies. It even has some washer-woman's boats. In its urns it preserves the ashes of all the celebrated people who have drowned, collected as it parted the seas, and it even has those of Joan of Arc which it quickly gathered after they had been scattered onto the Seine. It is an enraged collector with clumsy hands and often causes trouble at home. That is why it is forced to wander through the whole land by day and night, no matter what the weather, just like the Wandering Jew. No, no, a telephone call has just informed me that this is not entirely true. . . It seems that there are some sheltered valleys that know the wind only by name. Still it takes its revenge there by bringing down locusts and plagues and other catastrophes. This is what an old story from no-man's land says.

One day a beautiful and shapely little girl set out on the track of the wind. She knew how to seduce it and managed to twist it up so effectively that she could capture it in her bag which she held on a long thread. The wind rose up into the air and the bag went with it, lighter and lighter still. For many years the little girl took her prisoner for a walk. Unfortunately when the Fates decided to cut the thread which had attached her to life, the wind took advantage of the fact by making a run for it. So it is that ever since, in the squares and gardens, and even in department stores, there are children who walk around with little balloons dancing on the end of a thread. And perhaps this is why, when the weather is really good, it is because a little girl has captured the wind.

*****

first published in Lise Deharme *Les Poids d'un oiseau* (1956)
Le Terrain Vague
French original © Eric Losfeld

*****

LISE DEHARME (Paris 1898 – Paris 1979) Lise Deharme provided surrealism with one of its great emblems, as the woman with the light blue gloves mentioned in *Nadja*. She came into contact with the Surrealist Group in 1925 and thereafter became its 'good fairy'. Her large oeuvre (12 novels, 5 volumes of tales and 3 of poetry), of incomparable charm, has been almost completely ignored outside surrealist circles. She lived under the sign of the black swan.

OCTAVIO PAZ:

Marvels of Will

At precisely three o'clock don Pedro would arrive at our table, greet each customer, mumble to himself some indecipherable sentences, and silently take a seat. He would order a cup of coffee, light a cigarette, listen to the chatter, sip his coffee, pay the waiter, take his hat, grab his case, say good afternoon, and leave. And so it was every day.

What did don Pedro say upon sitting and rising, with serious face and hard eyes? He said:

"I hope you die."

Don Pedro repeated the phrase many times each day. Upon rising, upon completing his morning preparations, upon entering and leaving his house – at eight o'clock, at one, at two-thirty, at seven-forty – in the cafe, in the office, before and after every meal, when going to bed each night. He repeated it between his teeth or in a loud voice, alone or with others. Sometimes with only his eyes. Always with all his soul.

No one knew to whom he addressed these words. Everyone ignored the origin of his hate. When someone wanted to dig deeper into the story, don Pedro would turn his head with disdain and fall silent, modest. Perhaps it was a causeless hate, a pure hate. But the feeling nourished him, gave seriousness to his life, majesty to his years. Dressed in black, he seemed to be prematurely mourning for his victim.

One afternoon don Pedro arrived graver than usual. He sat down heavily, and, in the centre of the silence that was created by his presence, he simply dropped these words:

"I killed him."

Who and how? Some smiled, wanting to take the thing

as a joke. Don Pedro's look stopped them. All of us felt uncomfortable. That sense of the void of death was certain. Slowly the group dispersed. Don Pedro remained alone, more serious than ever, a little withered, like a burnt-out star, but tranquil, without remorse.

He did not return the next day. He never returned. Did he die? Maybe he needed that life-giving hate. Maybe he still lives and now hates another. I examine my actions, and advise you to do the same. Perhaps you too have incurred the same obstinate, patient anger of those small myopic eyes. Have you ever thought how many – perhaps very close to you – watch you with the same eyes as don Pedro?

★★★★★
originally published in *¿Aguila o Sol?*
English translation published in *Eagle or Sun?* (1969) New York: New Directions, London: Peter Owen
Mexican original © Fondo de Cultura Económica, 1960
English translation c. Octavio Paz and Eliot Weinberger, 1969
translated by Eliot Weinberger
★★★★★

OCTAVIO PAZ (1914, Mexico) After fighting in the Spanish Civil War, Octavio Paz joined the surrealist circle in Mexico, and when he became a diplomat in Paris he joined the French Surrealist Group. One of Mexico's most important writers, his luminous writings span the fields of sociology, political theory, anthropology, philosophy and literature. His poetry is incomparable.

ANNELIESE HAGER:

The Chain

Was it only a star falling from the sky? Was it a scream in the night embracing the agony of loneliness? I cannot tell, yet suddenly everything had changed.

Yesterday I wanted to buy the yellow rose. . . I saw it in a window full of flowers. . . but I passed by. . . and could not forget it.

Today I went there again. . . The window full of flowers had gone. Between two unfamiliar houses I noticed a narrow black opening. I squeezed through. I tasted the scent of the yellow rose on my tongue. I groped my way along. . . perhaps I would find it after all.

Was someone coming? There was darkness. I felt the breath of a mouth very close before me. I made a grab into the darkness – and suddenly I held the end of a delicate chain. Where did it come from? . . . the scent still lingered. . . and there was still this warm breath before my mouth.

The chain dragged me away – and it became light. I found myself in an old-fashioned town square with ancient houses and a column in the middle. From each window people were staring down at me – faces that were inquisitive. . . screaming. . . desperate and very quiet. Pain flashed through me as though I had been pricked by thorns. My hands held the chain more tightly. Its golden gleam drew me on.

Then a tall woman came towards me with swaying gait. I thought I knew her and went to meet her. . . Yet all of a sudden she abruptly turned and walked away! I watched her go. Her body and limbs were made of wood. Her clothes were sagging – I shuddered. I turned into the next best street. At the bottom a hand waved at me from out of a window.

Is that meant for me? Again I sense the warm breath before my face. I run and run. When I reach the window, it is being closed. I know the hand. . . but behind it dangles the mask of a man's head with barred teeth and hollow eyes. I clasp my hands over the golden chain – yet – where is the chain? Have I lost it? The hand again appears at the window. Is it possible that *it* suddenly holds the chain? I stare up – it picks up the mask, puts the yellow rose between its teeth and then takes them away into the darkness of the room.

Panic seizes me. . . I want to escape. . . but my feet, as though paralysed, cannot move. For a moment I close my eyes. . . Was it really the hand that held the chain at the window? Or was it my yellow rose?

When I open my eyes again, everything has gone. I stand and glare at a black lake. On the shore is a bench – when I am about to sit down the lake has gone and the bank is a high staircase with many steps. To the right and left black walls. At the very top a little light shines through a crack. I mount the steps, counting out loudly as I do so. The numbers resound from the walls. One becomes ten and four becomes eight. Three remains mute – when I announce the ninth step, I stumble and fall. I fall lightly as a feather spinning and spinning in the air. I fall into a hollow space without walls and glide into the frayed fabric of seconds. Here my hands become entangled and the fingers detach and the feet again climb the steps. While I. . . keep on falling.

Somewhere my mouth counts – seventy-five – seventy-six – seventy-seven.

Where am I? Do I exist any longer? Like the rose. . . the chain. . . the woman. . . the window. . . the sea. . .? I still feel the warm breath on my hair. It becomes a voice. . . hard and flat. . . like a stone. . . like a shriek. . .

There! Again the black lake – with a boat. A thin thread of blood trickles into the boat. When it is filled, it will take sudden flight – I won't watch it, since I know – it will be a gull. . . or hum like an engine.

It will fall as a star from the sky or embrace as a scream the agony of loneliness.

The numbers alone remain proud and immovable – an infinite chain.

★★★★★

published in *Die Rote Uhr Und Andere Dichtungen* (1991)
German original © Arche Verlag AG, Zürich, 1991
translated by Barbara Heins
★★★★★

ANNELIESE HAGER (1904, Posen) an important photographer as well as a storyteller, Anneliese Hager animated the Meta movement and has been a participant in COBRA, Rixes and Edda. She has translated Breton, Char, Desnos and Jarry into German.

AGUSTIN ESPINOSA:

Angelus

Only from a cloud, from a high tower, from a plane or from a ledge on a skyscraper would one see things as I saw them from an ordinary bedroom window that afternoon.

There was nothing particularly extraordinary about what I saw, yet it filled me with a fervent joy: a great white bird perched on top of a solitary, angular rock.

Perhaps the bird wasn't white, but merely grey, with all the colour drained out of it by distance and the darkness of the rock. However, whilst my memory of that is vague, I remember to this day its extraordinary size. It was – or at least it should or could have been – a vulture. Its head, as large as that of a two-year-old child. Its height, almost six and a half feet. Its beak, massive. Its tail, like that of a peacock.

Next to me stood a woman whom once upon a time I had often kissed but who now abandoned herself to the kisses of a dark young man who was smoking my cigarettes and using my matches as if they were his.

But what excited me most was the great white bird. I was about to aim at it with my pistol when, suddenly and stealthily, it took off in a flight so luminous and arbitrary that it seemed larger and more diaphanous the farther off from me it flew. Then I saw that it wasn't white but multicoloured and that what I had thought was one bird was in fact two. The light from the setting sun filtered through the four widespread wings like light through the Gothic arches of a cathedral, dappling them with different colours until they disappeared into the infinite. I tried in vain to fill my eyes with all these vague things, to find some way to banish from my mind the romantic idyll of

172

the girl whom once upon a time I had kissed and of the dark young man who was smoking my cigarettes as if they were his and using my matches, my balcony and my best armchairs as if they belonged to him.

I innocently consoled myself with the idea that, meanwhile, they were oblivious to the marvellous spectacle taking place behind their backs. They knew nothing of the four luminous wings, of the vast polychrome of the heavens and of the setting sun. Nor did they know about my pistol, which the flight of the great white bird had left cocked and ready.

★★★★★

published in Agustín Espinosa, *Crimen* (1934)
translated from the Spanish by Margaret Jull Costa

★★★★★

AUGUSTÍN ESPINOSA: (See page 81)

IRENE HAMOIR:

Adéla Romantique

Men carry their *shadow* like an apotheosis.

For myself I kept *Adéla* locked up in my room. If she had followed me outside there are those who might have taken her from me while others might have laughed at her. And so I kept *Adéla* locked up in my room.

One afternoon when I returned from holiday she told me she was bored of waiting endlessly for me: she wanted to go out in her turn and have fun in the fields. Glued to the curtains, she watched the city. She stood there with her back to me, completely naked, and her back had all the firmness and freshness of adolescence. She stood on tip-toe, stretching out her arms, extending them to her fingers. That pale, tender flesh, her hair with shimmers of skin, caused me to plead: "My little devil. . ." She turned around. O, *Adéla*, with her radiant breasts, and below her belly her little yellow and shiny virile member. Her cold eyes are forgetful of attention. I heard: "It's necessary to take risks," but who spoke, my God, where did that voice come from?

The door closed again on the faithless one. Anguish tightens the motionless room.

It was twice two weeks ago that night that my friend had left me. In vain I sought to find her (I probed everywhere, frequented dark rooms and deserted squares, spoke to the walls of avenues and the corners of alleyways.)

With my forehead of stone against the glass, *Adéla*, my dear shadow, won't you return to me from the blue gulfs that two-faced men – los hombres – have peopled. There is a town which is spread out into the far distance under a blanket of mist. A river cuts through its centre. A light of embers and a moon-like transparency bathe it in a veil of trembling soot. A dull rumbling mingles the sounds.

As I look for *Adéla* under this colourless form, my arteries are invaded with a leaden fear and nightmare begins to coil up inside me and cause me to close my eyes.

In a few moments the town will no longer be the same.

For hour upon hour I have awaited her return and yesterday I thought I had found her, but no – is this the wing of my black destiny? – once again I did not make contact with her. As soon as she appeared to me at the other end of the dejected path, I recognised my sister.

The light-coloured greyhound, raised on its hind legs, is wearing a full, loose-flowing, milk-shaded women's dress which covers its legs as far as its fine feet. In the right forepaw, which is secreted in the garment's loose sleeve, a large triangular dagger is brandished. The greyhound is at the exact corner of the street and whatever it strikes is hidden from me by the wall. Nonetheless, it is a being of flesh and blood that it hits since each time the dog strikes blood spurts and violently splashes it. Its whitish coat is striped with purple. And the head, the sweet head of *Adéla*, soon turns completely red.

I want to run but cannot move. Horror congeals me to the paving stones. A large black sun closes down the landscape.

I think it was in the peaceful park of Camperdu that I strolled, alone and sad, thinking about my young lover. The mild wind stroked the trees and lawns strewn with violets made every effort to be pleasing. Unfortunately my troubled heart could not accept this stillness. My heart missed *Adéla*: "My thirst with the eyes of a bird."

Suddenly a bird with beautiful plumage – a fantastic emerald of feathers stained with cinnamon, indigo, azure and light pink – pounced down on the sandy avenue. Aflame with joy, I chased after the bird but it took flight again before perching at the end of a young branch. Again I rushed forward, but it dropped to the ground and then rose again with a great flapping of its wings, grazed the sand in the avenue and went to land on the violet lawn.

I took up the pursuit again and the bird did a somersault among the flowers and flew further on. With its flying and my running, we went on like this for a long time before becoming very tired. The bird became ruffled, its gleaming plumage faded and its wings hung down like rags.

And so at last, in pitiable triumph, my palm fell on the bird and it lost its form. As I took the light panoply of feathers in my hand, it hardened, became a plant with dark green leaves, it hardened and became a bundle of thin blades. Careful to keep hold of my sharp prey, I hurried out of the park.

Behind me, the gate slammed shut. I had again found *Adéla*, my accomplice, the unformulated shadow of my sleep. . .

★★★★★
French original © Irène Hamoir
★★★★★

IRENE HAMOIR (Saint-Gilles, Belgium, 1906) In her youth was a circus performer before meeting Louis Scutenaire and becoming part of the Belgian Surrealist Circle. Her novel *Boulevard Jacqumain* was published in 1953.

LOUIS ARAGON:

Enter the Succubi

to André Breton

It would be wrong to suppose that very much light has been thrown on the phenomenon of the amorous impulse. Once night falls, men disperse in their droves. And there are loners in rural communities who, at the equinox, are said to don new garments and stroll down to the cities, where great beasts await them, fat and docile. All those agitated bodies cry out in vain from their hiding places, from paltry lodgings in the suburbs to the open fields which sing, to other bodies across the globe, immersed in floods of lace or the daily grind! Open wide your windows, sweet maidens: yet they let their gaze wander for but a moment, before closing the casement and turning back to their music. And yet a traveller had come to a halt by the river's edge. Hat in hand, he was watching the crowd pouring away through two holes in the air. Let me tell you something: there are so many wasted kisses that it is enough to make you cry poverty. And so, let us chase away those youngsters who are a perpetual insult to true love!

I have often wondered what happens to those weightless seeds which sail away from garden trees in spring. One watches them float by like clouds made out of snow, like a snowfall of caresses, like butterfly desires. But where do they go to? Beyond the fields and the cities, on the far side of the mountains, there is a peaceful park where, one fine evening, a single snowflake will end up on the female tree holding its boughs apart in expectation. All the rest have tumbled here and there among the furrows. I have often wondered what happens to those weightless seeds, so aimlessly scattered.

Often too I have felt my own solitude. As if a great fire had been quenched within my arms. What do I have to show for those thousands of caresses which silently possessed me? What have I done with all that power once granted to me and now taken from me? Unlucky fellow, you did nothing to guard your treasure. It was a treasure beyond comprehension, and it was rare for me to feel I had mastery over it, and then only when I was not using it. Lovers unsuspected, revealed by the very darkness. If only one could distinguish their heartbeats. For them, love retains all the wild ways of childhood. It is by no means easy, unlike mechanical love. I have often wondered what happens to those weightless seeds.

I grieve over the atrocious discordance of our desires, the capriciousness of their awakening. I have read volumes in the gaze of a father, while his child played innocently in the grass. Boredom reigned, and time and space, all about the house. And blood rushing to the head, and the whiteness of the little girl. I have seen college students who were fearful of death. And nuns deep in the labyrinth of shadows, with cloisters melting softly into the summer sky. Great shipwrecks of carnality, I know you through and through. So many unanswered appeals, so many marks left on the painful breast of night. They awaken, they rise, they step forth. The fragrance of flowers follows close behind. They step close to the walls. What are they hoping for? All they do is wait. Wait for a miracle. And without it, they return to the winding sheet where love mimics sombre death, the sheet so intractable towards a pleasure which has failed to achieve any shape.

I like to think about those things which are said to melt away in sleep. About giving up rest. About the hypocrisy of the sleeper. The sublime dissimulator. He exposes his body alone, and then, once vanquished, he becomes no more than the voice of his conquered flesh. Whereupon, prompted by this lapse, a great nocturnal shivering begins to move forward. Forward to the last corners of the shadows and the air. Reaching the places of disquiet.

Stretching to the febrile land of the spirits. Beyond the realm of the natural. Into the territories of the damned. And in that night some female demon, inhaling the tidal breeze, lets slip the stays on her infernal bodice, sucks in the human exhalations, and shakes free her fiery tresses. Whatever it is that lies slumbering in the depths of the whirlwind which has reached her, she can picture it all, and now she must break loose. In the mirror of the abyss, she carries out the strange toilet of one betrothed. I love to imagine her luminous ablutions. O purple shades of Hell, leave be this seductive body.

I have much to say on the subject of succubi.

Of all the opinions that have been voiced about succubi, the most ancient tells us that they are in fact female demons who visit people while they sleep. Doubtless there is some basis for this. Some I have met bore all the marks of hell. In which case they are rather beautiful to behold, for they have the power to adopt any form they choose. Frequently, even though about to leave their involuntary lover, they do not feel compelled to reveal to him their origin, which of course they took great pains to dissemble at the outset. Yet at other times they cannot resist the pleasure of an abrupt revelation, transforming themselves within the embrace they have engineered, so that their victim simultaneously experiences a delight which it is still too early to regret, and the horror of having succumbed to a demon's trickery. Either they suddenly throw off those faithful and familiar features which they have borrowed from a distant mistress, at which point the deceived lover accuses himself of a monstrous infidelity. Or else they manifest a hideous aspect that I find it hard to believe can only be characteristic of inferior spirits. Sometimes, with particular malice, they will disclose one of the features born of the artistic imagination which were seen as conventional attributes of the Devil, and in which men were wont to recognise the enemy of the deity (for they create the Devil in their own image): a hairy ear, a cloven hoof, a pair of horns... I have been told that female demons

179

reserved attentions of this kind for any pious young boys they might chance to find between the sheets. Now, it is by no means rare for this sort of angel of evil to fall helplessly in love with a man, who is henceforth entranced. The female devil returns as often as she can to her unfortunate companion. She oppresses him and, so it is alleged, she actually manages to regret her crime as soon as she has committed it. Succubi have been known to take stock of the ravaged created by their kisses, to lift up their transparent hands to the pale face of their favourite, to slowly stroke back his hair, and to make the night reverberate with spine-chilling sighs and lamentations of fate. But the very intensity of their transports obliges these insatiable visitors to temper their passion. They let several days go by before they come back; they allow the colour to return to the cheeks of that ravaged face. Then, as soon as the imprudent lover has found rest and abandoned himself to the shadows, as soon as his regular breathing can be heard from afar, there they come, back again, slipping in through the gate of dreams. There have been interminable debates as to how to rid oneself of succubi. It would appear that nothing, neither holy relics nor prayers launched by charlatans who drape themselves in the empty dignity of a phoney priesthood, nor yet the chimerical methodology of that psychiatrist from Vienna (for there is no point in only considering the techniques of one's enemies) nothing, I say, can protect a man against these oneiric consummations. Nevertheless, should it happen that he realises he is the repeated prey of the same demon, though this to be sure is by no means easy to determine, for in its cunning the demon invariably takes care to adopt several different guises, unless, once having become mixed up with mortals, it should want, crazily, to have its desire requited and should seek, by adopting an agreeable appearance, to elicit a passion from that body which had been its inspiration, then it is, so I am told, that the one who is possessed comes into possession of the desperate means not of rejecting the succubus in one fell swoop, but at least of deceiving her, and thereby of coaxing her into shaking off her appetite for him. It is at the very point when abstinence seems mandatory that the man thus stricken should throw himself into a frenzy of debauchery, in such a way that the nocturnal spirit should never find him otherwise than in a state of utter exhaustion, and thus safeguarded by impotence and pity. And yet, let him not suppose that he can make use of this therapeutic strategy in moderation: the succubi know so many tricks for restoring vigour in the feeblest frame that there are some, and these we call vampires, who can reanimate the very dead. If therefore he should devote his day to parsimonious excesses, there will be no guarantee of his safety that coming night, and dawn will find him lamenting his useless precautions. So if a man prey to succubi should make love, let him do so as often as he can. And once he has reached his limit, once his companion herself, even assuming he has chosen her for her endurance and her lust for pleasure, feels she can no longer draw from him the most fallacious ecstasy, even then let him have recourse to drugs to revive his powers, latent as they are. Though people will tell him that he is killing himself, he must persevere in this regime for seventy days without interruption.

Historical records throughout Antiquity and Christianity abound in anecdotes in which succubi are expressly named, or else can be inferred by an alert commentator. There exist treatises by specialists to which I refer the curious reader. Yet amid the diversity of all these tales, one notices that these voluptuous females of the nether regions tend to behave in two principal ways; between the two can be identified all conceivable intermediary positions, which in turn correspond to two contrary instincts, two tastes which are of equal strength, and which we might judge to be equivalent, were we to investigate their occurrence within ourselves. On the one hand, and these are the more numerous, there are those succubi whose pleasure consists in attacking men of impeccable virtue. I speak here not of men who are virtuous less for virtue's sake than out of natural inclination. No, the succubi choose those for whom virtue represents a continually repeated struggle. Those who spend their days wallowing amid vice yet never succumb to temptation while often admitting to feeling it. Oh dear, look out! Scarcely have their eyelids dropped than they are plunged into abomination right up to their necks. It has been argued that this preference corresponds to a calculated move on the part of the succubus, which somewhat surprises me: allegedly, she thinks this approach will assure her of lovers who are always solid and at the ready, so that, thrusting aside their chaste resistance, she can swiftly dispose of their steadfast modesty. I hardly feel this is the right explanation. Could a man outwit a succubus? One never sees him reasoning in this fashion. If he teaches his womenfolk to keep their eyes lowered, to avoid making love to the first person they fancy, it is not true that he does so in order to profit from an accretion of desires. By such actions he is teaching them to exercise restraint in the name of a God who, despite not always being the same, nevertheless always gives priority to the task of carefully verifying all acts of human congress.

The other type of demoness much prefers rakes to innocents. Such creatures are the most refined, being more concerned with subtlety in the modes of pleasure than with the quality of pleasure. The very imponderability of success is what gives it prestige in their heart. They have the knack of turning any rebuff to their advantage. It is quite common for them to leave a bed at dawn in which they have found no joy at all. No matter! The important thing is that they appreciate dealing with a body which has a superior sense of love, and see no ultimate need for it to procure crude satisfactions for them. They set little value in mere proofs of character. Not to mention the fact that, as everyone knows, one is more likely to be disappointed by a lover who has lived in total chastity than by another who seems worn out, extenuated by pleasure. This is why we feel truly at ease when we encounter those women who have dedicated their lives to the art of kissing and who are, so to speak, while somewhat depleted by love, equally renewed by love, and less exposed than others to the ravages of time; for their entire flesh is intelligence, they have the confidence to control pleasure, they sustain it within us. And nothing seems to tire them, nothing to obsess them. They have realised, don't you see, what it is all about. That is why those succubi of whom I speak appreciate most in sleepers a kind of genius of fornication, which they feel surpasses the qualities of ardent passion, as well as those, even less to be revered, of virtue. I shall not pass on to those whom they overwhelm with their favours the advice concerning frenzied debauchery which I took pleasure in relaying to the timid acquaintances of the earlier demon-esses of whom I spoke. It is indeed obvious that such tactics would get them nowhere with the second type. Moreover I imagine that our heroes of the bedchamber have no desire to banish from their dreams an obsession which is so flattering, and which revives in them the very impulse motivating their ardour. They exhibit none of those puerile and utilitarian attitudes typical of the phoney Don Juans of our age. Unlike the latter, they have no fear of losing control. They have sufficient taste for pleasure, and the good sense which comes of its practice, to greet it with the same good-will, whatever its source. Never do they contemplate that economising of effort which is less typical of true lovers than of those vain and ambitious ones who seek above all to show off their prowess and to exploit it to an advantage other than straightforward pleasure. When, suddenly aroused by the intensity of their sensations, they realise they are alone again, they do not waste themselves in empty curses, in vulgar and base expressions, as do those who had counted on improving their lot by holding back their energies. Rather they look to the care of their body with that same equanimity which characterises the loftiness of their heart. In so doing, they give thanks for the end of night, which has been so propitious for them. Their thoughts go out to the impalpable mistress who has just departed, seeking to recollect each one of her ephemeral aspects. Thereupon they await the hour when propriety will permit them to inform some woman of their acquaintance, sometimes even a lover, that the events that have taken place have been engineered only by the shadows, and are not due to any enfeeblement of their will.

It is however the case that modern observers, dating back, that is, over the past few centuries, have noted the high incidence of ugly women among succubi. This observation did not at first create much interest, given the state of demonological research at the time. It was commonly believed in earlier days that witches were not essentially any different from demons, so that it was deemed logical for witches to be succubi as well. However our knowledge has advanced radically since the advent of serious studies on witchcraft. There is now no doubt that witches do belong to the human race. Given this fact, why should one assume that ugly succubi must be witches, rather than simply women? If they are women, it is understandable that they should lack the power to cheat nature by adopting a beautiful appearance by choice, and the uglier they are, the easier it is to appreciate that they need to have recourse to the succubinal state if they are to satisfy the excesses of a transport against which their unfortunate appearance militates. This is not to say that female succubi are necessarily always ugly. But, according to connoisseurs, and in so far as we are allowed to invoke our own recollections, in accordance with our modest personal experience, it is highly unlikely that a very beautiful person, perfectly capable of procuring serious and agreeable lovers through normal channels, should have recourse to sneaking from chamber to chamber in a manner fraught with diabolical associations. This is a pity. I have actually taken steps, by dint of setting out in a somewhat didactic way a subject which men usually reserve for intimate confession, to encourage certain people I know and whom I judge to be extremely beautiful and well-formed to indulge in activities they have never considered before. And, given that a suggestion once made can follow its own path, I have not given up all hope of seeing them disembark some night in my dreams, with that unfeigned naturalness I have always found so beguiling. Should one ever encounter an acknowledged beauty who is exploiting this unusual channel as a means of holding sway over men who would scarcely reject her favours in a more accustomed context, one will almost invariably discover that deep in her heart she is nursing some piteous anomaly, such as an unhappy love affair or the memory of some distant crime. They are indeed disquieting encounters, when, in the very depths of sleep, you retain like a guiding star that minimum consciousness which a man needs who wishes to take the measure of evil in all its intoxicating majesty. Yet it is only rarely vouchsafed, this pleasure of an entrancing embrace. More often, human succubi are branded with the lofty seal of the hideous.

Hence there is about their love a character not to be found among the demonesses. With these last, the sleeper always forfeits all initiative: he may fancy it is he who is running after them, though he is in truth caught in their clutches. Certainly he will suppose that it is he who is the author of desire. Obviously this is by no means how things stand with such creatures. On the contrary, it is the demonesses who advance by night, step by sinister step. At first the sleeper cannot distinguish them from the other elements of his dream. Then they take on palpable form. At first their ugliness startles him, and he cannot imagine ever confiding in such monsters. He is taken aback by the familiarity of their manners. It is true that these ladies have very precise ways of communicating the aim of their endeavours. They do not waste time talking. There is about their silent approach, along with their fearful aspect, a prodigious animal energy which makes one astonished at one's own response, so that one anticipates defeat in the involuntary motions of one's flesh, and struggles in vain to divert from this all-powerful bestiality an attention which is already captivated and being led despite any detours to its ineluctable goal. For it seems that the horror of this bizarre coupling renders a voluptuous climax even more inevitable. We are not spared one single feature of the face or the body: these are truly hideous women, and indescribably vulgar. Yet they are women entirely dedicated to love. You will be forced to comply with their wishes. Once you realise this, you are finished. But what else could you do? Try and draw back: either some incomprehensible, and unfortunately selective, paralysis will grip you; or else withdrawal is useless, given that desire only mounts with each retreating step. It sometimes happens that one admits to an extraordinary weakness for ugliness. It sometimes happens that one feels less shame than one might have thought in a conjunction of this kind. It sometimes happens, yes indeed, that one trembles in anticipation of such a conjunction, exhilarated by the novelty of the adventure. It sometimes happens that pleasure blows anywhere it damn well chooses.

I would love to give full details of the diversity of the succubi, that is to say of the species I have just been describing. As for the other kinds, they can be found faithfully depicted in all the romantic keepsakes, identifiable as the offspring of Raphael or Sir Walter Scott. But I would need a whole lifetime to do so; and since they might find descriptions offensive, who knows if those delicate furies might not place me under some punitive spell? True, they are more often inclined to scoff at men's reactions. They are used to seeing grimaces on faces at dawn. They do not find them insulting. Indeed some succubi actually take pride in their ugliness. Likewise, in certain parts of the world, as travellers have told me, savages are known to take pride in beards and moustaches, which are a cause of shame among the civilised.

I have always longed to identify the succubi in ordinary life, and would have been delighted if some irrefutable sign allowed me, amid the hustle and bustle of the city, to recognise those women whose vocation is the furtive caress. But I have no means of doing so, and this saddens me. All the same, on a number of occasions, there have been very strong presumptions which have prompted me to suspect someone of being a succubus, someone in whom an ordinary person would have seen no more than a rather unattractive woman, a woman moreover preoccupied by her social situation, her work or some ethical worry, something seemingly at odds with the demands of succubinage. This sort of thing attracts me greatly. I like to keep in touch with a lot of ugly women, because of this curiosity I have about them. I would even admit that this might be the root cause of certain wild impulses which have frequently disconcerted my friends, and which have made them see me as someone crazy, perverse, who knows what else? – There are a thousand expressions in our language which refer to a failure of discrimination in an amorous choice which I might see as entirely justifiable. I mention these things solely to back up what I have said, in an entirely disinterested spirit, scientific even, and by no means to excuse certain lacklustre relationships which have done little for my social image. Even less do I seek to boast of them. Despite this, I believe it would be of profit to humanity if certain critical spirits, like myself, were to set out, once and for all, everything they know about this much neglected topic, drawing up exact descriptions, names, dates, every last detail of the transaction. We would then be in a position to make some very illuminating comparisons. It is impossible to suppose we would not come closer to the truth. Then at last we might be able to determine what it is that distinguishes succubi from other women, what it is that gives them away in the daylight. That would be a signal benefit of which, without my expiating further, it is clear what would be the happy consequences for anyone inclined towards pleasure. Not to mention the fact that we would then be free of a good many moralisers, who would be compelled by the accumulation of evidence to renounce forever those unconscionable theses which poison our existence. All at once our vices would appear innocent when set against certain virtues. And a lot of insignificant people would suddenly have

187

access to that mystery of which it is only just that they should partake and which we have had the meanness to deny them because they are ugly, and because we see them, simply and idiotically, as simple and idiotic. I revel in the thought that these words might help bring about such a revolution in our attitudes. May this declaration hasten such an outcome by glorifying the succubi while promoting public awareness of them. May it also confound those sombre souls who never dream of love, and who claim they are reserving themselves for some sublime exploit in the future!

As if one could do what one wanted with one's own body!

*****
originally published in *La Révolution Surréaliste*
reprinted in Aragon, *La Défense de l'infini* (1986) Paris: Gallimard
French original © Editions Gallimard, 1986
translated by Roger Cardinal
*****

LOUIS ARAGON (Paris 1897 – Paris 1982) Dazzling poseur who played a major role in defining surrealism in its beginnings. Dalliance with communism turned to fullfledged opportunism in the thirties and made of Aragon one of the most discredited figures of contemporary French literature who, in betraying surrealism, betrayed his own inner sensibility. His early writings nevertheless remain fresh and electrifying. His *Paris Peasant* has long been recognised as one of the great texts of surrealism. His equally brilliant *Treatise On Style* has recently been published for the first time in English translation.

NELLY KAPLAN:

Beware the Panther[1]

Your animal eyes tell me (red velvet)
What genius itself would not even dare imagine

Pierre-Jean Jouve

I have lived with him for as long as I can remember in the highest part of the Louvre Palace, an attic with just a small window that has a direct view over the Tuileries. No one has the least suspicion of our existence.

In the beginning I thought he was my father. Perhaps he was a bit strange, but it was difficult for me to draw such distinctions when my experience was limited to what he told me during the long twilight on summer evenings.

Once when he had a bit too much to drink I learned the truth of my existence. I discovered that one day long ago my mother had been burned publicly at the stake, despite her innocence, and that she had managed to hide me and entrust my care to the man I had considered to be my father. He it was who had promised to look after me until the distant century when she would be able to return to complete my education. So it was that I was saved from sharing her horrible fate. As for my father, my true father, he had been savagely beaten to death in the forest, though not before having slashed the faces of twenty men with his splendid claws. His pelt was sold in I know not what hideous market. I feel very proud of him.

I am also beautiful. The Little Red Man who, by habit, I

---

[1] The French title 'Prenez garde à la panthère' is also a play on 'Prenez garde à la peinture', which generally is not warning us to beware of painting, but is the sign used for 'wet paint'.

still call Father, was adamant: I am blond, tall, slender and my golden green eyes and my smile would be the delight of those curious beings that Father calls men. I have never actually seen them, save from a distance when I look out of the window. I find them quite gracious.

Father does not want me to go outside. He is afraid that when I come into contact with them the strange magic of my ancestors would awaken in me a terrifying metamorphosis. But he is aware that one day I shall go out. It is so written in the secret books we deciphered together to distract us during the long hours.

My relationship with Father is very special. As I understand from the books of the humans, which I sometimes read to amuse myself, we had merited their condemnation. Father is right. These human beings really are idiotic creatures who understand nothing.

Father is very kind to me. He has taught me how to use my powers, how to anticipate the moment of my metamorphosis; he had shown me how contemptible men are and thousands of other things. He loves me passionately. I am fond of him too, but have no one to compare him with. And I anticipate the day I will descend to the Tuileries. It is so written in the secret books we deciphered together to distract us during the long hours.

Tonight is the evening humans call 11th April. Father had revealed to me that it was on just such an 11th April, all of three centuries ago, that my mother had been burned publicly at the stake, despite her innocence, just a few hours after I had been born, at the same moment my father, my true father, had been savagely beaten to death in the forest, though not before having slashed the faces of twenty men with his splendid claws. Father told me I must never forget these two murders. I have so promised.

But it must be *so* sweet outside. It is spring and from the window I can cast my reveries into the gardens, now free from the horrible brats who frequent them during the day. All that remain are a few couples and some solitaries, dreaming idly like me.

Today is my birthday, and in my honour Father has prepared some exquisite philtres. Already I feel a little tipsy and this exhilaration, combined with the April breeze, gives to everything an unexpected sweetness.

Suddenly I knew. This was the day. Tonight is the night I *must* go down and confront the perpetual enemy.

Father also realised it. He looks sad, but knows that there is no force on earth that can stop me. It is so written in the secret books we deciphered to distract us during the long hours.

I put on a tight fitting dress which father had woven with shades of gold and clouds. My eyes gleam with impatience and my body burns with expectation.

I cast the necessary spells to transport myself outside. Immediately I am there. It will soon be night. As I walk through the gardens I feel free, detached, almost happy. The few passers-by all look round at me as though dazzled. Father must have been right: I am very beautiful. But I also get the feeling that they are afraid of me. It is an unperceived fear: the fear of the unwonted. So they hurry on their way. I smile. I have all the time in the world. Night is mine, together with a substantial part of the future.

It is now that I see him, sitting there on one of the benches. He seems to be about thirty-five in human terms. He is handsome and must be rather tall. A sudden wild desire to caress his disordered brown hair passes through me. Oh yes! I would love to bury my fingers in his hair and make him press his head against my body. But father has taught me to be patient. I must not frighten him. I pass slowly in front of him, feigning indifference. I feel his transfixed and astonished glance follow me. I sit down facing him. I stare at him and for a long time we play the eternal gambling game of seeing who will be the first to lower their eyes. It finally ends in smiles, since neither of us will admit defeat. He offers a tentative 'good evening'. I reply to his welcome. He rises. He seems to hesitate about coming over, but finally does so. Is it not a little strange to find ourselves in a situation like this on such a charming spring evening? Yes, of course. And yet, is this not what was destined for me? And how!

His eyes are alert and intelligent. I like him at lot. I would never have thought a human being could be so attractive. I am particularly pleased that, unlike the others, he shows no sign of being afraid of me, and that if he had not approached sooner it was merely through fear of displeasing me.

It is becoming dark. One of the park attendants passes without noticing us. Soon afterwards he announces that the gates are about to be closed. We do not move. We smile at each other. The gardens belong to us.

He tells me about himself, about his hopes and what he does in his life. I also tell him about myself, a new life I invent, for Father had always insisted that one must never frighten human beings with *our* truths. A strange feeling passes through me. Finally I bury my hands in the disordered silk of his hair and feel him trembling. I caress his head, run my hands over his face, and kiss him. I like this man so much I could almost forget who I am and enter into the short span of his human life, so tempted am I by this passionate experience that I could stay with him forever and love him as furiously as I do tonight.

My dress of gold and clouds becomes unfastened beneath his hands and falls. He caresses my skin and explores my body as madness seizes hold of us. We roll entwined on the grass torn apart by our kisses and I discover the raptures of human love.

From time to time he seems amazed. Does something in my gestures or swooning betray my true nature? No, it is my beauty that has overwhelmed him. He worships my fury and my embraces. We love each other as mother and father must have worshipped each other hidden by the forest, three whole centuries ago. The perfume of the jungle penetrates into my blood. This is no longer a garden. I feel myself transformed, my skin colours, my eyes become cruel, as my hands twist strangely and tear at his shoulders. The oaths of vengeance rise in my memory, but I cannot bring myself to perform the final act. Because I love him, as my father must have loved my mother in the forest and because, despite my skin, despite my eyes, despite the blood which my loving claws have caused to spurt from his body, he still shows no fear of me. Because he loves me as I love him, because he still kisses my mouth, because he possesses me many more times, as he did at the beginning when the perfume of the jungle had not yet returned to my veins. . .

Only the two of us know what has happened on this night of 11th April.

Now he sleeps, drawing me into his arms. The first rays of sunlight caress his hair. I withdraw from him, put on my dress, and arrange his clothes to cover his wounds. I watch him sleeping for a while before leaving at last.

I did not kill him, but I had come close to doing so. It was only because he was not afraid of me that I spared him.

Now I return to my high dwelling in the Louvre Palace. I can still taste his blood on my lips and my body still trembles with the strange movements of the forest at the memory of his caresses, the forest to which I shall one day return.

The Little Red Man is waiting for me and I read the look of anguish on his face. He is worried he will lose me. He knows that nothing will again be the same between us, that the memory of man will always haunt me, and that from time to time I shall descend to the garden to taste blood and caresses. He is afraid that one day I shall remain down there, as almost happened the previous evening. He is wrong to be concerned. I shall always keep my oath, and it is written in the books that I must remain with him, my bizarre and unique Little Red Man of the Tuileries.

But those of you who read this story, beware. There will be many more occasions on which I shall descend to the garden at night.

And so if one evening a beautiful young blond woman with eyes the colour of the jungle sits down at your side, rise and leave immediately, if you still have the strength! For you would be unable to do anything other than fall in love with me and I would love you as no other woman has made love before. And with good reason.

But you will face the risk that, in the midst of our embraces, I may suddenly remember that it was your kind that burned my mother publicly at the stake, despite her innocence, or that I shall think about my father, savagely being beaten to death in the forest, though not before having slashed the faces of twenty men with his splendid claws. And if then, *seeing me as I really am*, I perceive the least sign of fear in your features, I would be unable to spare you.

★★★★★

published in *Le Réservoir des sens* (1988)
French original © Nelly Kaplan and Éditions Jean-Jacques Pauvert et Compagnie, 1988

★★★★★

NELLY KAPLAN (Buenos Aires 1934) Abandoning her studies in economics, Nelly Kaplan came to France on an impulse as a representative of young Argentinian cinema. Decisive encounters with Abel Gance and André Breton changed the course of her life and she became Gance's assistant on *Magirama* and *Le Sunlight d'Austerlitz*. Mainly known as a film maker (her 1971 film *La Fiancée du Pirate* has a cult following), she has also published a scandalous novel of feminine revolt, *Mémoires d'une liseuse de draps* (1973).

JOYCE MANSOUR:

Dolman the Malefic

Like the black and icy spiral that sighs on certain stairs, as well as in certain coffins, mediocre buffoons beckon with forked feet and sulphurous breath, delighted by their broken springboard over the abyss, never content in their pranks, intoxicated by the spasmodic burning of passion, they persist buoyantly in their grins. They are of little significance in the demonic hierarchy and do not have the power to affect anyone's mind.

Completely different are the high wire demons who are named Métastases, the codicil of a vanished race. They are magnificent in malediction: incestuous and morose, they spread doe-footed plague, toads and ulcers, these libidinous flowers. Disdaining common mortals, they are only interested in those who belong to the elite. Mendacious and with hooked noses, they embody infamy in its pure state with a virility capable of disturbing the tranquillity of even the most virtuous. Dolman belonged to this grade.

Before he rose in the morning, Dolman tore his eyes out of their orbits and, as birds of prey do, they darted towards the unknown. Indiscreet and destructive, everything maliciously touched with beak or wing was held for a long time in a state of paralysis. So Dolman knew the biting sadness the old tree felt when broken by the wind; he was able to find the sensitive part of arthritic rocks, and, an incredible thing which he absorbed merely through observation, the sweet velvet sensation that passes through a feminine thigh when she is caressed by the companion who walks at her side. The world was spread out luxuriously in front of Dolman. He satisfied his hunger with what was served by a hundred terrified villagers. Each night a good refreshing sleep tilled his eyelids. His secret, which was unknown even to himself, was that he had the faculty to possess everything he saw from within. Even so this undeserved life left him unappreciative and in a desperate state. His clothes hung from his body like so many rags from the moon and he even wasted away with boredom. Sometimes he languished with his eyes closed for whole days before the most beautiful panorama held in symmetry by the women who worked the fields with rumps in the air and beaded with jewels of rain. Mountains of water fell in a cascade on his pupils in their frivolous chassis fringed with gold.

In certain rocky lands, far, far beyond the horizon of the possible and forgotten in the putrefaction of Genesis, a man was born who was of the most exceptional nastiness. Dolman surpassed even the most horrible. His mother, set like an omelette of pious dread, died as she gave birth. His father was a courageous fisherman who did not have a particularly strong character and was by no means sure of his paternity. With a shrug of the shoulders he went off to the Orient without the least regret and left no instructions for the welfare and upbringing of the child. For ten years Dolman rotted away in a hut without so much as opening anything other than his mouth in the form of a furnace. Moonlight sealed his dreams with emotive trifles and he lived very simply, nourished on vermin. A normal child would have died, but Dolman had the extraordinary ability to flourish on his furtive bestiality with no need for a family. His only contact with the outside world was a bat. It dutifully changed the air from time to time and the child, enveloped in the moistness of chaotic mists, recognised it by its small rending cries and the fact that it smelt like a lonely old lady. The rest of the village ignored the child-larva that crawled in the solitude of its hut as people try to forget the leprosy that disfigures the face of a beloved. So the years followed each other stealthily over the mountains and the plain without leaving a trace in the fields of snow. This lasted until the day when the sun rose late by an hour and in its drunkenness forgot to pass its purifying index-finger over the hut in which the child lay. In a trice the village emptied for, in spite of the late hour, the heat and the noise, night seethed strangely in the crib. "We are going to have to pay! Sacred fire pulses in his veins! It's every man for himself!" This was what the sages announced, and men, women, cooks, children, houses, goats and boats all fled like a shot to the mountains and summits sprinkled with sanctuaries. They set out without dispersing, without putting their ideas into order, in an opaque group of minds, with legs dislocated by the swarming of fear, shadowed by a forest of fists they brandished above their heads to protect them from the evil eye.

Dolman woke. He heard the flight of the villagers to the north and as he experienced the cold lucidity of high places he felt the whirlwind of the demented shadow which seemed to want to open his eyes without understanding these fingers which cruelly turned back his eyebrows with stitches and hooks. As he opened his eyes, he cast his first glance like a hernia gushing forth from an abdomen. Visually he took in his hut with its tiles engraved with anathemas. Pale and bronzed with morning confusion, he lurched into the sun barely sure of his legs as night followed in his wake outside the cabin, far away from the pomp of nightmare, as hesitant as a gasping in the sackcloth of mist. The child chased the last filaments of night from his shadow and all at once possessed, with an inflexible look, sky, forest, village, sun, the invisible air, the insect nibbling away at his toe, the puddle of muddy water in which a pig wallowed; he absorbed it all by osmosis, as he went by. . . in short, everything that surrounded him, and the air as far as the eye could see, with a single inflexible look. He felt his spine stretch under the shock of the cataleptic skeleton of giraffes and, with stupefaction and delight, allowed his eyes to skim over the savannah, and felt himself become in turn grass, reeds, earth, wind, earth, earth, EARTH! He was married to the fir trees and their branches, rumblings,

197

birds and roots entered him without offering the least resistance. In the winking of an eye he absorbed the trees that had been struck by lightning. A tree himself. . . but his eyes still roamed far. . . He knew far away women, clacking on the roads that led to the summit between llamas with their heavy necks of phallic signification and the men who groaned at their sides. Worn out, Dolman stumbled on a stone and covered his frenetic pupils with his palms. Shaken by a sneeze of exaltation, he experienced his first dizzy fit.

Meanwhile the villagers had reached their goal and immediately offered a prayer to the valley as they returned on their tracks without too much haste. Honour was saved.

Later, in fact some twenty years later, Dolman discovered sex. He was first kept busy with the exploration of his own body with the aid of a microscope and set-square, but then as he became less timid, he devoted himself to the young girls who dared to stare at him with this air of suggestiveness, with eyes moist and with those faint smiles that were their specialty. He operated at a distance. With his sparkling eyes he pierced the plump forms, soiled the light-coloured tunics, caressing their wounds for as long as his nerve held, without proceeding to the least exchange of blood, or taking any account of the breaking of the hymen, until his victim became frenzied, trembled in front of him and convulsed herself, naked, avid to allow herself to be devoured by these indefatigable eyes. Being a formalist, Dolman was careful not to transgress the rules of hospitality; everything happened during the day and without raising a finger on the juvenile ghouls, without a word, and consequently, with no fear of reprisal. Dolman loved the experience of being a girl. He lay in wait for the first buds as they emerged under linen bodices. He fixed on the recently nubile girl in such a gracious way, impregnated himself with her peppery breath, and with his pupils held fast on her nipples bound with red velvet as he was careful to think about something else and, wham! their silky breasts would stir on his own chest. In so far as he was an aesthete, Dolman was very demanding and so, in order not to force his body, that had become flabby through nights spent alone, to follow the rambling of formalities, he employed an old man called Chimera, who knew how to deal with civil justice while remaining unscathed. Dolman placed his order for flesh without raising his eyes to the diadems of figs in order not to efface from his skin the fresh vision of his desire and to be sure of not interfering in the old bag with dilated pores, with discoloured spit and knowledge of Latin named Chimera. The latter feared the workings of magic, and departed without challenging the choice of his master, even though he was a question of his own daughter. He returned without delay, bringing delights, dribbling and proud. Spread-eagled by the gnarled arms of the servant, the victim offered no resistance in the mud. Covered with shame, each hesitating facet caught fire as the eyes of Dolman animated it, the girl sprang forward on the circuit of female orgasm.

Dolman varied his pleasures. An indescribable mockery in his ferret's eyes, he sharpened his senses at will on the satin backs of his victims. Cruel, the spicy brunettes with small breasts and pubic hairs twirled in acrostic caused him a visual rage tempered with melancholy, a veritable landslide of sadistic anger. He plunged into them in a blaze of blood. He let himself be penetrated by means of his victim's terror; rumpled like her he shivered with fear, cried, touched her bulging belly, incandescent with hysterical flames, on thin adolescent flanks. He practised sacrilegious onanism with relish on the body of a pale effigy freshly delivered from the arms of conventines with buttocks pricked with rose. A more cunning Narcissus, he possessed himself in the feminine. As a necrophiliac, he disinterred his mother and spent an unforgettable night conversing with her under the moon wearing long mauve suede gloves, in the company of white sauce flavoured with capers and holy wafer. Without remorse and without repose, he never tired of himself. On each inch of his interchangeable body he flattened his pupils and sighed with happiness so deep did he find its truth. His desire ran in long murderous gutters towards the victim of the moment, who always ended by struggling at his feet stripped of modesty and prepared, yes prepared, under his unpitying eyes, but without being vanquished. Then Dolman would laugh silently. Chimera loved these occasions since Dolman would often throw him the leftovers, thanks to which the old man took his wife, a co-religionist, a relation and his daughter under the ironical eye of his master, tired of being someone else.

So the adolescent knew all manner of things. He learned the language of good nutrition, the texture of Oriental silks, the flight of the most intrepid birds, the thought of sages and the digestive system of volcanoes. And he became tired. He was tired of women, of landscapes scattered with warriors, with the cries of cats, of insects, of himself, of everything else. He tried very hard to rekindle his enthusiasm by all sorts of alluring perversions but the delicate breadth of his unfettered penis no longer interested him. The rhythmical distance of the mad with their unstable mouths barely amused him. Murder drew from him no other reaction than a cynical sneer. Softened by boredom he bathed his eyes in bowls of fresh blood, in the necks of chopped up pigs, sliced by the attentive thighs of an ephebe. He soaked completely in artificially purulent wounds, tried to lose himself in abominable orgies of frenzy that almost always ended with the bloody death of the actors or the birth of a mutant: boredom still ceaselessly imposed itself.

A hundred times each day he cast his fly into the air, as he knew how to do, in quest of an idea for new distractions but it was without effect, until the day when his right eye saw the reflection of the sea gleam in the sky. The awakening of desire was immediate. He wished he could be wave, fish, water. He wanted to be dune, foam, algae. On their backs, across the mountains and plains, the villagers transported him to the faraway beach. They reached the goal considerably thinner after a month of forced marching. Without wasting time in thanks, Dolman immersed his haggard brain in the waves. In accordance with his wish he did become sea, algae, fish. He drowned his sorrows in the moving jelly and from then frittered away under the moon like a whale, washed of all terrestrial nostalgia.

This happy age did not last long. Dolman became tired of his aqueous image and again set the community on its way. The villagers, covered in sand, tore their children from the coconut trees and wailed on the forest paths. Dolman was filled with anguish. He returned to his hut and old habits without pleasure. Dissatisfaction consumed his meninx, and a desire to flee inflated his lungs like a blood clot. Death bought a lottery ticket in his name.

... And the Devil intervened, could not accept the escape of one of his creatures. He left his tower of silence and rushed forward, determined to enclose Dolman in the always changing perspectives of a suffering that had no escape. He could not allow the crushing of the mire, for he had too great a need to consolidate his reign. He therefore turned up his lips and prepared for battle, leaving nothing to chance, for the unexpected is the father of laughter and laughter liberates, lightens, and tears the handlebars away from demonic paws.

Dolman was relieving his soul's distress in a small terracotta bowl when he felt a burning in his shoulder. "Don't cry any more, I'm here," said the Atrocious One as he sat down. In his agitation, Dolman banged his bowl against the water jar, but the Great Profanator eyed him without malice. The man would have wished to slip to the ground like a leaf and to allow himself to eat the face of the Unnameable One that he did not know, did not see, but knew to be crouching in the shadow like a spasm in the emunctory of a woman, ready to break him in a bandaging of ice. He threw more logs on the fire. "Leave this corner with the mottled hangings of horror" said Dolman in a guttural voice. He was afraid, and in spite of himself his lips proffered insults, then impudent, he undressed in the wink of an eye and wanted to stand astride the invisible face. He knew, in fact, it was necessary to chase away the Beast before the yeast of ordure rose into his throat and suffocated him, but a strange exaltation prevented him from doing anything. "I am too great, your eyes cannot detect me", said the Beast, whose breath smelled of cloves. "You could never settle in me, the demented sower, my omega would swallow your tiny bird brain before the completion of the slightest sacrilege." "The Devil?" suggested Dolman. "None other, The Dark One. The one who glows red in the half-light. The execrated tabernacle of the Poisonous One." The voice swelled up from one moment to the next. Dolman turned up his sedentary man's sleeves and controlled his totem with its haunting glares. He wanted to protect himself, to create a diversion, to flee. "I'm not game," he said. The Devil rubbed his hands with absinthe juice to avoid a too sudden warming of his senses and took advantage of the silence to escape conventions. "I do not mean you any evil for the moment" he said, sliding his hand between those of Dolman, along the slippery wood of the object held between his bended knees. "I will give you my totem, my virility, in exchange for a single look at your secret," said the man as he sank the object into the straw that was saturated with fetid humidity. The Beast groaned and drew back his hand. "I am the void. The hullabaloo of new impressions ceases in my presence. I banish routine, the shaken crash of life falls and grinds in a vacuum on the frontiers of my silence. What more do your want?" It was true. Dolman sank like a boat in the hollow of a wave which, mysterious, deep and tranquil, never rose up again. "I thought your empire was animated with loathsome passions. I was afraid of the cold, of the atrocious solitude, of remorse," he said as he placed his hand on the enamelled arm of his invisible visitor. "I thought you suffered eternally." The Other did not reply but pointed with his finger to the setting sun. The sky perforated with refined birds grinned and was extinguished. Night fell like a sledgehammer. The finger returned into its leather case. The moment of disenchantment could not be far away. "I would like to understand you," he said sadly. He staggered as he allowed himself to fall on the bed like a mast pounded by the wind. "You are close to me, closer at this moment that any of those who knew me in bygone centuries," the Delightful One said tenderly as he squeezed the man's chest without taking heed of his recoil. In the darkness Dolman remained fearful. "I want to know you, become part of your skin." In spite of his fear he remained persistent. "I will give you my goods, my hut, my fertile entrails, my beach. I offer my hatred in exchange for a single participatory glimmer." "You belong to me. I am so near to you," said the Frightful One in an uneasy whisper, "touch me, feel my musk sweat on your clothes." He ran his fingers down Dolman's body, and a smoke of coal and satisfaction spiced with puss provoked his victim's senses. "I want to understand you." Dolman knew he was clumsy but, as he cherished frankness in his dealings, he could not refrain from protest. The Horrible One breathed like a walrus. Dolman hid his face in the folds of the groin. The hour stiffened on its pedestal. The man retorted savagely: "A single look without reticence or recoil in your haggard eyes, a moment of happiness before vanishing." He had to wait for the reply, which was: "I want to be a father." Spoken in a pitiable way, Dolman could not believe his ears. "What?" The voice was engulfed in mud riddled with cloves of garlic and whistled: "It is essential for me to become a father, even if only of a louse." "Let me think about it," said Dolman on all fours "and come back in the morning." The voice was insistent: "Let me stay near to you, I like it in this hut!" "No! the man cut him short and the Tender One gave up, making threats, but defeated for the moment.

Dolman lay down and slept and woke without having found a solution, without even being capable of dreaming about it. It was twelve hours later when the Frightful One reappeared. "And?" Dolman soothed the shadow with a crushing gesture. "I will be your swan." The Beast stood erect. "Take off your shirt, your hairs and surliness. Sing the charms of hallucination, the whirlwinds of pillows, the icy belly of night. You are the terrible spouse who has always been awaited." As he opened his mouth, Dolman found that his voice was absent. "I am lost," he thought. "I have been outmanoeuvred. How could I have hoped to stand up against Fear?" He crawled towards the staircase of the Husband.

The Devil coiled around the bound breasts with a perspicacious tentacle of sweetness and plunged his tongue sharpened with neurosis between the entwined legs. Dolman smoothed his long hair and sighed, his belly the carrier of sparks, stank of excrement. The Beast caressed his stiff thighs and rubbed his face with a moistened paw before saying: "With my lance dipped in adrenalin, I will palpate your unstable womb with offspring. In my turn I will be a creator."

Swooning and discomfited the Vile One fell on to his side. "I will keep you company tonight." And he slept without letting go of the sophisticated tips of Dolman's breasts with his teeth. "See! Know!" Dolman opened his eyes of the last chance, collected together his limbs as best he could to re-kindle the fire. He put his flushed face close to the Hairy One. Nothing. He understood nothing, saw nothing. "Perhaps I have lost my gift of discernment?" He threw open the door and stared at the lake of pure reflections. He possessed the icy water, felt the waves change into petals of foam as fishes went by, heard sounds scented with fluvial harmony resonate in his entrails. Incapable of integrating himself in the delicate velocity of the Shadow, there remained for him only one possible escape: death. He no longer saw the sky marbled plum-blue, and the gigantic fluffy artichoke pressing its crest between the sheaves of fire barely interested him. He was nothing, the Other continued. "Come," whistled the Adorable One between lips of slush, and Dolman submitted to the call, tearful and distracted. "Be happy," said the Ignoramus as he underlined in blue the miserable grove in which a last cry was raised on hind legs. Dolman opened his legs and felt the splashes of lava that preceded the final sneeze. "Be happy," repeated the Ignorant One when Dolman expired. "I will be eternally present." "Will I see you?" hiccuped the man whose head was already in the beyond. "The one who comes will have my face." "Will I see him? Will I see him?" In agony he took a last look around and died.

The Devil waited and waited, jumped with both feet on the distended stomach, used a lever to open the jaws, scraped the womb without being sure of its location, called out in a raucous and excited voice. Nothing. He took a glove, two rusty forceps, a camel's hair and operated on the dust without waiting for an autopsy. At the far end of a drawer he heard a slight sound. He encouraged it, cajoled it, and finally caught it. And so in this way war was born.

★★★★★

First published in *La Brèche: action surréaliste* no 1 (October 1961)
reprinted in Joyce Mansour: Ça, Editions Soleil Noir, 1970
© Actes Sud, 1991

★★★★★

JOYCE MANSOUR (Bowden 1928 – Paris 1986) Born in England of Egyptian parents, Joyce Mansour spent only a few months in her country of birth before her parents returned to Egypt, where she became a leading athlete, a champion runner and high-jumper. Her first volume of poetry, *Cris* was published in 1953 and thereafter she lived in Paris, becoming one of the most active members of the Surrealist Group.

RIKKI DUCORNET:

The Monkey Lover

(an authentic tale from Baclava)

My husband, that ridiculous worm, had an upside-down
head, being profusely bearded and totally bald. As he slept,
I liked to imagine that the red beard was a wig, the bare
dome a chin, and the open mouth, so terrible in slumber, a
pistol wound in the forehead. Had he been a better man,
such thoughts may never have entered my head. But as
things were, these visions tormented me until there was no
peace for either of us. The man was a pig, his chin
inscribed with nasty scrawls of nicotine, mustard and chocolate – for his mouth was forever full of things dark and
viscous as was his brain. And although young enough to
be his daughter, if I had ceased to laugh whenever I
chanced to see myself reflected in the glass or catch a
glimpse of a toad lurching across the porch in the moonlight, it was because my laughter excited him and my
smiles made him gloat with pleasure. He thought then that
I was happy. . .

"Are you happy, Saida my little fishcake?" he would
dribble, taking my ears in his paws and pretending to box
them. "Are you happy my little blue fig?" Grabbing my
childish breasts in his terrible paws that smelled of a goat's
testicles. "Come sit on my knees and play the tongue game
with your Papa."

His name was Dung Baba. Promoted by fate to Chief of
Police, he loved his job which provided the flesh he toyed
with as a sow toys with a walnut, rolling it back and forth
through the dust with her snout until all at once exasperated
she smashes the shell and swallows the meat with one noisy
gulp.

My husband's savagery was notorious. Persons who had

206

been caught sleeping under the bridge or secreting chick peas in their pockets were brought to him twitching like worms in puddles of mud. He trussed them to oddly stained poles. He humiliated and maimed them in a thousand unexpected ways.

Of these truths I knew little, swaddled as I was in my child-bride's shifts and fear of the monster, the web of my father's lies and my mother's resigned mutterings. In Baclava a girl must take what Allah tosses her way with a scraping and a bowing and a blinking down at her feet.

It is said that Allah owns a filing cabinet. Sealed with the blood of the hymen, all marriage contracts are kept therein. When with a smart clap of thunder the drawer is slammed shut, nothing can open it, not even death. A widow, no matter how young, must never look again upon a man, be he her own brother. Locked in the kitchen, she is forbidden everything: visits, speech, self-love; forbidden to pass the milk and dates through the little window in the wall no bigger than a book of verse lying on its side.

I called Dung Baba's house the cage; in his kitchen, my dreams decayed. The house was circumscribed by a high wall of earth and date pips; rooting in the earth the pits had formed an impenetrable barrier. As is customary, I picked stones from the lentils and scraped the dung from my master's boots which were set out for my attention, nightly. If at dawn the boots were imperfect in any way, Dung Baba invented a punishment. Such was my life.

I was lonely, childless. I pleaded with Dung Baba for a little monkey to play with, but he refused angrily, grumbling that animals were as detestable to him as men. Next I prayed to Allah whose ears are deaf; then did I beseech his fallen twin, the Devil Hornprick, who sits upon his thorn of fire, gloating upon his constellations and counting his bloody seeds.

In Baclava it is said that Hornprick once caught a glimpse of the First Woman as she sat singing to her snake in her chamber of sacred mud. Dazzled by her sight, the light of love and lust, he fell. He is still falling. For all eternity her breasts orbit his dreams.

Hornprick listened to me. Without delay he sent me little Kishkishkat the monkey. At dawn he leapt over the wall. I was breathless with the wonder of his small beauty. My furry grasshopper! Even his voice was small. It was easy to coax him to eat dates from my lips and soon he let me fondle and caress him. I knew love and laughter. In time I gave birth to a beautiful daughter.

But for her oval face, her buttocks and the palms of her hands, Naatiffe was covered in soft pink fur. If she was my treasure, Dung Baba feared and hated her; as he pricked his teeth with his great knife, he plotted to kill us both. But Hornprick, who sees and hears everything, broke off a sharp piece of his crown. He gave it to Kishkishkat and bade him to cut out Dung Baba's heart. This heart – shaped like a European urinal – was no bigger than an onion. Tumbling to the floor, Dung Baba's body deflated like a bladder of spilled wine.

We escaped to the Tower of Invention where the Devil sat waiting; his black crown, broken in countless places, stood as tall as a date palm upon his head. There he bestowed upon Naatiffe, Kishkishkat and me the three infinite oceans, so that we might live in peace. And it is we who have parented all the gentle whales which inform the world with enchantment, sobriety and tenderness. . .

★★★★★

published in *The Butcher's Tales*
© Rikki Ducornet and Atlas Press, 1991

★★★★★

RIKKI DUCORNET: (1943, New York) Has published four novels, *The Stain* (1984), *Entering Fire* (1986) and *The Fountains of Neptune* (1989) and *The Jade Cabinet* (1993), which comprise a cycle exploring the elements, earth, fire water and air respectively. A fifth novel, *Birdland* is in progress. She has also published six volumes of poetry and illustrated works by Jorge Luis Borges and Robert Coover. The definitive edition of *The Butcher's Tales* will be published by The Dalkey Archive in 1994.

CLÉMENT MAGLOIRE-SAINT-AUDE:

Vigil

The dead girl was lying on a narrow bed. She was black and beautiful and seemed to be asleep, delivered, one might say, from the cares of living.

★

It was night in an uncertain alley in Bel-Air.

★

In the mortuary chamber, the gathering seemed crushed under the strain of oppressive and mysterious sorrow. The neighbours had gathered on the porch and the dead girl's mother was chatting in a low voice with the corpse attendant. The latter was smoking a cheap cigar and spat out tobacco. Her breath stank of garlic.

★

It was whispered that the deceased had not succumbed to sickness, and it was confidentially said that she had expelled her last breath without suffering.

★

They said it was not a natural death.

★

Drinks were being served in the corridor. I left Teresa's room (the dead girl's name was Teresa) and went, on the insistence of the 'madre', to sit between her and the corpse-attendant, who immediately asked me, in an authoritative tone, for a light for her cigar. I struck a match and, as I brought the flame closer to the attendant's face, noticed that she had the eyes of an owl (or a witch) with sharp animal teeth and hands that were horribly calloused. Our eyes met sharp as lightning before I turned to the maid who served cinnamon tea. I drank it and followed it with a glass of clairin and some coffee. I shook the dregs out of my pipe and carefully re-filled it with a marvellous Splendid tobacco that had the aftertaste of chocolate.

★

At midnight an angry man ran from the adjoining alleyway. He was a half-breed with a belly like a pregnant woman's. This thug was lashing out with vehemence at a young girl in a transparent nightgown. She was a very beautiful dimwit, with a mottled complexion and the looks of an angel. She was insensible both to the flailings that lacerated her body and to the blood that stained her clothes around the shoulder. In the distance a dog howled sinisterly at death; and without one knowing from whence it had come, a mongrel as white as milk raced in from the alley and started to lick the girl's feet.

★

My friends Laurent P and Gaston F called me over to share a bottle of Barbancourt rum with them. I left the dead girl's mother and the corpse-attendant to their gossip, offered my apologies, and joined the drinkers.

★

I sat down in an armchair in the kind of corridor adjoining the dead girl's room, at the opening to the apartment, and so I was face to face with the deceased.

In her white dress heightened around the bust with lace flounces, Teresa seemed to be awaiting first communion; in her eternal stillness there was nothing mournful. She did not have a chin-band and her full and straight skirt barely fitted her.

★

There was on her lips the outline of a smile with an imperceptible hint of mischievousness. Her hair, raven black, covered her forehead.

★

But as I examined her face (I only had to stretch out my arm to be able to touch her body) something caused me to shiver: the eyes were not completely closed and, from beneath the eyelids the dead girl seemed to be looking at

210

me... and to look at me, in fact, with such fixity that filled me with a sense of panic. I tried to move but an intolerable cramp paralysed my movements. I wanted to speak but was voiceless.

★

And Teresa still looked at me.

★

At me alone.

And my own eyes felt magnetised and were unable to detach themselves from those eyes from the other world.

★

Nevertheless I did manage to swallow a glass of liquor which Laurent pressed to my mouth. I hiccuped. Gaston brought me some lemon water which I gulped down breathlessly at intervals.

★

My hiccups continued in growls.

★

I was given aspirin. In spite of the sedative, I still felt sick. I was sweating, ice cold, and the dead girl looked at me, and still her eyes, now half-open, were like those of the living... and I saw her pupils, which were hallucinatory...

★

Candles had been placed by the deceased's bedside. Suddenly the flame of one of them flickered, revived as though in response to the breath of a hidden presence, and then was extinguished.

★

The other glimmers of light, as though waiting for such a signal, followed suit.

★

In the half-light that followed, Teresa opened her eyes wide. They were strangely beautiful eyes, and had a sensual gaiety that was unseemly to the point of cruelty.

★

With a great deal of effort I managed to rise, like an automaton, in order to close the eyes of the dead girl...

211

There was a terror that chilled my blood, and a wisp of smoke escaped from my jacket.

*

An indescribable serenity suddenly permeated my soul as I lifted my pipe to my lips.

*

All the guests had left.

*

For half an hour the Cathedral bells had rung.

*

In the East the stars paled.

★★★★★

published in 1956

★★★★★

CLÉMENT MAGLOIRE-SAINT-AUDE (1912 Port-au-Prince – 1971 Port-au-Prince) A founder of the review Les Griots (1937) which played an important role in the development of Haitian culture, Magloire-Saint-Aude met André Breton and Pierre Mabille in 1941 and, in a society greatly influenced by surrealism, was the only Haitian to fully adhere to the surrealist movement. His uncompromising work was dedicated to exploring the limits of language and its possibilities of communication until he was consignedy to silence after the accession to power of his once friend François Duvalier.

HENDRIK CRAMER:

The Mirage-Child

A man and a woman met by the wayside. After exchanging a few words they wandered into the forest, fell to the ground and made love.

Six weeks later the woman went to look for the man and told him: "I'm pregnant." The man replied: "Wait a little, dear. You could be wrong." At the end of the fourth month they went to see a wise-woman who performed an abortion. The woman delivered her of a foetus that was already in an advanced stage of development. That evening the man and woman left the village. The man carried the foetus in a bag hidden under his coat. They took the road that led to the lake. The moon was very red and very white. At the shore of the lake, the man tied the bag to a stone and threw it into the water.

As they returned to the village the woman told the man: "I feel very sad." They got married. It was a happy marriage and the woman soon brought into the world a very handsome child who looked like his father. The parents did everything possible to provide for the happiness of their child, and the latter, who had a docile and cheerful character, seemed to love his parents.

When he was six years old the father started to take him with him on his walking trips. It then happened one evening that they came, by chance, to the lake side. The moon was very red and very white. At the place that had been marked by sorrow, the little boy stood before his father and said: "Father, this is the place where, seven years ago, you threw me into the water. Since I have never felt content on this earth, I would like to go back there." He waded into the water and vanished. The father jumped in after him but was unable to save him. Filled with despair he returned home and employed workers with the machinery to dredge the lake for weeks. But the only thing that could be found was a foetus inside a bag attached to a stone.

So it was that the man and the woman recognised that the child they loved had been a mirage-child.

★★★★★

first published in Le Grand Jeu issue no 3
reprinted in Hendrik Cramer: Visions et naissance
French original © Editions du Rocher, 1988

★★★★★

HENDRIK CRAMER (Utrecht 1884 – Neuengamme 1945) Cramer was a great traveller and raconteur, an amateur ethnologist in the best sense, fascinated by folklore, with a special interest in Haitian voodoo and Hindu concepts of being. A decisive encounter with Véra Milanová in 1926 introduced him into surrealist circles and he participated in *Le Grand jeu*. His only book, *Vizioen en Geboote* (Vision and Birth) was published in 1940. Active in the Resistance he was arrested by the Gestapo and died in deportation.

JEAN FERRY:

Rapa-nui

I arrived in Easter Island on 13th February 1937. For thirty years I had waited for such a moment. For thirty years as the years of my life unfolded, I had experienced an overwhelming desire to see Easter Island, but never expected to do so. I thought it would be too difficult to arrange, that my wish was nothing but an extravagant dream. And now, on 13th February 1937, just to show that if we wish hard enough what we desire can come true, I set foot on Easter Island soil.

For thirty years I had been thinking about this, and one can well imagine I had planned my itinerary out in advance. Moreover I had no time to lose as the Chilean training ship which had brought me was only putting in at port for two days. If I said I trembled with emotion, beneath that oddly pale sun, I would not be lying. It was difficult to convince myself that this was not just another dream, the one in which I dreamed I arrive at Easter Island trembling with emotion under an oddly pale sun. But no, it was all true, the wind and the black cliffs, the rumblings of the three volcanoes. It really was the case that there were no trees or natural springs. And in accordance with the rendezvous fixed since the beginning of time, the immense statues waited for me there on the slopes of Rano Raraku.

I know I would be fooling people if I did not admit that the realisation of my desire did not also bring with it a frightful feeling of disillusion. I should mention that, faced with the sisters of Breaking Waves, I recognised that it was not worth expecting so much, or coming so far for something so simple and so real. I could complain about the insects, about the dirty little Pascuan who offered me some statuettes with hollowed bellies that had barely been carved the previous evening. So much the worse for those desperate for origins. And the person I was at the bottom of the crater is nobody's business but my own. Simply, I knew why I was there and why, for thirty years, I had so obstinately wanted to visit the island one day. So, finally here I was. . .

But apart from the fact that I have wanted to go to Easter Island for the past thirty years and that I am sure something does await me there, not a single word of the preceding account is true. I've never been anywhere near Easter Island and don't suppose I ever shall.

★★★★★

published in *Le méchanicien et autres contes* (1951) Paris: Gallimard

French original © Editions Gallimard

★★★★★

JEAN FERRY (see page 40)

ROGER CAILLOIS:

The River Amour

"In a few moments we will be flying over the River Amour." The intercontinental aircraft flew over interminable Siberia some ten thousand metres down below, a vast, vivid green sponge unable to absorb all the water in which it was engulfed. It was already possible to perceive the river, below the wing, running violet in the emerald softness. Divided into two branches, it framed an escutcheon of pure vert, sown with large mauve – or sometimes, when clearer water reflected a cloudless sky, turquoise – tears. No human trace was apparent over the abstract expanse, a landscape that invited meditation even more than the gardens of sand and stone I had just visited in the Kyoto temples. There the priests rake and weed every morning to preserve the dryness and give a facade of immortality. Here it is the inverse: an ocean of earth irrigated to saturation point with no need of man's solicitude. Neither enclosed by four walls nor put forward to anyone's reflection, it is traversed only by means of a powerful wine-coloured vena cava or vena portae which is branched by thousands of vessels forked like the bristles of neurons. A calm and scintillating web of tincture, it is more than a saltire on the planet in a dazzling gown, the deeply etched lines of the earth's palm that has no expectation of a palmist's oracle.

A thin sandy beach, as everywhere sand-coloured and taking a delight in proclaiming its own materiality, without neglecting its course, set off its plum bluish tint. A flow without motion, life embodied, it is more durable than man and yet can still run dry. More than the arid gardens of asceticism and ecstasy, sustained with subtlety to manifest how vain desire, work and application are, I think about the meticulous paddy fields which are to be found over the whole cultivated part of the land. With its back relentlessly bent over astute, indefatigable fingers have transplanted the nourishing cereal foot by foot in infallible rows. Successive pools of water have been arranged along the hillsides in slight submerged terraces. They served to perpetuate the profile of the original landscape, which has barely changed. But the vast concentric curves which extend the length of the slopes betrayed an imperceptible effort, as discreet as the caress that concludes by glazing a rebellious coat.

There is not the space of a hand that would be rendered productive by the patience of millennia. And like the pools of the River Amour, the sky is reflected in its fertile ponds. This time it is reflected between the fine equidistant clusters, established by the industrious insects that are nourished by them. Each year they begin an identical labour which is set in motion within them by the stars or the calender. From this height one could not make them out. In any event what would be the good of noticing them? They are dark and nullified, indistinguishable from the nature of which they are both a part and which, at the same time, they shape – like the wind that moulds it, like the waters which flow slowly through it – hollowing out their buckles with the time before them, like the River Amour in the solitude of Asia.

"His head haloed with the River Amour." This phrase suddenly came back to me. This is all I can still remember of a poet's complaisant description long ago depicting a young giantess relaxing over the entire extent of the earth. Was it necessary to add a giantess to the earth? It is itself a splendid giant. It is a grandiloquent and redundant rhetoric to lay the body of an imaginary giant over it. Much better to take it as it is, in its inconsequentiality, without ceremony, without mediation, with its mosses, lichens, peat-bogs, its incessant canker, and the multitude of swiftly replaceable being which stirs on its surface. I do not distinguish between the swamp, in which it unfolds alone, and the smooth cirques of those steps organised by my species for their subsistence. The priest's bare gardens certainly have their place in the general scheme – a desiccated image of nature that is not as natural as they seem to think. Too harmonious and calculated, certainly too remarkable to be a simulacrum of emptiness. And what does the trick of the fifteen stones, of which one only ever sees fourteen at the same time, prove but the futility of human ingenuity?

I dream with more piety of my obstinate ants, with more reverence of the slow River Amour – slow and lilac coloured – which lazily drains life towards an icy sea; the solemn, treacherous River Amour, whose Siberian syllables only imitate a simulacrum of the French word for love.

★★★★★

first published in Roger Caillois *Randonées* (1986)
French original © Fata Morgana, 1986
translated by Guy Flandre, Michael Richardson and Peter Wood

★★★★★

ROGER CAILLOIS (Rheims 1913 – Paris 1978) Joined the Surrealist Group as a precocious nineteen year old. Sociologist fascinated by the phenomenology and perception of the natural world, Roger Caillois wrote on a wide-range of subjects. His *Necessity of Mind* has recently been published in English translation (Lapis Press). He discovered the manuscript of Jan Potocki's *The Saragossa Manuscript*, published by Dedalus.

JULIEN GRACQ

The Cold Wind of the Night

During the evening I waited for her in the hunting lodge by the banks of the Dead River. The perilous winds of the night shook the fir trees as the shrouds rustled and the blazing fire crackled. The black night was lined with frost as if wearing white satin beneath an evening gown – outside coiled hands ran from all about over the snow. The walls were large dark curtains and over the steppes of snow, a white tablecloth spread as far as the eye could see, the mystical light of candles rose in the way that fires take off from frozen ponds. I was the king of a people of blue forests, like a pilgrimage with its pennants drawn motionless across the shores of a lake of ice. On the ceiling in the vault the cyclone of black thoughts was animated one moment then, like a fabric's watered silk, paralysed the next. With my elbows against the fireplace, attired in full evening dress, I fingered my revolver with a theatrical gesture and, in idleness, interrogated the green and stagnant water of the very old looking-glass. Occasionally a strong gust would cause it to cloud over with a condensation as fine as that on the decanter but I would see myself emerge from it anew, spectral and fixed, like a bridegroom on a photographic plate emerging from the surging growth of the foliage. Oh, hollow hours of night, so much like a journey through delicate bones borne into the air and passages of the rapids! But suddenly there she was, sitting erect and dressed in her long white finery.

*****
first published in *Liberté grande* (1946)
French original © Librairie José Corti, 1946
*****

JULIEN GRACQ (Saint-Florent-le-Vieil 1910) Brought up in Nantes, Gracq trained as a geographer. His first novel, *Au Château d'Argol* (1938) established him in the forefront of writers connected with surrealism. His other narratives, *Un Beau ténébreux* (1945); *Le Rivage des Syrtes* (1951); *Un Balcon en forêt* (1958), have all been translated into English. His other work, pungent reflections on the experience of literature in its widest sense and travel accounts of startling originality, remain unknown in English.

ANDRÉ PIEYRE DE MANDIARGUES:

Clorinde

in memory of Tasso

Without a feather, without a plume, Clorinde has put on
(a grim omen) the rusty and black armour.

Jerusalem Delivered

You sleep like an ox. Yesterday evening you got drunk
again, and now the vapours of rum have caused the flies to
turn somersaults around the overhead egg serving as a
counterweight to the lamp. Dawn breaks as the gas lamps
fade outside the window whose shutters you forgot to
close. On the marble top of the chest of drawers, beside the
narrow bed where you lie, a number of curious tiny
objects are collected under the glass bell inside which I can
make out three or four desiccated butterflies, some phalae-
nae and a hawk moth, a once resinous piece of wood now
corroded by the larvae of I know not what insect, and
finally, on a strip of moss, a tiny iron helmet no bigger
than a thimble and inlaid with old gold, which an armourer
might recognise as being of ancient Germanic craftwork.

Life is now, for you, a thing of the past. The days ahead
of you are numbered. You drink, you sleep, you roll up in
the horse-blanket on this mattress without sheets. As the
concierge knocks at your door you hastily grab a book
within reach of your hand or pretend to write, even
though the page remains blank, since you fear the secret
judgement of this snooping woman you have never heard
speak and who resembles a bundle of blackthorn. And
since you will soon be dead and you will never be able to
do so yourself, I am going to try to note down on these
scattered sheets of paper what you confided to me that
night, after I had, at your entreaty, accompanied you

home, and before you had taken possession of this now empty bottle that the slope of the floor causes to roll towards me each time I try to kick it under the bottom drawer of the dressing-table.

It was a very warm day at the beginning of last autumn, in a pine forest where you were walking with the vague idea of gathering mushrooms, despite the fact that it was not the season, when you suddenly noticed, on an earth mound, an object which suggested the form of a castle with ramparts, crenels and turrets, such as one might see in Victor Hugo's drawings. In fact it was only a piece of wood embedded in moss and blanched by several winters' rains and riddled with cavities caused by corroding larvae. Your curiosity caused you to tear it away from the moss and turn it over and over for inspection, shaking and shaking it so that it cast off a dust as fine as flour. Inside you heard a strangely metallic clinking, and from one of the holes a shiny living creature which you first took to be an insect fell out, maybe a large cricket, for you were unable to believe your eyes and admit the existence of a tiny knight dressed from head to toe in flashing armour of reddish gold. Standing now on what seemed to you part of the ramparts, he unsheathed a large sword, grasped it in both hands, and made vigorous thrusts which pricked your fingers uncomfortably.

You watched with amazement and fear, for he seemed perfectly capable of cutting your thumb to the bone (or even splitting your thumb nail open, an idea as painful as the reality). As you tried to evade the blow, a nervous gesture of your hand served to unsteady the support and the little warrior fell from the top of your chest to the ground and crashed against a pebble. You saw him lying there unconscious.

You immediately bent down (so sharply that you nearly fell flat over him) to pick him up. As he lay in the hollow of your hand, fearing serious injury if not death in the fall, you sought to help him by opening his armour. Your fingers rather clumsily sought the spring that released the helmet: when the visor was raised what was the unexpected marvel revealed to you but the sight of the most ravishing face of a young girl.

Taking great care not to scratch the beautiful unconscious face with the contact of the steel you drew the helmet completely off, unhooking the breastplate held by a strap which opened from behind like certain corsets and, as you held the little woman by the waist as delicately as you could, you threw off the rest of her armour, something that recalled the way you extracted the meat from the shell of a Norway lobster. The creature was now dressed in nothing but a chemise, which you felt was a very fine material but which, in relation to the scale of the body, was really a coarse fabric, a chemise that descended only halfway down her thighs and barely concealed the rounded form of her golden bosom.

Life soon returned to her and as you sat on the ground to examine her more easily, the little warrior jumped from your hand to your knees and then darted into the moss and tried to hide. But the unevenly projecting twigs hindered her way and you had little difficulty in recapturing her. She struggled with fury, and her very black and very luxuriant hair which fell to her collar-bone shook back and forth, beating your fingers with her fists and trying to bite you. To quieten her, you tore two strands of wool from the bottom of your jacket. The first, still red in your memory, you tied around the creature's back, while you attached the second, a pretty blue, by her ankle to a pebble heavy enough to preclude any possibility of escape. As you knelt beside the moss to which she was fettered she seemed, even though she could not extend her arms, to be entreating you. Instead this made you want to see her naked. You took a penknife out of your pocket and held it suspended in the air before you cut open her chemise (without forgetting the shoulder straps), from back and front and up and down and its shreds were carried away by the wind, and you returned your prisoner to her cryptogam bed.

She lay on her back, closed her eyes, and adopted the

resigned expression of women of the larger species (this was how at that moment you thought of your own kind) when they realise that shame or even the pretence of it has become futile, and so abdicate any sort of modesty. No obstacle was offered to your glance as it fixed on her bosom in which you glimpsed a true Tamil splendour in cup and weight, whose girth could have been encompassed by a ring, and flitting over the smoothness of her knees and thighs, plunging into the obscurely buckled triangle of a fleece whose lustre and vigour appeared almost bestial. As though it was not enough just to look, you put your monstrous nose against her stomach: her body exuded a perfume that resembled mignonette in bloom. What would you not have given to have been able to reduce your own dimensions to those of the little creature, to collapse and became her equal on the moss at her side, and take her in your arms, since your actions had apparently served to place her at the mercy of anyone who came along if he was the same size as her.

At that moment at you needed to give release to your desire, which was so strong that you trembled with powerless rage before the little body. And certain of being able to find your prisoner again, you fled into the forest like a man who had lost his senses, and grasped the trunk of a pine in your path before falling into the ditch and tearing at the mossy carpets and kissing the bare earth between the honeysuckle, plantain and horsetail roots. When, with your frenzy extinguished, covered in mud and vegetal debris, you returned to your prisoner, who you considered as much yours as a hedgehog or lizard captured during a walk, you found she had vanished. You had no doubt about the place you had left her. Neither the thread of blue wool nor the pebble had moved from the bed of moss. However, the former had been cut to three quarters of its original length and was bathed in a spatter of fresh blood.

Not for a moment did you suspect the pinewood ants which ran quickly through the nearby dry needles, since there was no sign of any bone on the ground, and it is well known that these insects devour large prey to the bone and do not carry it away, but with indescribable horror you suspected the beak of a bird. Especially distressed, with your conscience tormenting you, you visualise the woman's naked body in a warbler's beak. Why, you ask me, do impostors write stories or rhyme songs that, with the same lack of imagination as naturalists, have so capriciously given the warbler a reputation for delicacy and good grace which is contrary to what should be apparent to everyone? Its song is nothing like as beautiful as people think. Only the name properly describes how malign it really is, far from the imaginary world created by poets. It is only necessary, you went on to declaim the three words "weasel, wolverine, warbler. . ." to immediately recognise the tortuous deception and implacably cruel and carnivorous character of this bird of prey. You bent down to look for a vestige of what you had lost, and found the little helmet which you put in the handkerchief in which you had intended to place the warm and living warrior before taking her home with you.

What had happened to the rest of the armour? All your efforts to find it came to nothing.

And now your life has become a pitiable thing. What everyone vaguely dreams about and desires was granted to you, one beautiful autumn day, under the pine trees in the Landes, but you spurned it through the delirium of your senses. Nothing else can come to you but death. As you wait for it to take you, you get drunk like a beast, on rum, and you sleep.

*****

published in André Pieyre de Mandiargues, *Soleil de loups*
(1951) Paris: Robert Laffont
French original © Editions Gallimard 1979

*****

ANDRÉ PIEYRE DE MANDIARGUES (Paris 1909 – Paris 1991) One of the finest storytellers of surrealism and a sensitive writer on art, Pieyre de Mandiargues' récits *The Girl on the Motorcycle* and *The Girl Beneath the Lion* have been published in English, as has his collection of tales, *Blaze of Embers*.

ALBERTO SAVINIO:

The Garden of Eden

The shop stood at the junction of Via Tolomeo and Via Copernico. A laughing little devil tickling his left ear with the tip of a thin, long tail wrapped around his body announced it from a sign. The shop was called 'Beelzebub's Whims', and these whims were spread out in two display-windows, one on Via Copernico, the other on Via Tolomeo, to entice passers-by. They were mainly trick objects: a fake fly on a fake sugar cube; two fake fried eggs lying like a pair of yellow spectacles in an earthenware pot; some fake slices of salami arranged on a plate; a glass of ruby-red liqueur which, when one tried to drink it, turned out to be solid and stuck to the bottom of the glass; and some miniature toilet bowls for use as ashtrays; tiny chamber pots also destined to receive the combusted part of a cigarette and its residue, a fake folded telegram known as the 'American joke'; a blister which, placed under an armchair cushion would emit indecent cackles under the weight of a sitting person; some perfectly imitated human excrements; and finally, fixed to the window at eye level, a backlit plate of opaque glass, on which the Chinese shadow of an Arab dancer gyrated her hips in a tireless belly dance.

Of all the objects exhibited in the two shop-windows of 'Beelzebub's whims', it was above all this little self-propelled silhouette which attracted the eye of the passer-by, stopped him in his tracks, invited him to enter.

A ploy by Mr Codro, the owner of 'Beelzebub's Whims', revealing his profound understanding of the human psyche. Mr Codro knew that a motionless object, however peculiar, is less alluring than a moving one, however insignificant; in which respect man is very similar to monkeys, dogs and chickens. "Keep moving, o man, and the eyes of your fellow-men will fasten upon you." Indeed, a double ploy on Mr Codro's part, as he also knew that to enter that emporium of his, full of objects of unacknowledged necessity, one must loosen a certain inhibiting restraint and arm oneself with a degree of boldness equal, if not superior, to that needed to enter a chemist's and ask for condoms.

We have reason to believe that the location of 'Beelzebub's Whims' between Via Tolomeo and Via Copernico, at the junction of two opposed world views which nevertheless together exhaust the problem of the universe, had been chosen by Mr Codro with great deliberation, to signify that his shop and the objects it contained were beyond any cosmic notion, beyond any terrestrial or celestial mechanism, a little limbo in which tricks and games lived in purest anarchy, free of all divine and human law.

However, we are talking here of things of the past, of dead things. Mr Codro's shop no longer exists. A voracious urban plan devoured it quite a few years ago, deforming so significant a junction of two streets, that meeting of two opposed world views which together exhaust the problem of the universe; splitting that metaphysically precise corner so fertile with unexpected encounters, rounding it, smoothing it in a porticoed half-circle barred by four basalt columns; suppressing into the bargain the name of Copernico on one of the two streets and replacing it with that of an unknown "Egino Tancredi, poet, 1890–1917"; so that, if not all over the world, at least in that small part of it, the cupola of the Ptolemaic sky had again descended like a lid with stars nailed to its vault, leaving men's bodies breathless and denying their souls freedom of flight.

Here we are talking of dead things; and to measure how long it has been since these things ceased to exist, suffice it to mention that Mr Didaco, otherwise known as the Almighty, is now sixty, while at the time of 'Beelzebub's Whims' he was only five. And yet it was precisely at that tender age that Mr Didaco's destiny began to take shape –

that destiny which eventually won him the nickname of the Almighty – and precisely on the day when the mother of the then little Mr Didaco entered Mr Codro's shop to buy her child a fake miniature tree, which from the window facing Via Tolomeo displayed its small conical shape to passers-by, placed, like a candle extinguisher, on a short ochre-varnished trunk, which rested in turn on a little green painted disc. Did little Didaco's mother have to overcome any obstacles of a moral nature before entering Mr Codro's shop? Probably not. The shame a man feels on entering the Emporium of Uselessness is not shared by a woman; and should she have felt any, this woman was a mother and no obstacle can stand between a mother and her child's happiness. In this story everything is connected by a subtle but very close counterpoint. It is no coincidence that the little tree which first determined Mr Didaco's destiny was displayed in the window on Via Tolomeo, rather than on Via Copernico; Mr Codro's destiny is strictly Ptolemaic; in other words, based on fiction. Ptolemaic says it all; it means above all fixed and unchanging, that is to say different from real life which is by nature changing and temporary. It means: not according to natural truth, but according to man's desire and the pretence inspired by his fear of dying and his desire for permanence. A motionless world, the cupola of the sky over it, and in the middle of the sky a god, the master and conductor of those few 'internal' movements which suffice to the life of this colossal toy. Yet this toy is neither the work of nature, nor of chance, but of man, and this is all that matters. This toy was not born out of a rudimentary or erroneous astronomical concept, but of man's precise will to oppose natural life, which is all movement and transition, and hence continuous death, and to build for himself a world which would fully guarantee solidity and permanence. Man does not want to feel like one who is thrown in at the deep end and can't swim. What does it matter that expanding knowledge later reduced that earth, that sky, that god to an absurdity? Building nevertheless remains man's ideal, that is, the keeping alive of the necessary fiction of immobility and permanence; and man continues to build, with his hands and his brain, with machines and with art; to build, build, build; from the smallest object to God: man's supreme masterpiece.

The first impression the little tree bought in Mr Codro's shop had on little Didaco was one of fear, because the similarity of the little tree's cone of leaves and the cocoa-butter suppositories with which Didaco's mother occasionally stimulated the intestinal functions of her child, sadly prone to constipation, made him fear that the little tree too would constitute a threat to his anal orifice. But as the days went by and the object of that threat did not materialise, little Didaco's fear gradually subsided, and once fear had subsided, little Didaco liked the little tree's conical shape, so similar to a mosquito-fumigating cone. And he liked the cone-like little tree even better after one day, at dinner, his father talked about conifers, and with an expansive gesture of the hand in which the fruit knife shone, evoked the image of huge forests of resinous trees; afterwards little Didaco, his head full of trees, withdrew to his play-room, and there, alone with his fantasy, imagined the endless vastness of the vegetable kingdom, the earth's hair, beard, its fuzzy surface; in the valleys, in the plains, on sea-shores and river banks, on the hills and the mountain slopes, he saw solitary trees, trees in pairs, in trios, in quartets, in groups; and the immense crowds of trees, against which the crowds of men and the herds of animals are but paltry minorities. The third impression the little tree had on little Didaco was an impression on 'thought', together with the revelation that man's life is divided into two 'adversary' worlds, the natural world which is changing and transitory, and the world built by man, which is unchanging and fixed. As autumn began to take shape, he saw that the trees in the garden started to lose their greenness, and he saw, on the other hand, that his little tree did not lose its leaves, nor did they lose their greenness; and suddenly his sympathy and his faith went to the world of which his little tree was part, the unchanging and fixed world, Ptolemy's world; and for the first time Didaco felt himself to be a man, that is, a builder and a preserver; or, more precisely, a builder of preservation; more precisely still, a builder because of his will to preserve.

We do not pay enough attention to the objects we place in children's hands. The shape, the type, the colour of an object influence the child's character, direct his mental attitude, determine his destiny; as demonstrated by the example of Mr Didaco, known as the Almighty, who became the greatest taxidermist in Europe only because one day, when he was five, his mother went into Mr Codro's shop and bought her child a fake little tree shaped like a candle extinguisher.

After that little tree, the first beginning of his Ptolemaic world, little Didaco wanted another, then another again; and after the little trees he wanted other simulated representations of the real world: little sheep, little donkeys, little dogs. And in his play-room, little Didaco gathered a minute but complete animal and vegetable kingdom and spent his days admiring it. Later, no longer satisfied with the little trees, the little sheep, the little shepherds bought by his mother in toy shops, he wanted to make them himself; and in the fabrication of fake trees, fake animals, fake men, little by little Didaco acquired extraordinary knowledge and skill. Later, when he reached the age when one thinks about an occupation or, as people say, about one's future, the idea of preserving things was so rooted and developed in him that he firmly declared he would choose no profession other than that of the taxidermist. He learnt the finest embalming techniques, and even perfected them and invented his own. He studied Herodotus to learn the three methods the Egyptians used to mummify the dead, turned to the petrification of corpses, experimented with Gerolamo Segato's secret, made a few brilliant discoveries, which preserve the colour and the look of life in the bodies removed from motion and transported into immobility. His fame grew, and brought him wealth. For Mr

Didaco taxidermy was not a profession but a passion, the love of a life that escapes the fate of life, of which man himself is the master. He was happy when distressed men and especially elegant, tearful women knocked on the door of his laboratory bringing a dead parrot, a dead poodle, a dead Siamese cat, and entrusted him with those beloved little pets, so that he, with his expert preparations, would save them from the decay which is itself movement, and thus in a sense a continuation of life, and 'fix' them in an unalterable state: upright on their little paws, their muzzle glossy, eyes gleaming and fixed, ready, one would think, for a leap which, luckily, would no longer come. But why wait for dogs, cats, parrots, to die their natural deaths, in other words, to reach the end of their decline and their own destruction? "This way," Mr Didaco lamented, "we collect animals deformed by old age and disease". One day, he paternally suggested to an elderly lady as she invited him to admire her minuscule and precious Pekinese, that he could kill it in the most painless and merciful way, in order to fix it forever in the perfection of its health and youth. But the elderly lady, far from accepting his amiable proposal, grabbed the precious Pekinese with her right hand and grasped it spasmodically to her heart: with the left hand she rang the bell and, the servant appearing on the threshold,peremptorily ordered him to escort Mr Didaco to the door. "How men let themselves be seduced by life, which is transition and mutation, and therefore death! I offer them unalterable and fixed form and they, the madmen, reject it!" But Mr Didaco's greatest satisfaction was the embalming of men: a few of his operations were universally talked about: F.T. Morrison's, the famous American billionaire, for which Mr Didaco had to travel to the United States; Miss Arabella Teck's, killed by her jealous seventy-year-old lover two days after she had been crowned Miss Universe, which required Mr Didaco's second trip to the United States. Much was also said about the invitation Mr Didaco received from the Soviet government in 1937 to go to Moscow and contribute the light of his science to the conservation of Lenin's mummy which was beginning to disintegrate. Mr Didaco's greatest satisfaction, we were saying, was the embalming of men and, had he been allowed to embalm living men, that is kill them so as to embalm them in the full bloom of life, Mr Didaco's ambition would have been fully accomplished.

When Mr Didaco's financial circumstances allowed him to do what he wanted regardless of expense, he finally realised his life's grand project. It became an object of curiosity and the destination of numerous pilgrimages, a wonder in the house of the taxidermist: in an immense conservatory Mr Didaco had recreated the Garden of Eden, gathering together perfectly stuffed animals, plants, also stuffed, and in the centre he had placed the tree of good and evil, rich with its fatal apples, around which the tempter snake wrapped its coils. It was Mr Didaco's relaxation, his relaxation and delight, his delight and reward to walk in that miniature Eden, wrapped in an ample cloak, snow-white beard flowing on his chest, snow-white hair flowing on his shoulders, among the motionless and docile animals who looked at him with innocent glass eyes. Even his bearing, his gestures, his voice acquired a divine calm. He spoke briefly and paternally. The gesture of opening his arms as if to embrace men and things had become familiar to him. He was above human events.

Someone once called him the Almighty, without a shadow of irony and as if to give him the name that most befitted him, and the nickname stuck. Within a short time, the only name which distinguished Mr Didaco was the Almighty. And Mr Didaco naturally felt like the Almighty, without effort or affectation, a creator god, a demiurge.

What effect did demiurgism have on Mr Didaco's sex life? As love also initiates the renewal of life, and consequently it too is a cause of death, however indirect, Mr Didaco kept himself away from life, as from everything that is part of the flux of natural life. This notwithstanding, when he was already in his late years, and had earned the nickname of the Almighty, one day, suddenly, no one

233

knows why, Mr Didaco married a woman thirty years his junior: Teresina Saliscendi. But the union of Mr Didaco, alias the Almighty, and Teresina Saliscendi remained sterile, it is not clear whether because of his old age, or because the birth of children in a way marks the death of their parents. Still, in order to make his young bride fit for the edenic environment of which she was to become a part, Mr Didaco changed her name, and of Teresina made Eve.

The more successful the taxidermy business became, the more difficult it was for him to find assistants to follow him in his work. Eventually, after a long search, Mr Didaco found a gem of an assistant in the person of a bold young man, much skilled in the science of corpse preservation, Gerolamo Saltincasa, whose name Mr Didaco, ever faithful to his principles, changed to Adam.

One day, Mr Didaco received a letter which was a long cry of anguish. It came from Genoa and bore the signature of Contessa Santa dell'Aquasanta. The noblewoman announced the death of her beloved Bull with heart-rending words, and exhorted the illustrious Professor Didaco to rush to Genoa without delay, so that at least the mortal remains of the beloved could be preserved, now the dear soul had flown away. If the Contessa Santa dell'Aquasanta is a believer and a church-goer, as her name and social condition would lead us to believe, we can understand how the noblewoman managed to reconcile the precepts of religion with her faith in the soul of the 'beloved Bull' who, as far as Mr Didaco could make out, was a bulldog. On the other hand, though, it was precisely that hint to the soul of the 'beloved Bull', that is, to his canine soul, which induced Mr Didaco to go to Genoa, he who never travelled except in the most exceptional circumstances and with the promise of huge fees. After all, Mr Didaco could leave in all tranquillity; even if his absence were to last for several days, his assistant, Gerolamo Saltincasa, alias Adam, would competently replace him.

Bull was a magnificent bull-like dog. His coat tawny, his muzzle duly obtuse, with powerful jaws, he lay on snow-white linen, between four lit candles, on a table in the middle of the parlour at the dell'Acquasanta residence, watched over by the Contessa Santa dell'Acquasanta herself, black in her mourning clothes, the very image of grief.

"There he is," said the noblewoman, lifting a white and disconsolate hand towards the cherished corpse. And after a pause, "How can this be! He who was Life! Movement! Joy!"

"So much the better," whispered Mr Didaco, but fortunately the Contessa, deafened by her grief, did not hear these words, and added imploringly: "For pity's sake, Professor, don't torture him too much!"

Mr Didaco prepared the enema of corrosive liquid to inject in the dog's entrails, but as he approached Bull's anal orifice with the beak of the enema two savagely gleaming bloodshot eyes opened wide and the dog leaped up on his bent, muscle-knotted paws, grabbed the injecting instrument with his powerful jaws, crushed it like a straw, and was about to hurl himself on the man who was preparing to administer him that treatment and punish him for his audacity. Urgently summoned, the vet could not explain such an extraordinary case of catalepsy, but the Contessa Santa dell'Acquasanta saw the reviving of Bull as a miracle, and rejected all other explanations. As for Mr Didaco, the indirect cause of that miraculous resurrection, he received from the jubilant noblewoman three times the sum agreed for the stuffing, and despite the insistence of the Contessa, who wanted him to be her guest in the palace for a few days and bear witness to her joy, he caught the first train out and returned home that very evening.

The house was silently asleep. Mr Didaco tiptoed up to his room, took off his travel clothes, put on his cloak and went down again to the ground floor for his habitual walk around his reconstructed garden of Eden before going to bed. He opened the door very slowly, with all the respect warranted by the venerability of the place. In the quiet light which illuminated the little Eden through the glass wall the plants and the docile animals were motionless, each in its place on the velvet lawns: the ox, the camel, the ass; and to complete the edenic family, Adam and Eve, that is Teresina Saliscendi and Gerolamo Saltincasa, lay entwined at the foot of the tree of knowledge deep in sleep, and their bodies had the pale phosphorescence of naked bodies in semi-darkness.

What did the mind of Mr Didaco, alias the Almighty, feel at that sight? Jealousy? Surprise? Indifference? We do not know, we will never know. Nor will we ever know how Mr Didaco managed, without waking them, to transport Teresina Saliscendi and Gerolamo Saltincasa from the sleep of love to the sleep of death.

"I chose the thinnest needle in my laboratory, a completely painless needle, and injected the sleeping couple with a powerful anaesthetic." This is what Mr Didaco said at the inquest and repeated to the Court.

He added: "You should have seen them, My Lord! Adam and Eve! The exact image of Adam and Eve! And how thoughtful! I had created my Garden of Eden, they had provided it with its inhabitants."

In a cage at the Assizes, Mr Didaco, alias the Almighty, hesitated in his rapture; then, suddenly, shaking his divine snow-white head, he started to speak again:

"Beautiful! So beautiful! But then I thought: in a while these two will wake up, they will stand up, leave the tree, put their clothes on again, and the spell will be broken. Could I allow such a thing, My Lord, could I allow it?"

This was the pure truth. Certain that under the effect of the anaesthetic Gerolamo and Teresina would not wake up, Mr Didaco proceeded with the embalming: he drew on all of his art, surpassed himself, accomplished his masterpiece; and finally, having saved the two bodies from decay and having made their beauty immutable, he arranged them again, cold and white, at the foot of the tree of good and evil. Then, his work accomplished, Mr Didaco picked up the phone, and invited friends, acquaintances, clients to come and observe his garden of Eden, finally completed by the presence of Adam and Eve.

And men, women, children filed past Adam and Eve lying at the foot of the tree of good and evil, and praised, admired, marvelled. Some also wanted to touch, but then Mr Didaco, alias the Almighty, would intervene, wrapped in his cloak, his snow-white beard flowing on his chest, his snow-white hair flowing on his shoulders; and with a paternal gesture, in a calm voice he admonished that it would not do to touch the first two humans as they slept in the sweetness of sin.

At last someone understood and the spell was broken. And Mr Didaco left the celebration which was to have been the apotheosis of his career in his cloak, flanked by two carabinieri.

More God than ever. Between two angels.

*****

Published in Alberto Savinio: *Tutta la vita* (1945) Casa Editorice Valentino Bompiani (Milan)
Italian original © Angelica and Ruggero Savinio de Chirico
translated by Marina Aldrovandi

*****

ALBERTO SAVINIO (Athens 1891 – Rome 1951) Savinio's first love was music before he visited Paris in 1910 and became part of the circle around Apollinaire. He participated with his brother Giorgio de Chirico in the 'metaphysical school' in which he was regarded as the most important writer. Began painting in 1925 and became friendly with the surrealists in the late twenties as his brother was becoming estranged from them.

MARCEL MARIËN:

The Other

The savage murder of Dora at the hands of her husband Josef Fransic did not unduly surprise anyone who knew them. Everyone was aware the couple led a twisted life that had got worse over the years. No doubt Dora's death was a shock but only to the extent that all death is shocking. No more than that.

Yet the couple had begun married life happy enough with the banal bourgeois existence that accorded well with their own aspirations. It had been one Saturday evening at a dance that Josef had stared at Dora and she had returned his look. She was twenty-five and he was thirty. He asked her to dance. He danced badly and so did she. A fortnight later they went out together, and even though their dancing was even worse, they did speak a little more. At least sufficiently so that they married three months later. They set up home at Zizkov, on the outskirts of Prague, in a small newly built one storey house with a garden which Josef cared for diligently.

But the marriage lines soon began to distend and the sky above the marital bed clouded over. Was Dora or Josef to blame? This was the crux of the problem. Apparently it all began one day when Josef took his wife to task during dinner. He playfully complained that his soup was cold, even though it was patently piping hot as steam was rising from the plate. Dora did not argue with him, but merely nodded in agreement even as she needed to blow on each spoonful to cool it down before sipping it.

Thereafter, and apparently for no reason at all, similar inconsequential incidents occurred, which Dora always accepted, no matter how unfair they were, without the least demur. Warming to the game, Josef began to assert the most preposterous things: that Berlin was in Mexico, that cows ate meat, that the lungs are to be found in the place of the kidneys while the latter resided in the toes and other cock-eyed stuff.

He even once dressed up as an outrageously made-up woman and invited Dora to undress and take him like a lesbian, something she did with such finesse that Josef recoiled before the suggestion that immediately came to his mind that Dora's sentiments and feelings in the perception of life were completely different from his. On the contrary, this was something that might have been so different from the reality which, in their eyes, was the thing they least shared.

There began a period of rapid deterioration that led to extreme violence, since Josef had acquired the conviction that only relentless torture could cause the veil behind which Dora breathed without really existing to fall, for suffering is the only touchstone of reality.

He started by slapping her, hitting her and then slowly began to engage in a more horrifying cruelty. He whipped her, bit her, burned her and ceaselessly brutalised her in so many ways until tears and blood flowed. Dora reacted to the pain but made no complaint. In fact there was not even the slightest hint of reproach in her eyes, and this caused Josef to seriously doubt whether she really did feel the blows.

Perhaps the fact that she loved her husband to a degree that forbade all protest no matter what his wicked conduct explained her exemplary resignation. This was in fact exactly what the torturer sought to determine without a glimmer of success no matter what he might do.

The overflowing desolation of the household increased until the outside of the house offered visible stigmata of the tragedy unfolding within its walls. The neglected garden, abandoned to wild grass, the dirty window panes and the yellowed curtains, spoke to passers-by of the drama taking place behind the sinister facade.

This hell had lasted for a year when Josef, having tortured his wife for so long, having transformed her breasts into pin cushions, became fully convinced that all her cries were merely a sham. All that remained was to kill her. It was the only way he felt he could put an end to her act.

Josef lay Dora down across the bed, with her head extending on one side, and then held her down by the hair as he supported her so that her head remained aligned with her body. With eyes closed and lips sealed, Dora allowed him to do as he liked. Then, with a handsaw, without stopping for a moment, her husband cut through her neck. A plaintive cry rose from Dora's throat which was cut short by the saw as it penetrated deeply into the flesh and blood gushed out, engulfing the bedside rug. The executioner completed the beheading and his wife's head fell to the floor.

He dropped the handsaw and stared at Dora's almost naked body lying lifeless and headless on the bed. Whether through desire or remorse, whether some unknown emotion was triggered by the occasion, whether he still needed to test the depths of the reality he had effected with his own hands, he then lay on top of Dora and made love with her headless body for a long time. His arms under her armpits, he gripped her solidly against him, palms clenched against her shoulders, chin lodged in the wound in her neck, while his gaze drowned in the enormous bloody stain that soaked into the rug. When the act was over, he had the distinct impression that the still warm flesh of Dora shuddered. And so, even decapitated, even dead, she continued to be faithless. He put his bloody clothes back on and turned himself over to the law.

By special authority the guilty man was allowed to attend his wife's funeral. He had not requested it, but the examining magistrate had required him to accompany his victim to her final resting place. Josef did not recoil at the sight of the laying out, first of Dora's body, then her livid head with closed eyes, in the quilted coffin. The head was placed on a round cushion surrounded with lace, a few centimetres from the neck which was hidden by the shroud. Afterwards the undertaker, with a solemn and sombre expression, fastened down the coffin lid with a crutch key.

Josef watched the whole ceremony handcuffed to a plain-clothes policeman without uttering a single word and showed no sign of affliction. In truth he was sober and deeply moved, but remained in prey of his doubt about Dora's real existence. He tried to imagine his own funeral but was unable to do so. Although he was a murderer, as he was still her husband he was asked if he wanted to go to the expense of a tombstone, to which he mechanically agreed, and left the undertakers to do what they thought best. He was invited to throw a spadeful of earth on to the coffin and his warder took him back to prison.

The trial took place at the Prague assizes two months later. Josef's impassivity conferred a fixed air on him, which must have weighed in the balance since the jury passed a verdict of extreme severity. The judge, however, reduced the punishment from death to thirty years forced labour.

What Josef thought during those three decades none could have known since he maintained a complete silence, isolating himself from the other prisoners and refusing all confidences. He broke stones, extracted coal, drained marshes, and made slippers and toys all with the mechanical application of a well-oiled machine.

It was with the same indifference that, one rainy autumn day, the door was opened to free the sexagenarian he had in the meantime become. As there was no where else for him to go, he returned to Zizkov where his house, which had aged as he had, still waited, empty and cold, for him. He took no notice of his neighbours, or of the people he passed in the street who, for their part did not recognise him as the affair had been forgotten.

Josef started by putting the house in order and waited there patiently for the continuance of existence. After a

241

few weeks he opened a drawer and his eyes caught sight of a photo of Dora. Since the crime its author had seemingly not thought any more about her, as though by expelling her from the land of the living he had at the same time chased her out of his memory.

Yet the portrait made a considerable impact on him. Dora was smiling in a way he could not recall he had ever seen her smile. Memories came flooding back to him and filled his mind, back and forth, until he was overcome. How could he ever have doubted her? How could he have ever questioned the sincerity of the cries he had torn from her by his monstrous tortures? He recalled the first day when he had burned her thigh with the tip of a lighted cigarette and again heard the scream she had emitted, so loud it rang in his ears as if she was there at his side again, invisible but quivering under the torture.

Then there was the time he had pushed her down the stairs with a thump and when she got up found she had sprained her foot. As she groaned with pain, how could he have thought her tears were simulated?

Josef was smoking. He drew on the cigarette to revive the end and on an impulse applied it to his bare skin. He cried out and immediately pulled away the incandescent tip. Next he climbed to the top of the stairs and threw himself down to the bottom to convince himself how painful and bruising the fall must have been. His wife certainly had existed and he had been the one who had martyred and executed her so ignobly!

In the meantime night had fallen bringing with it a single thought which became an *idée fixe* that gripped him like an ineluctable order. He took a lantern, a short ladder, a pickaxe and a shovel from the cellar and loaded them on his bike. Then, without a moment's hesitation, he rode off into the shadows in the direction of the Olsany cemetery.

The tomb had been left to the elements for thirty years and was surrounded by nettles and thistles. In spite of the erosion of thirty years and the ravages of inclement weather, the faded name of Dora Fransic was still readable with, below it, her dates of birth and death. The slab was heavy. Josef was able to move it only with difficulty. He started to dig the earth. He shovelled in silence. The moon projected a wan glow on the cemetery while the lantern, suspended from the tombstone, illuminated the work of the profanator. Somewhere in the night an eagle-owl hooted dolefully.

After twenty minutes the shovel hit the coffin. Josef's head now vanished under the ground. The effects of exertion combined with age exhausted him. He felt as if he was going to meet his own death. Nevertheless he managed to free the last layer of earth from the lid of the coffin. It was of an excellent quality and had resisted the storms of time but even so had started to rot away. With his pickaxe, Josef soon broke the cover open plank by plank. He gazed inside the coffin, the upholstery of which had retained the pristine quality of the day of inhumation. He recognised the round and immaculate cushion, and let out a cry of despair or triumph.

The lantern discharged its pale light into a wide-open coffin that was completely empty. For Josef this was the startling and irrefutable proof that the *other* had never existed!

★★★★★

published in *Figures de poupe* (Jean-Claude Simoën) 1979
French original © Marcel Mariën 1979

★★★★★

MARCEL MARIËN: (see page 115)

ALBERT MARENČIN:

For the Last Time

I had sought out the most beautiful words in my memory during all those years I had put them together as I separated them again, displacing them and repeating them over and over in my mind and rehearsing the effects they had on me, but when I wanted to communicate them to the person to whom they belonged, the empty wine casks around me suddenly began to rumble and this dark rumbling drowned out my words.

When the racket had died down I was able to make myself heard again: "You are my breeze, my storm, a dust of stars in my eyes, a wave on the sea in the desert of my life."

There was a cracking in the receiver and I could hear her voice: "Speak louder. I can't hear a thing."
The line was then cut.

On other occasions I was just about to say something very beautiful and tender but also brutal and cruel so my words gave her everything a human being could experience; I imagined her listening to me with eyes closed and a dreamy smile, and suddenly she would look fearfully at me, trembling in misery and fear, but straightaway I reassured her and dissipated her concern by giving her such a feeling of confidence that she clung to my chest and completely abandoned herself to the voluptuousness of oblivion and I then hit her harder, until she sobbed and shed tears . . .

I wanted her to perceive only me, and with the whole of

her being: I wanted to empty her like a house in the process of removal, throw all the rubbish out into the street and establish myself and completely fill her majestic rooms and mysterious hiding places: I wanted to thank her and have revenge for all the delights and sufferings of love, I wanted to love her and torment her, bring her to the point of fury and despair and dementia and at the same time to the heavens of bliss but as I opened my mouth to say all these things to her, each time a cloud would burst, a jackal would cackle or a hippopotamus would roar, and the crash of thousands and thousands of breaking windows would be heard.

Then one day everything became silence.

"Listen to me, my love," I said.

She kissed me and cuddled up with her whole body tight against me and said: "I'm listening."

And the same thing happened: at the first word I spoke all the musical instruments in the whole world screeched out from somewhere on high, a church organ fell on the tin roof, from its entrails the deafening cacophony of pipes sprang forth in a death struggle which on the stairs re-sounded like a hurricane of wild horses pulling a rack chariot filled with drums and violins. This time I did not remain silent and, with a stronger and stronger voice, I howled out every word and every phrase that had accumulated within me for so many long centuries.

She watched in an assured way as I tried to make myself heard above the terrible racket and how the veins in my neck were inflated and she looked at me with a face that always retained the same mysterious smile.

I became furious: "Listen to me, wretch," I shouted.

And without waiting for her reply I shouted into her face as loudly as my strength allowed the most beautiful declarations and the most disgusting curses: I shouted out that I could not live without her and that I detested her, for she had absorbed me and wanted to transform me in her digestive system into shit, but I refused to give myself to her and instead of my sperm I would infuse a mortal venom into her entrails.

"Do you hear me, whore?"

"I'm listening," she whispered in my ear and held herself tighter against me. Speak then, speak, please, just for one moment. . . . But I still did not succeed in finding a single word in my memory; the last sighs of the pipe organ and the jolts of the chariot were still to be heard; I was waiting for what would happen next with horror when a great silence fell.

2

First a crazed leopard bounded towards me; then someone threw a sack of burning coke onto my back.

At the same time I felt that the earth was falling away beneath my feet and I was being enticed into a yawning chasm. . . I was not able to set myself upright to overcome the monster and did not even have the strength to hold out my hand to grip on to something. I pressed my forehead against the wall and called out to the passers-by: "Save me, comrades. Help me to defeat this monster before it crushes me."

In a moment, in spite of the deep night, a crowd of onlookers gathered but none of them helped. They all remained standing there, silent and motionless, some distance away. I could only see their feet. I noticed from the form and model of their shoes that they belonged for the most part to old people. But there were also several young women among them. "Perhaps she is also there," I thought. The idea that she might also be a witness to my sufferings and humiliations caused a sense of shame to suddenly pass through me.

"I beg you," I said, trying to keep a calm and reasonable tone. "Call the fire brigade or get a fork-lift truck to come and help free me from this thing. Sorry to be wearisome, but I really can't do it on my own.

But even then no one said anything.

"They are all indifferent and unfeeling swine," I thought. But why was she also silent? She was ashamed, just as I was. Or else she was doubtless enjoying herself. . . Otherwise how could she fail to recognise the torment I was in.

I felt my strength abandon me. At the same moment a whistle sounded and immediately I found myself face to face with a man in uniform who presumably, if appearances could be trusted, was a policeman.

"What's going on?" he asked in a severe tone. "What are you babbling on about?"

I told him what had happened: that a crazed leopard had pounced on me and then that someone had, doubtless as a joke, thrown a sack of burning coke onto my back.

"Well! Well!" He made a face. "I think we're exaggerating a little, aren't we? If a crazed leopard had pounced on you there would barely have been time even to scream. And all this about the sack of coke, how do you know it is burning coke if it's in a sack of jute?. . .

His contemptuous and uninterested tone revolted me.

"Why should I want to drag a leopard, even a tame one, on my back, or even a sack of coke? I really had far more important things to do."

"Really?" he asked mockingly.

"I am a poet," I replied.

I then tried to add something but the policeman burst into such a roar of laughter that I could not have cried out any louder. And his laugh was so contagious that the whole crowd of onlookers, which until then had remained silent, also started laughing. I turned around without understanding. Tightly aligned side by side around me were men's feet in old shoes, old women's legs covered with varicose veins, young women's legs in light sandals, and above their legs a sonorous laughter burst forth. In a choir of several voices, I tried to distinguish her little familiar laugh, that laugh I loved so much, although others couldn't stand it. But it was all in vain. On the contrary I noticed her legs (they were in the foreground) and her long pale calves each of whose veins and mysterious light blue meanderings I knew by heart.

I raised my head for a last effort.

Yes it really was her, but she was not laughing. Everyone around her laughed good naturedly. She was the only one who did not laugh. And in the same way as I did, with a final effort, she raised her head to look at me, for like all the others she was bent under a monstrous burden which drew her towards the ground. Each person carried an object on his back, whether it be a kitchen sideboard full of crockery, a piano, a carriage door with a hinged flap, a cut down willow tree, enormous sacks containing God knows what, large pieces of fresh and bleeding meat, moist halves of cows and pigs. . .

As for her, she carried on her back a sort of sack that looked like a deflated balloon. Inside was something rugged but alive and ceaselessly struggling. Judging from the movements and sounds it emitted, it could well have been a pig.

Our looks met for a moment. Then, under the weight of our respective burdens, both of our heads were lowered.

When I told this story years later to my friends they all thought it was a dream or an invented story and overwhelmed me with questions about it. They asked me what I was trying to say, and looked for symbols or allusions everywhere and tried to analyze everything with the aid of some key.

To this day nothing I have ever discovered adds anything by way of explanation. What's more I do not consider this sort of thing very helpful. In the whole story, there was only one moment that seems important and that was when our glances momentarily met and a smile appeared on her exhausted face that was contracted by unhappiness. And until that moment I had dreamed of her. And at that moment I saw her for the first time in her real amplitude. For the first and last time.

*****

published in *Surréalisme* no 1 (Editions Savelli) 1977
© Albert Marenčin

*****

ALBERT MARENČIN (Bystrom, Czechoslovakia, 1922) Collagist and writer, translator of Breton, Jarry and Apollinaire into Slovak, Albert Marenčin established contact with the Czech Surrealist Group in 1964, as a result of which the first properly Czechoslovak group was established. Worked as a scriptwriter for the cinema before losing his position in the purges that followed the 1968 invasion.

ZUCA SARDAN:

This Book

The reader discovers this book languishing on the shelf and distractedly picks it up. He is puzzled by the cover made from jacaranda wood and the pages made from pressed vine leaves, about a thousand or so of them.

The reader leafs and leafs through these green leaves and finds nothing. He can find no writing, not a single word. . .

Time passes and the leaves begin to turn red and start to fall and fall, scattering themselves on the floor. Someone comes to sweep them up. A window opens, there is a gust of air; the leaves whirl up and fly, whispering, out of the window, one after the other. All that remains of the book on the table is the cover made from jacaranda wood. Suddenly the cover gives a somersault in the air, falls off the table and rolls about on the floor. It gives a stifled laugh.

And then a skein of wild ducks flies clattering over the reader's house.

★★★★★
published in *Os Mysterios* (1981)
Brazilian original © Zuca Sardan
translated by Margaret Jull Costa
★★★★★

ZUCA SARDAN (Rio de Janeiro 1933) lost his childhood somewhere and since then doesn't know whether he is himself or his shadow. Tried different jobs and finally became a diplomat, Counsellor Saldanha, who went around the world for some thirty years losing important documents and stamping the wrong papers. . . Meanwhile his shadow became instructed into poetry by surrealism and he wanted to be a Stephane Mallarmé (or perhaps he didn't). Plays with papers to create stories, drawings, mysteries and cantos which he distributes erratically.

LISE DEHARME:

A Strange Night

For not particularly pleasant reasons my friend Ariane and myself had decided early in December to get some fresh air at the seaside.

We chose an odd little hotel on the Normandy coast, the only one in the tiny locality that had remained open. It was perched on top of a deserted cliff, at the start of a sort of fissure descending with a rapid declivity in a debris of flint and shingle to the sea.

It was run by a rather odd family whose behaviour seemed to us, from the time we arrived, rather baffling. It was too late to go back. There were no other guests but us. In December, you understand, a short stay at a seaside resort, which wasn't too warm in the middle of summer, only tempts people who are themselves a little strange.

We had taken a room with two beds. The wallpaper was coming unstuck and the roses that decorated it were as pale as their dead sisters in the garden. We cheered ourselves up with stories about islands where heat, flowers and dances abounded, where women's teeth are, between their red lips, like a double row of shells: they still venture to laugh no matter what for they have not completely learned the stupid misdeeds of civilisation and its fear of an 'ignoble death'.

Oh yes!. . . The inanity of our conversation caused us to laugh when suddenly we felt the shiver of winter and night.

We went down to the ground floor. I should mention that it was a mediocre hotel in which only the windows gleamed, and large drops of rain beat with a sinister sound.

The owners, the family, the boy put away quantities of

cider as they stared at us meanly. The little we heard of their conversation was hardly comforting: "We need to put the old-bag in no 3 because the wind could carry her off tonight. . . I would prefer to be alive in prison than dead in freedom. . ." said the woman. What on earth did she mean? It almost seemed as if these hoteliers worked according to a set plan. "No, not that. . . We have already done too much. . ." replied the husband to his wife's suggestion made in a low voice. They seemed to be playing roles which were not theirs. The wife resembled a leek and came from a horrible world of disquieting vegetables. The sister-in-law was a big white rabbit. Frankly the meeting of rabbit and leek was disagreeable. The husband, brother-in-law and boy merely seemed dangerous, as if prepared for trouble, their arms invisible.

We were in one of the rooms pompously called 'living-rooms', probably because it was impossible to live in them. Insistent currents of air ran right through the wicker-chairs. To prepare for bed and try to dissipate our uneasy feelings, we each had a double whisky, as though we were in an American thriller. Miraculously it was good stuff. "What idiots we are to be so taken over by appearances." We were under the salutary influence of whisky and suddenly everything seemed perfectly normal. Dinner was good. Unfortunately we were the only people in the dining room. In the distance a foghorn groaned miserably.

I don't know if it was the effect of the alcohol, but the decor, which at first we had not noticed, then caused us to burst out laughing: artificial nasturtiums, climbed up the walls, mingled with equally artificial roses with petals speckled with fly dirt. It was pretty gross. We passed from laughter to terror which, like love and hate, are close relatives.

The hotel family continued its strange conversation and mysterious preparations. We heard a few phrases like: "Salt is not too bad, but milk is more effective in this sort of operation." The brother-in-law was more cheerful: "My mother died without leaving me a cent." "It's disgraceful," added his wife. "There's worse," said his sister-in-law. "Without knowing it, I ate my little child." "Did you enjoy it?" asked the hotel-keeper "Don't you think I have since forgotten the taste? But I was incredibly unhappy for seven whole days." "Indeed," rejoined the other.

They sat down for dinner. They drank lots and lots of water. Ariane and myself were a bit disgusted. Our soup was too thick, thanks very much, but theirs was like water – almost pure water. One of them put a chunk of butter in it but that changed nothing.

Around eleven we went to bed, and it was then that things really got ridiculous.

A dog scratched at the door. I love animals and opened it: no dog. Nothing. Then about one in the morning there was a frightful din in the fireplace. Caught between fear and curiosity I investigated: instead of wood there was an accumulation of bones in the fireplace: tibias and femurs that burned with a sweet warmth. I pressed the hand-bell but, of course, no one came. I have to say we felt a little ill-at-ease. Suddenly the burning bones passed into the room and danced around us, grinding in a most disagreeable way. As I looked closer I saw there were masses of small holes in the ceiling from which hung barely visible threads to which the bones were attached.

At about three a dozen black cats appeared in the room in a veritable sabbath. Again they came, I presume, from the fireplace.

Then the door banged open and four bedizened laqueys appeared carrying the shaft of a magnificent sedan chair. Inside a splendid old lady, dressed divinely in eighteenth century fashion, before whom they bowed down low. A special detail was that she was completely covered with small green mice. The latter panicked at the sight of the cats and raced here and there to escape. Four cats with blazing eyes pounced on the woman's naked shoulders. The mice raced towards us but in spite of our efforts to save them, the tom cats soon devoured them. Game, after all, is game.

In the distance the foghorn punctuated the scene. No appeal for help could come from our contracted lips. Besides, who would we call? Only the wind and rain might have answered such a call. Probably we would appear to be two mad women, it was not something about which to call for help, after all. There was probably no danger.

Suddenly Ariane, who lay in bed very pale but also calm, began to scream. Forgetting my own terror I rushed forward: a small grey snake with triangular head was moving over the sheet towards her with a forked tongue like the pistil of a lily.

On my bed, a severed hand lifted up the covers to disclose a large bloodstain on the sheet which blossomed like a crimson flower. The hand scurried around the room with crab-like grace.

The rain still fell in squalls. A horrible face appeared at the window, so much more atrocious for being the face of an admirably beautiful woman, but with an expression of incomprehensible hatred. The corner of her mouth was turned up in a horrible grin as her eyes stared at us through the glass.

I pulled open the door and shouted so loudly I thought I had torn the veins in my neck. The white rabbit sister-in-law appeared a few minutes later. "Why are you making such a row," she said, rubbing her haunches. Breathlessly I told her what horrors has been happening. Ariane had collapsed on the floor of the corridor. The white-rabbit shook with laughter. "Is that all! But *it's quite natural. It is winter, after all. We have to something to amuse the guests*. Don't you like it?"

★★★★★

published in *Cahiers Bleus* no 19 (1981)
French original © Centre Culturel Thibaud de
Champagne, 1981

★★★★★

LISE DEHARME (see page 166)

RAUL FIKER:

World

Lasciate ogni speranza, voi ch'entrate! Dante

I

With a grinding noise that signals that the machine has broken down, the lift stops between the twentieth and twenty-first floor, and St Simon Stylites finds himself suddenly and definitively incarcerated. He shows neither surprise nor irritation or, rather, it is the man in the white suit, his feet firmly planted on a rubber mat (feeling somewhat insecure because his trousers are too short and consoles himself with odd associations that lead to thoughts of Achilles), who, on finding himself trapped in a lift, is briefly touched by such emotions. But this has little to do with St Simon, who conceals behind his fine, angular face, partially covered by a geometrical goatee, the immeasurable magnitude of thousands of desires which will one day give him an importance barely comprehensible to a thin man wearing a white suit, whose immediate (and therefore only) concern, on finding himself trapped in the lift, is to get to the twenty-ninth floor where he hopes to sort out certain matters relating to his person. St Simon Stylites, on the other hand, feels hopelessly lost, breathless. But he was feeling like that when he got into the lift and even before that, when he was walking towards the building, grasping in his hand a little piece of paper containing an address, and long, long before that, when he was still very young and discovered the third person singular and all that implies. Thus, St Simon does not experience the situation as something unexpected, nor even as a potentially pleasing new aspect of his tragedy. The Stylite experiences moments of real terror, his fear fills everything with such intensity that he has a profound sense of his own existence, or at least he thinks he does.

II

After about ten minutes, the Stylite is already viewing his situation as something that has been in existence as long as he has. He has always been inside that lift and he will spend the rest of his days there. The walls of varnished wood, with their obsessive knots, have always been his only landscape. And the gaps around the door that leads to the twentieth and the twenty-first floors, where the terrible eyes of his implacable judges are hiding, were always both his fear and his motivation. St Simon Stylites is incarcerated, this is his protection, and from it is born his extreme vulnerability.

III

Opposite the saint is a panel of buttons, amongst which, imposing itself provocatively on the gaze of the Stylite, is the red emergency button. But the tragedy of St Simon Stylites is too grandiose – it is after all a tragedy – to be shattered by the simple act of pressing a small plastic button with his finger. That is how the Stylite thinks of an alternative offered by the emergency button, and his relationship with it oscillates between fear and rage. The saint wants nothing so much as to leave his prison, it is terribly distressing to be enclosed in a space less that a yard and a half square in a lift of such small proportions as the one in which Simon finds himself trapped. There isn't enough air or freedom of movement, and then there's the solitude, which is awful, and the silent eyes that watch him, inexorably waiting, in order to condemn him, for the slightest hint of some attitude unworthy of a saint and any gesture will do, clicking his tongue, for example, or picking his nose, and a tear would certainly qualify. So the saint moves with extreme caution, not even his thoughts seem safe and, overcome by this, his stomach contracts and he abandons himself to fits of shivering and unbearable tension. And this is to be his situation for the rest of his life. How could it be possible then – or even probable (probability does not exist for the protagonist of a tragedy) – that a tiny gesture, like pressing a button, could literally save him? Besides, that is a truly hateful, discreditable prospect. For such a possibility might diminish, render inconsequential, the tragedy of St Simon Stylites and, more than anything else, he is a man living a tragedy. Perhaps he would prove unable to be anything else; everything pales into insignificance before tragedy – before his tragedy in particular – and it is that which places him on a completely different plane. Above all, it confers importance on him. That, thinks the saint, is absolutely vital. As for the man in the white suit, who is merely trapped in a lift, he would not hesitate to press the button. St Simon Stylites cannot be that man. And so, perhaps without realising it, the saint hates the button.

IV

He needs to make some grand gesture for the benefit of the eyes peering through the cracks. Those eyes are fundamental components in the Stylite's tragedy. Whilst, on the one hand, they represent a constant threat, on the other hand, and possibly more importantly, they are the means to St Simon Stylites' consecration. In this way, the saint begins his work: a huge column – that will really impress them, as it will the saint – on top of which he will install himself, once the arduous construction process is over. Arduous because the materials used in the enterprise consist of fragments both of the lift and of himself, St Simon Stylites.

★★★★★
Brazilian original © Raul Fiker
translated from the Portuguese by Margaret Jull Costa
★★★★★
RAUL FIKER: Participated in the Brazilian Surrealist Group from 1964 to 1969.

The Man

It is now a matter of making a man, thought Letizia to herself. Oh it couldn't be any more difficult. Instead of the hard work being above, it would just be down below, that's all. In truth, fabricating breasts is a real problem. You need to assemble segments of tissue in the form of a half-melon twice over. And then there is the problem of fixing them to the torso. . . it's awkward! A man was definitely needed, since the assembly of women had become boring with never varying conversation: housework, food, babies and sickness. A man would be a nice change. True I do already have one male with my little Paul, but serious conversation is not his forte. He is still only five years old; the poor chap will only ever be five years old.

So, should the gentleman have a moustache or not? How do you see him, Letizia? Large or small brow? Arched — was she not clever enough to do anything? A strong nose or not? He should be a little taller than the women, but there was no need to exaggerate. Well, I have an idea! What if I dress him up in Edgar's clothes, in the navy officer's uniform? That would be a good talking point when they all met as he could tell everyone about his travels.

As a child, Letizia had already created animals filled with old stockings, as well as little primitive dolls whose physiognomy particularly interested her. She was eager to embroider the eyes. An element of chance had been involved, which was nice. Whether they were sad, laughing, or staring, they gave her a great sense of delight and, as she was able to relate to them, she felt she had created a human being; in a moment, even without a mouth, it would be able to speak to her.

Since the death of her husband Edgar she had brought nine women and a child into the world, all life-size. The former were all dressed in her own clothes, skirts, blouses, stockings and shoes she no longer needed, and so they seemed quite old fashioned ladies. For the child Paul she found a wealth of clothes at Woolworths to equip a young schoolboy.

Although she had always been alone she did not find it easy. She liked her husband well enough but did not love him. He was a sailor who went on long journeys and each time he returned home he became more of a stranger, but for her it was a pleasure to wait for him and prepare herself for it in stages. After he died, there was no longer any pleasure in waiting, and it became a solitude with no hope and devoid of the slightest consolation.

In the three months that followed her widowhood, she had dreamed of surrounding herself with mannequins who would take her voice for she needed to speak and hear something. She had no relatives. Her neighbours were suspicious and the shopkeepers taciturn. There had only ever been a few friends and relations and after Edgar's death, after a few weeks sympathy, she never saw them again. Anyhow, she was not especially fond of them. She was afraid of others, of their words, their possible coldness, of everything that might cause her pain.

So there were her creatures: Reine, representing the daughter she never had, her fictive sister Ronnie and first cousin Leonora. She invented them all, giving to each a past and a well defined character. Old Aunt Lucia, for example, and the six ladies who came to visit on Thursdays and Saturdays. One of them was Madame Petiot, to whom Paul belonged. He was her only son, since she had the misfortune to have two aborted pregnancies and, worse, to lose her little girl at the age of only two years. Since then she had remained in mourning.

In the course of time, Letizia became something of a ventriloquist. It was tiring but she managed to simulate a climate that made it possible for her characters to communicate, whether it be chit-chat or more serious conversations, the latter rising up from her intimate being in which her 'inner' life inhabited. So she could say things she might have thought but not formulated. Often she even proposed themes and the discussion went at a good pace. They drank tea, some preferred whisky and, since they did not really drink, the hostess had to gulp down all their glasses. Naturally after an hour her spirit knew no bounds and she could rejoice – even if a little tipsy – at the thought of having organised a pleasant afternoon. Or perhaps someone had a tantrum which made Letizia very angry and she would cram the visitor responsible back into the cupboard where she would spend the week waiting for the next reception date, and then only if she deserved it. Only the family of Reine, Ronnie, Leonora and Aunt Lucia had the right to remain on the living room sofa all the time, and they would sometimes follow their parent into the kitchen to watch her eat or do the washing-up. They take up so much time, said Letizia – that suits me fine – but they have to watch their waistlines. With Lucia, who was older, it was okay, but with Ronnie still being young, it was not serious. It's true that her boyfriend had recently abandoned her and she had barely recovered. After all, as I run around after them I use up so much energy it gives me an appetite.

The man was born one day, rather late, in fact since Letizia had suddenly hesitated, for there was a sort of shame involved in anticipating control of a body not like the others. Finally there he was, completely naked, with a smell of new chiffon. The only thing still to be done was put to on the wig, thread by thread. In fact she liked him just as well as bald as a coot; he already possessed a turned-up moustache, green eyes and rather red cheeks. She baptised him Gontran and he was an old admirer of hers, an intimate friend of Edgar. So much had to be done! All the coquetry, the hints, the flatteries and all that. . . She herself had to behave with circumspection when she had a tête-à-tête with him and, on occasions, the relatives would be sent off to the bedroom.

"Do you remember," Gontran said. "The time we dined together at the restaurant near the Madeleine... It was during a period of my leave, when Edgar was in China."

She said: "I remember... but let's not talk about it."

"I know why you don't want to talk about it. It's because that was the day I dared tell you I had been very much in love with you a few years earlier, but that I no longer was... Certainly it was another way of making a declaration of love, and it is that which embarrasses you..."

She would laugh and pass her hand through his hair to smooth it down, or would re-arrange the folds in her dress harmoniously, as if she was receptive to what he had said and in her confusion wanted to hide the fact. She also rejoiced in the fact that, with this knowledge, they would say something else face to face.

Well now, to add a little piquancy, she would also imagine that Miss Bramble, her English doll - who always ended each sentence with an 'isn't that so?', which Reine mischievously counted up "that's already six, mama" – that this Miss Bramble was attracted to Gontran and that this was something that did not displease the latter. For he started to appear other than at the times of his own visits. Letizia became jealous, and her resolution finally ended in a feeling of resentment.

"You are a real ladies' man, my dear Gontran," she affirmed.

"Why do you say that?"

"You know very well what I mean. Moreover, I expect that on Tuesday I shall be away and will not be able to see you."

Yes, she must retaliate and he would accept her reproach, conscious of his infidelity. Even so, she was still sure that it was she he loved, and that he had only succumbed because the English woman had put on the charm.

She had created such a complex little world before Gontran had even entered into the circle. When she saw him now, sitting on the armchair with a cigarette between his fingers, his legs wide apart, she felt troubled by the protuberance of his sex beneath his trousers. She had herself sewn, modelled, and held these parts between her fingers without experiencing the least emotion, and the shame at the beginning had been purely cerebral – but now... Of course it was only wadding, supported , if rather inflated, under the man's trousers, but it seemed so lifelike! The worst thing was that it never changed position, that it was offered to her permanently and drew her look towards it.

After this the conversations did not have the previous ease. Gontran spoke stutteringly about navigation in general and Letizia went red when she felt he was about to say something else. They had only one further meeting together, after which she preferred to invite him together with the women. In any event, she was uneasy. Her words became listless, so the whole group was weakened. In the end she started to ignore Gontran altogether, or at least she had to make a special effort. That happened on several occasions before she made a decision to parcel him up in a bundle of old newspapers and consign him forever to the cupboard, on the highest shelf which it was only possible to reach with the aid of a stepladder. Wounded and humiliated, she started to drink more, what's more, to spend whole nights in a tobacco haze into which she abruptly plunged. These were cigarettes she had bought for Gontran. Afterwards she started to buy them for herself and was soon purchasing entire cartons.

For a few months the sessions followed each one in indolence. Letizia had perhaps become a little thinner and she argued a lot and did not invite everyone.

Summer came. Madame Petiot left for her holidays with young Paul. Some family tragedies crashed down on the other *habitués*, and Letizia remained in the company of her daughter, sister, cousin and aunt. She found this more peaceful, for she had been allowing herself to become incredibly tired. So tired that one evening she experienced a fleeting malaise. Vague stomach pains and an impression of cold that she combatted with alcohol. She went to bed and the following day, in spite of a heavy feeling of lassitude, the pains did not return.

They spoke very little, played cards together, and did needlework. It was very pleasant. Letizia became less agitated, but had little appetite and no longer did much cooking.

On another evening, a new crisis seized her, one that was more violent. She groaned and gripped her neck. She felt an icy sweat run along the length of her temple and cheeks. Fanciful but lucid, she reached the top landing and managed to open the door. Almost flat on her stomach on the door mat, she called out several times but there was no answer. She lost consciousness and remained there for a good few minutes. When she recovered, she closed the door and went back to the living room, where she collected all the mannequins together. In turn she took them all to her bedroom and placed two of them on a sofa and the others around the side of the bed. She lit a few candles which she put on the floor around her bed and then got undressed and slipped under the sheets in a state of exhaustion.

"I'm not well," she told her dolls. "I am going to have a third attack and then that will be the end. I am so cold. . ."

It took a long time. She stretched out her hand on both sides, seeking the hands of the dolls. Each time she found one or other mannequin, the contact of the material thrilled her. As she thought about the flesh and blood faces of Edgar and her friends of long ago – supple faces that changed and sometimes got hurt, but that it did not matter. She felt tears in her eyes. She who had known so well how to get along with these innocent dead people, who she activated as best she could, longed at that critical moment for true affection, for eyes which moved, which expressed, implored and gave.

Around midnight, after having choked and experienced some intolerable pain, her movements ceased. Her breath stopped and she suddenly died.

The body of the doll Ronnie, which had perhaps been badly secured on the bed, fell down with her nose to the sheets. She appeared to be crying.

*****

published in Gisèle Prassinos: *La Lucarne* (1990)
French original © Editions Flammarion, 1990

*****

GISÈLE PRASSINOS (see page 127)

ALAIN JOUBERT:

Night Windows

IMAGE: *Night Windows* (1928) Edward Hopper

SOUND: *Strange fruit, She's funny that way, Fine and Mellow* by Billie Holiday

On that Sunday evening New York was calm. A mist as warm and humid as a sheet taken from a sweatroom enveloped the city. Summer had already lazily made itself at home for a few weeks and many residents haunted the streets late into the night seeking an unlikely freshness. Those who did not even have the courage to go out lived with windows wide open and the lights that pierced the facades of the buildings acted to provocatively draw one's gaze to them. Neglecting all reserve and modesty, everyone was placed on display framed by narrow windows, playing a role very much their own for the benefit of neighbours and passers-by in a room in which what was unveiled completely escaped them, since it was submitted to the re-interpretation – or phantasms – of the watcher-to-be.

I was among those watching. On the fifth floor of the building facing my apartment, at the corner of the street, three wide-open windows silhouetted three pale rectangles inside a room carpeted in green. I noticed the corner of a bed, a radiator, the door frame and the end of a chest of drawers that had been painted red. The transparent curtains – probably nylon – of one of the windows were at times swallowed up by the night, raised by a shaft of warm wind as thick as whipped cream. Lifting, Medicine ball, Orchestra, Murmur. These words of no apparent significance floated in my mind, uncertain flotsam of the shipwreck of my sensibility and will. Sitting on a chair with both arms folded under my chin and placed on the edge of the window, I held the room in my gaze with a mixture of detachment and despair. A woman in a mauve satin slip entered one of the rectangles. She trailed through the room with the sloth of a Chinese fish in a bowl, without future. Her gestures were those of a drowned woman filmed in slow motion and her slip, completely drenched with sweat, accentuated this impression. This apparition transfixed me. For a long time nothing the window could reveal escaped my gaze. When the woman in the mauve satin slip vanished for a moment behind one of the sections of wall separating the windows an incredible anxiety seized me, as if my life depended for now on the existence of this woman, or rather on the 'vision' I had of her existence. What if she did not re-appear!

I was 'hooked'; she was the alcohol my senses desired, the drug my nerves needed to remain calm. Lifting. Medicine ball. Orchestra. Murmur. . . An invisible thread of extreme tension connected us from above the street without her knowledge and against my will. Street sounds mingled in long sonorous trails, sticky with heat, which flowed from the windows and if sometimes a jazz tune or some bars by Judy Garland could be recognised in the passage, it served better to underline the essential anonymity of the sounds. For a moment the woman in the mauve satin slip remained in the middle of the central window of her room, with two hands placed on the ledge, and with her head leaning over the street. Her body swayed slightly from stem to stern, in a motion which soon quickened to the point of disequilibrium. The whole of her weight suddenly veered outwards and the woman rocked into the void without a cry. I barely had the time to realise what was happening under my eyes than a murmur, created from multiple vibrations, cries, the breaking of tyres, banging of doors, exclamations of all sorts rose towards me in a rotating way, like waves created by a stone thrown to the bottom of a well. I hesitated. Standing there facing the window, with head looking over the street, I saw a swarm of frantic bodies running this way and that while a mauve satin slip stained the greyness of the sidewalk. It was as beautiful as fear! I swayed slightly from stem to stern in a motion which quickened very naturally, against me, against my will, to the point of disorientation, until the whole of my weight suddenly veered outward, until the void absorbed me. The sound of the Salvation Army's brass band, playing a little further on at the crossroads came to me in a flash.

My rehabilitation progressed. Several hours a day, I practised exercises in suppleness with the aid of a bag full of sand whose weight served to restore my muscles. A few weeks had passed, as if between parentheses, since my leap into the unknown, into vertigo. This morning, they would take off the bandages which still covered my face, this face in too much of a rush, which one evening was fascinated by a mauve satin slip. The scissors, the stares, a mirror, the care, the panic! Another looked at me, eyes in my eyes, another face with porcelain skin, smooth and tight, cold, coming from somewhere else. The face of the void itself.

    Murmur, orchestra, medicine-ball, lifting.

*****
published in the collection of the same title
by Arabie-sur-Seine, 1984
French original © Alain Joubert
*****
ALAIN JOUBERT (Paris, 1936) Alain Joubert joined the French Surrealist Group in 1955 and remained an active member until the dissolution of the group in 1969. Otherwise his life revolves around the pivots of cycling, jazz and the cinema. According to Philippe Audoin he maintains an 'elegant equilibrium on the razor's edge of dandyism'. His object-montages have been widely exhibited.

MARIANNE VAN HIRTUM:

Proteus Volens

Ouch! Without noticing, Proteus Volens stepped on the piano leg. "Now I shall have to take it to hospital," said Proteus. This was all the more so in that the piano, even though it was black, began to bleed with red blood. "It's not normal," said Proteus. "It must have something wrong with its heart."

The street was blocked because of a demonstration by discontented eggs demanding a salary increase. How could he possibly get the piano through the cortège of eggs?

Some of the eggs were broken. That always excites the desire of the good bourgeois to see dogs lick up eggs. No sooner thought than done: the good bourgeois were down on their knees, on all fours, licking the eggs.

Bad luck. . . bad luck as always (it is very well known that the bourgeois are not lucky), these eggs were not very fresh. Some of the bourgeois were nauseous. Others vomited. Even graver: around a hundred had turned into apples. (Naturally, this did not please the apple trees, and some suffered fractures, whether of tibia, femur or hip. . .) Finally everyone reached the hospital. I say 'finally', since thanks to the crush caused by the arrival of ambulances in the midst of the cortège of eggs, good bourgeois, dogs and the poor piano accompanied by Proteus Volens, together with the crippled apple-trees, it took some decades to clear the public way. The road system, the commission of public ways and the police's regulatory system changed very quickly. Strangely only the piano had not aged.

One could, after so much investigation and with so many forms filled out, find a convenient bed in the waiting-room. Proteus Volens, astride the piano, led the charge.

The battalion of surgeons made its entrance, welcomed by a crowd of eggs that had collected together in a gigantic omelette made rotten by the years. They are what we call today the 'eggs of the Thousand and One Nights'. They are served in Flat Iron restaurants.

This is how one reaches the higher grade of surgeon.

From birth the children destined for this remarkable profession are scrubbed all day long with the most refined spices, and then prepared with grammar books perfumed with synthetic pineapple. Next comes apprenticeship. The most promising learn how to ride wheelbarrows and Arab flies as meek as lambs. (The sun did not always shine on the legend.)

"Long live Proteus Volens," was the cry heard in unison. But since this is only a parenthesis let's return to the surgidogs.

The surgidogs had the faces of angels. This was what distinguished them from the common herd – I almost said from mortals! – but we know very well that surgidogs are immortals. How would they not have their place under the famous Dome of orange-flavoured Sugar. They also have long blond hair like the little girls of our dreams.

The surgidogs have no mamas: for the most part they are orphans from generation to generation. The Great Council of Orphans got on best in the management of their musical instruments. For the surgidogs are so gifted! From the trombone to *trompe l'oeil* to trompe-cul, although the latter instrument presented great difficulties of adaptation.

Let's be with our own time rather than with that of others: of yours, theirs, hers. (Would that the time of hares be over!)

Surgidogs eat barley sugar in their lost moments. This spare time could no more be recovered than barley sugar sent into the celebrated time machine, than what is found gleaming in polished copper, the halls of the most modern financial institutions marked by no other epithet than the twist. Which is why one must twist and plait these barley

270

sugars sticks to accomplish the most complicated operations.

The piano was placed on the largest of all the operating tables and the operation began. In the first act a Marseillaise in mustard sauce was heard, played by pipes dressed to the nines, (it was Sunday, after all).

Proteus Volens and his piano were now operated upon.

Some eggs came out of the radiolarian to the aid of the musical instruments necessary for the operation. The apple trees sat down and called on the help of occult forces. With arms folded, they did not make a sound, but counted the precious minutes with the redness of their apples, accentuated at each moment and lighting the field of operating apple-trees.

The dogs were asleep, digesting in peace the surgidogs they had gorged themselves on, with dessert of good bourgeois stuffed with rubbish.

Total silence was necessary for the success of the operation.

The children cavorted in the street, since the fire had burned down all the schools and the letters dispersed in the wind created a poem that could be recaptured only by birds whose hearts were pure.

Proteus Volens also put his hand on his heart, for he was resting. With a smile he thought about the piano whose keys were made of the best loaves lovingly moulded by the proud fir-trees with their own hands.

The day ended in well deserved euphoria.

The chariot of triumph was drawn by four pangolins arched like canopies, by two elephants bearing complete sweetness, by an anteater from a far-away grassland, who held the moon on his nose and the sun at the end of his raised tail.

All this while a film was shown about the American Indians in the only area of Paris still standing after the avalanche: the district of thinking Dawns. The houses there are bagpipes and the sheets are made of red currants. The squirrels played, sitting in a circle with old magicians. For nourishment, the only thing necessary was to open the window, for then storks appeared bearing honey and rubies which are the best type of meat. The flowers fastened to the trees were chattering handbells. It was fine to be in that wonderful district.

In truth, Proteus Volens and his piano had dreamed about it for a long time. Of course the dream, unlike virtue, is always rewarded.

Spring had come!

It came out of the night, but what is night? Is it a part of time or space? No one knows. Is it not perhaps one of the innumerable elements of the universe in which we try to live? (Some try desperately, others just live – very, few of them, it's true, but there are so many we see who do not live at all!)

Spring is the only revolutionary whose revolution has succeeded. That is why we do not place the Phrygian cap on it. It has no cap of any sort. Not even a nightcap: since it was the victor, like one who has effected his own metamorphosis, the only one, once again, who would be the operation himself, who would have effected his own cure, all by himself.

Would you too like to be cured?

Then I will give you the recipe. It is necessary to walk. To cross the incredible and dangerous night without seeing it to maintain its whole Magic. Close your eyes in order to be able to see nothing. (Everything is so ugly around what is not that night). Keep your arms close to your body so as not to touch anything, since the only thing touchable is from within.

Then walk straight ahead, almost for eternity.

Go out of the night while remaining within it: that is the secret of metamorphosis.

P.S – The piano, which is completely black, is red-blooded, since it is now cured.

*****

published in Marianne Van Hirtum: *Proteus Volens* (1991)
French original © Hourglass, 1991

272

translated by Guy Flandre, Michael Richardson and Peter Wood

*****

MARIANNE VAN HIRTUM (Namur, Belgium 1935 – Paris 1988) Joined the French Surrealist Group in 1956 and remained a key member until the dissolution of the group in 1969. Her writings and drawings bear witness to a life lived in a sense of enchantment.

ELISABETH LENK:

The Man in the White Gloves

Schizophrenic Dialogue

Ego: My face appeared to be worn down. Images spread everywhere. The man in white gloves was here. I designed for myself a persona and watched myself in this persona. This persona was called Alterego. At times I looked at her from the outside and thought: it is but a mask. But sometimes I crept into her and looked at the world through her eyes. Although she represents me, she is unable to see, I secretly thought. It is through me that she sees. I carried my persona with me like a doll, but she was too heavy to carry and unwieldy and one day I simply cast her away. Now I lacked my suit of armour and felt like a snake. It was in this strange, almost skinless, condition that I lay beside a spring and saw before me a wonderful face. The face was not that of my persona which I knew and saw in my mirrors every day. It enraptured me, it was all movement, flowing and pure like water from the spring. I fell in love with myself. These eyes, to which I had become accustomed as my eyes, disappeared. Instead I beheld hundreds of dancing lights, all smiling mysteriously, and I smiled back, or was I the one who smiled first? And yet I did not throw myself into this spring, I did not jump into the smiling river. In time I recalled the doll which I had left standing at the shore. I took her persona on again and stumbled through life with her. This persona, which I have created for myself, is no longer my ideal though. But I got used to her, I inhabit her. When I do not bear this burden, I lack something. And only sometimes, in ecstatic moments, I see a streaming light somewhere inside. Perhaps it seeks to show me the way. If I didn't have to bear this big unwieldy doll, I would follow the light.

Alterego: I find Ego presumptuous. She imagines herself to be the substance inhabiting me and looking through me. But so far she has only led me astray. She claims to bear me where I want to go, but we only ever go where she wants. Besides Ego was the one who fell for the man in white gloves. I felt indifferent to this man. However, she masked herself with me and made eyes at him. And he thought he was dealing with me. He trusted my stiff and dry manner. He thought I was reliable. But it was really Ego who had, through me, winked at him in her provocative way.

I admit I too was impressed by the man in white gloves. Especially the first time I saw him or thought I saw him. At that moment the sea, my stick and his heartbeat seemed to me one. Immediately he touched me like a vision. Later he drew both of us, Ego and myself, across into his 'realm', as he called his peculiar world. We were both completely under his spell. He was our folie-à-deux. That first day I saw only his dark coat and that inimitable posture, something I had never observed in anyone: elegant and shy or, more precisely, futile. It was as though he did not really exist, but was only a suggestion: indeed, only his light gloves were clearly distinguishable and it seems as though they were what touched me first. Or better: I was touched in passing by his gloves and that unique glance. Perhaps he sensed that he had impressed both of us, but more surprising was that he understood straightaway that there were the two of us. Because we are not visible at once. Only for the two of us there is no doubt about this duality. Normally the glance that meets us from outside perceives us together as a single person. The man in the white gloves alone penetrated our secret. When Ego, shocked, was in floods of tears, which she was capable of, she was truly and purely fluent; yet I sat unmoved and dry-eyed, and he winked at me as though I was his accomplice. The moment Ego cast me aside was terrible. She wanted to get rid of me, I sensed that. I remember it as though it happened only yesterday. I felt like an empty shell, devoid of life like a deserted house. By contrast, she had rapturously slipped away and was lying down. She stared at something that beamed towards her. I believed that I saw a face, a face I knew from somewhere... Then a deathly pain went through me, as though something inside me had torn and, from that moment, forced its way onwards.

On this memorable day of separation and reunion the man in white gloves had not yet appeared to us. I recognised the face: even though the flowing distorted it beyond recognition, it was quite clearly my face. Later one she called this movement: my smile.

Ego: I hate Alterego. She believes it was her face I saw at the spring and fell in love with. She takes everything away from me, my experiences, and even the man in white gloves. Oh, I could kill her; I often dream of that, of a genuine pleasure-suicide, a yodelling scream, grotesque and incredible to the very last minute. Society which just a moment ago had been laughing loudly, appears to be asleep now. I have switched the light on. Much I thought had been lost lies around here. Why am I seized with this excitement? I will strangle her, or she me. I am longing for this satisfaction, this feeling of calm, for the indifference of this passionless, at best somewhat contemptuous, glance. I cast it at myself. The way I am masked prevents me from having to see myself any longer. It looks strange. There is just the cloth I wrapped around the eyes. The eyes cannot be seen.

We are both I-obsessed, that is what connects us, but it does not bring us closer. Our duality flows from an obscure spring.

Hannover, 1991

★★★★★
published in *Droomschaar* no 2
German original © Elisabeth Lenk
translated by Barbara Heins
★★★★★

ELISABETH LENK participated in the activities of the Parisian Surrealist Group during the 1960's, making an important contribution to the 'Heidegger controversy'. Now lectures at the Free University of Berlin. Published *Das springende Narziss André Breton poetischer Materialismus* (1971)

Dedalus Anthologies

Titles currently available are:

The Dedalus Book of Austrian Fantasy: *the Meyrink Years 1890–1930* – editor Mike Mitchell £8.99
The Dedalus Book of British Fantasy: the 19th century – editor Brian Stableford £8.99
The Dedalus Book of Dutch Fantasy – editor Richard Huijing £9.99
The Dedalus Book of Decadence (Moral Ruins) – editor Brian Stableford £7.99
The Dedalus Book of Femmes Fatales – editor Brian Stableford £7.99
The Second Dedalus Book of Decadence: the Black Feast – editor Brian Stableford £8.99
The Dedalus Book of Surrealism – editor Michael Richardson £8.99
Tales of the Wandering Jew – editor Brian Stableford £8.99

forthcoming titles include:

The Dedalus Book of Belgian Fantasy – editor Richard Huijing
The Dedalus Book of German Fantasy: the Romantics and Beyond – editor Maurice Raraty
The Dedalus Book of French Fantasy – editor Christine Donougher
The Dedalus Book of German Decadence – editor Ray Furness
The Dedalus Book of Polish Fantasy – editor Wiesiek Powaga
The Dedalus Book of Russian Decadence – editor Natalia Rubenstein
The Second Dedalus Book of Surrealism – Michael Richardson

The Dedalus Book of Decadence (Moral Ruins) – editor Brian Stableford

Every aspect of *The Dedalus Book of Decadence* (*Moral Ruins*) received praise, from the brown and gold of its cover (Times Higher Educational Supplement), the introduction (The Independent), the choice of stories (City Limits), and the whole book (Time Out). It was a critical and commercial success, which featured in the Alternative Bestsellers List.

A few comments:

'an invaluable sampler of spleen, everything from Baudelaire and Rimbaud to Dowson and Flecker. Let's hear it for *luxe, calme et volupte*'

Anne Billson in Time Out

'*The Dedalus Book of Decadence* looks south to sample the essence of fine French decadent writing. It succeeds in delivering a range of writers either searching vigorously for the thrill of a healthy crime or lamenting their impuissance from a sickly stupor.'

Andrew St George in The Independent

£**7.99**   ISBN 0 946626 63 4   288pp   B Format
(new edition June 1993)

The Dedalus Book of Austrian Fantasy – editor Mike Mitchell

"Subtitled '*The Meyrink Years 1890–1930*', this is a superb collection of the bizarre, the terrifying and the twisted, as interpreted by the decadents and obsessives of *fin de siecle* Vienna. It features big names like Kafka, Rilke and Schnitzler, but more intriguing are the lesser-known writers such as Franz Theodor Csokor with the vampiric '*The Kiss of the Stone Woman*', Karl Hans Strobl, whose '*The Wicked Nun*' begins as a ghost story but twists and turns into insanity and Paul Busson, contributing an uncanny tale of feminine sorcery, '*Folter's Gems*'."

Time Out

"Divided into five sections (Possessed Souls, Dream and Nightmare, Death, The Macabre, Satire) that tell you all you need to know, the stand out works are those of Gustav Meyrink, Strobl and Schnitzler and Franz Csokor's wonderful, mad chiller '*The Kiss of the Stone Woman*'.
The best stories faultlessly follow the traditional template of deepening mystery grafted onto time-honoured methods of signalling narrative action. Recommended"

City Limits

£**8.99**   ISBN 0 946626 93 6   416pp B Format